HELL AND ICE

ANDREW WARREN

B

Boldwood

First published in 2016 and 2018 as *Devil's Due* and *Cold Kill*. This edition published in Great Britain in 2025 by Boldwood Books Ltd.

Copyright © Andrew Warren, 2016

Cover Design by Head Design Ltd.

Cover Images: iStock and Shutterstock

A CIP catalogue record for this book is available from the British Library.

Paperback ISBN 978-1-83703-887-9

Large Print ISBN 978-1-83703-886-2

Hardback ISBN 978-1-83703-885-5

Trade Paperback ISBN 978-1-80635-328-6

Ebook ISBN 978-1-83703-888-6

Kindle ISBN 978-1-83703-889-3

Audio CD ISBN 978-1-83703-880-0

MP3 CD ISBN 978-1-83703-881-7

Digital audio download ISBN 978-1-83703-882-4

This book is printed on certified sustainable paper. Boldwood Books is dedicated to putting sustainability at the heart of our business. For more information please visit https://www.boldwoodbooks.com/about-us/sustainability/

Boldwood Books Ltd, 23 Bowerdean Street, London, SW6 3TN

www.boldwoodbooks.com

FOREWORD

The events of *Hell and Ice* take place before *Tokyo Black*, when Caine is hiding off the grid in Pattaya, Thailand...

PART I

DEVIL'S DUE

1

The tiny grill spat grease and smoke into the tropical air. Its blackened metal rods were covered by a thick, charred crust, the petrified remains of previous meals. But the smell emanating from the strips of meat cooking on its surface was mouthwatering.

From the shore, Sarah leaned over the wooden railing of the narrow walkway and waved to get the attention of the tiny Thai woman working the grill. The grill was set up on a small boat, one of several that were docked in the muddy waters of a shallow canal that crossed through the Pattaya floating market. The market was a popular tourist attraction, and a bustling crowd of people shifted around her.

As Sarah waited for the woman, she caught a glimpse of an older man wearing cargo shorts and a Hawaiian shirt that looked one size too small. He was eying her legs as she leaned over the railing. Her slim, lean body was tanned from weeks of travel, and she knew the tiny cutoffs and faded tank top she was wearing did little to conceal it.

She was grateful she had kept her tan, despite the cloudy, gray skies that loomed over the market-place. She had arrived in Thailand two weeks ago, and in that time the sun had barely peeked out from behind the thick, gloomy curtain.

She ignored the lecherous man, and soon he disappeared into the crowd. She waved to the old woman again and finally caught her attention as she handed a Styrofoam plate of food to another tourist. The woman's face was dark and lined with wrinkles. A green embroidered shawl was draped over her working clothes.

'Sixty baht, sixty baht,' the old woman chanted. Sarah did some rapid currency conversions in her head. Two plates of food would cost her about three Euros, which would just about buy her a can of soda back in Germany. She held up two fingers.

The old woman nodded and prepared two plates

for her. Each plate was stacked with rice, a small cup of cucumber salad, and three skewers of the sizzling meat. Sarah handed the woman six twenty-baht notes, and a ten-baht coin. 'Keep the change.'

The old woman smiled and nodded and slid the plates over the railing to her. Sarah inhaled deeply. The meat smelled delicious, but she couldn't quite identify what it was. 'Chicken satay?' she asked.

The woman shook her head. '*Jarakay, ka.*'

Sarah had no idea what that meant, but she knew the proper response when ordering food in Thailand. She smiled and said, '*Aroy.*' Delicious. She grabbed the two plates and continued down the wooden walkway of the market.

To her right, the long strip of water wound its way between the two sides of the market. The canal was crossed by several arched wooden bridges. Crowds of tourists made their way across each bridge, usually stopping in the middle to take pictures of the boats in the water below.

The canal was man-made, and the water was a dark, muddy brown. Its dull, flat surface only served to highlight the explosion of colorful fruits, seafood, silks, and other goods that filled every boat and stall in the market.

Sarah took a deep breath as she absorbed the sights and sounds around her. She felt alive, the most alive she'd felt since finishing university. The idea of returning home, of finding a job in some law office in Hamburg filing papers and reading court documents, seemed like just another cloud on a distant horizon. What kind of life was that, compared to what she had experienced in these months of travel? The warm, tropical climate, the thrill of new people, new places and, most of all, new possibilities... At that moment, she knew with absolute certainty that this was the life she wanted.

Her train of thought was suddenly interrupted as she felt a hand squeeze her ass through her torn, cutoff shorts. She shrieked and spun around, dropping one of the plates of food in the process. Remembering the leering old man in the Hawaiian shirt, she raised her hand and prepared to deliver a strong slap to whoever had groped her.

She looked up and lifted her sunglasses off her face. She was staring into the warm brown eyes of Guenther, her university mate and traveling partner. *After last night*, she thought, *Guenther is quite a bit more than just a mate.*

'Arshloch!' she screamed in German, beating his tanned chest with her tiny fist. 'You scared me!'

Guenther was shirtless, and his skin still held a golden tan. A black tribal tattoo snaked around the lean, athletic muscles of his right arm, and a shell necklace hung from his neck. Sarah watched the muscles move beneath his skin as he threw back his head and laughed. She found herself thinking more about the previous night. That feeling of being alive, of infinite possibilities on the horizon... Guenther was part of those possibilities now, too. She couldn't deny she was hungry for a repeat performance of their intimate physical gymnastics.

'*Liebling*, if you haven't relaxed by now, what am I gonna do with you when we go someplace really crazy?' he asked.

She let her fingers linger on his chest. 'I know, I know. Sorry, this pervert was stalking me before. Just got me on edge, I guess.'

Guenther looked deep into her blue eyes and brushed a wisp of blonde hair from her face. 'Well, who could blame him, eh? I was getting an eyeful of you myself. You know I love those little shorts.'

She laughed. 'But look what you made me do!' She pointed to the spilled food on the ground. 'That's your lunch down there. Enjoy!'

She scooped some rice into her mouth with chopsticks. Guenther reached for her plate, but she turned her back on him. 'Oh no, clean up your mess first.'

Guenther grabbed the plastic plate off the ground and used it to scrape the fallen mess of food off the walkway and into the canal. A school of tiny black fish darted to the surface and nibbled at the morsels as they sank into the water.

He tossed the plate in a garbage can, and the two walked through the market. Guenther threw his arm around her shoulders and grabbed a piece of meat off her plate. He popped it in his mouth and chewed. 'It's good,' he said, his words slurred as he continued to grind the meat between his teeth. 'What is it?'

Sarah shrugged. 'Chicken satay, I think? I got it from one of the boats. The woman who served me called it *jarakay*.'

Guenther swallowed and scanned the market stalls. '*Jarakay*, huh? Think I need a beer.'

'A beer, now? Why?'

'Because *jarakay* means crocodile, and in Thailand one does not eat crocodile without a cold Singha beer.'

Sarah laughed. 'Oh, that's a rule, *ja*?'

'It is now. Guenther's rule on eating crocodile in Thailand with a beautiful girl.'

Sarah leaned into him and kissed his cheek. 'I like this rule. Let's go.'

They shared the plate of food as they walked arm in arm through the market. Guenther spotted a small stall that was selling beer from a cooler, and he broke off. 'Be right back. Don't eat all the crocodile without me!'

Sarah watched him waiting in line at the food stall. His legs were lean and strong, the result of months spent surfing and hiking around the world. She looked up at the cloudy sky, and decided that, once they left the market, they would be spending the rest of the day in their bungalow by the beach. They could go sightseeing again tomorrow. After all, there were infinite possibilities on the horizon. What would it hurt to spend one more day in bed, satisfying their passions?

She heard the high-pitched sound of a child crying. Spinning around, she saw a little Thai girl, no more than five or six years old, stumbling through the crowd. Her simple tan dress with blue and pink stripes looked handcrafted. *Maybe her mother is working on one of the boats, and she wandered off*, Sarah thought. No one was stopping to help. The crowd simply pushed past, oblivious to the crying child.

Sarah tossed the remaining food in a garbage can and walked over to the girl. Kneeling in front of the child, she put a reassuring hand on her shoulder. 'Hey, it's OK. Are you all right?'

The girl looked at her with small, deep brown eyes. Her mouth seemed to struggle to form words. Sarah pulled a napkin from her pocket and brushed the tears from the girl's puffy cheeks. 'There you go. Are you lost?'

Sarah saw a flash of movement over the girl's shoulder. She looked up and saw the old man, the one who had been leering at her earlier, moving across a bridge toward them.

Sarah knew that, in addition to the beauty and energy that she thrived on, Pattaya had a dark side. Prostitution and sex tourism were common. If one was seeking perversions, anything imaginable could be found in the city's dark alleys and seedy bordellos... For a price, of course.

Was that why the girl was crying? Was this pervert in a Hawaiian shirt chasing her?

She took the little girl's hand and stood up. 'Come on,' she said. 'I know someone who can help.'

The girl continued crying but dutifully followed along, her little legs moving as fast as she could to keep up with Sarah.

The two made their way back to the food stall. Guenther smiled as he walked toward them, taking a long swig of beer from a frosted Singha bottle.

'Who's this, then?' He smiled at the girl, and for the first time, she stopped crying. Sarah melted, knowing how reassuring she found that smile herself.

'I found her crying over there.' She pointed toward the bridge. The man in the Hawaiian shirt was there, rummaging through a box of seashells perched on a rickety souvenir cart.

'That's the guy I told you about, the one who was stalking me. I think he was following her,' Sarah said in a hushed whisper.

Guenther looked down and spoke to the girl in broken Thai. '*Mae?* You lost your mother?'

The child stared at him in silence. Guenther spoke a few more words to her, but it was clear she could not understand him.

'What do we do?' Sarah asked. 'We can't just leave her here.'

'Excuse me, I help you?' a singsong male voice asked. Sarah and Guenther turned to see an older Thai man standing next to them. He was tall for a local and looked like he was in his forties. His navy-blue polo shirt and khaki shorts looked crisp and brand new, and his body was lean and athletic. He was carrying a large canvas duffel bag that was slung over his shoulder on a leather strap.

Above his dark brown eyes, his brow was furrowed in concern. 'Heard little one crying. She lost?'

Sarah looked the man up and down. She turned to look at the Westerner in the Hawaiian shirt, but he was nowhere to be seen.

'Yeah, man, we think some pervert dude was stalking her,' Guenther said. 'She looks scared.'

The older man kneeled in front of the little girl and spoke to her in Thai. Sarah couldn't understand what he was saying, but the tone of his words sounded reassuring.

The little girl stared at him with wide eyes and nodded. She continued to grasp Sarah's hand.

The man reached into the pocket of his shorts and pulled out a small plastic bag of dried fruit. He opened the bag and held it out to the girl. She gingerly reached in, grabbed one of the fruits, and stuffed it in her mouth. The man looked up at Sarah.

'Dried plums. They my favorite when I was her age. Taste like candy.' He grunted, stood up, and dusted off his knees. 'She too scared to speak, but she must be lost. There's a police box at end of the market. I take her there; they find parents.'

He reached his hand toward the girl and spoke to her again in Thai. '*Maa gàp phŏm ná.* Come, come, little one.'

The girl looked up at Sarah. She looked back at the man, shook her head, and shuffled behind Sarah's legs.

'Look, she's scared. She doesn't want to go,' Sarah said. 'Let's just call the police, and they can meet us here.'

Guenther gave Sarah a condescending look. 'Babe, come on, you want to wait here all day for the police?'

Sarah stared daggers at Guenther, then turned to the older man. 'No offense, sir, but we don't know who you are, and she doesn't seem to want to go with you.'

Sarah saw a ripple of anger cross the man's features. He seemed about to speak, but then hesitated. He nodded. 'Yes, yes, of course, you right. Sorry, just want to help the child. Tell you what. I go to police, bring them back here.'

He lowered his duffel bag to the ground. 'You wait here with child. Watch my bag, OK? Very heavy! I be right back.'

The man wandered off down the market. Within a few seconds, he was lost in the shifting crowd of tourists and vendors hawking their wares.

Guenther pursed his lips and uttered a low whistle. 'OK, that was a little odd.'

Sarah shook her head. 'I don't know. I don't see the Hawaiian shirt guy anymore, and something about that other guy was weird.'

Guenther laughed. 'Jeez, babe, don't be so paranoid. You don't trust anybody!'

She looked down at the child, who returned her gaze with wide eyes. She lowered her voice. 'OK, then why did he leave his bag? They say you're never supposed to take a stranger's bag. What if it's full of drugs?'

Guenther hefted the bag off the ground. 'Well, if it is, we hit the jackpot 'cause this thing weighs a ton!'

'That's not funny!'

'Come on, let's check it out.' Guenther pushed through the crowd and walked to the side of the market, where the constant stream of people thinned out to a low trickle. Sarah and the child followed, hand in hand.

'Guenther, I don't like this! Do you know what the sentence here is for drugs?'

Guenther turned his back to the crowd. 'Keep

your voice down!' he hissed.

He unzipped the bag.

The little girl began to cry again, and her face turned bright red. Sarah pressed up against Guenther to peer over his shoulder. 'Well, what is it?'

'Just a second. Can you quiet her down?'

Guenther rummaged through the bag, pulling out a bundle of cheap T-shirts. 'It's just stupid T-shirts, tourist stuff... Oh, fuck!'

Kneeling, he gingerly set the bag on the ground. Sarah caught a glimpse of electrical wires and two large, clear cylinders taped together. Each cylinder was filled with a yellowish, crumbled powder. A red LED light attached to one of the wires was flashing.

'What the hell is—' she began, but Guenther grabbed her arm.

'Sarah, shut up and run!'

Sarah scooped up the screaming girl and ran. She'd gone only a few steps when suddenly everything she could see, hear, or feel was blotted out in a giant ball of orange fire.

She screamed, but the sound was silenced by the explosion. She felt her body moving and had just enough time to realize she was not running. She was flying through the air. Her skin was burning, but she felt no pain. Her eardrums and eyeballs ruptured from the shockwave, and the blood cells in her lungs exploded as her body was torn apart.

As the pinpoint of white light that was her consciousness dimmed out, a dying thought flickered through her mind. This was true infinity... Infinite blackness. Infinite darkness. Infinite possibilities reduced to an infinity of cold, black space.

2

A light but steady rain washed the grime and residue from the roofs of the go-go clubs and beer bars that lined either side of Soi Six, part of Pattaya's infamous red-light district. It was early October, near the end of the rainy season for Thailand. Normally, the afternoon sun would have already heated the air to a stifling ninety degrees or more. Instead, the unending drizzle of rain cooled both the climate and the wallets of visiting tourists.

Today, once again, the rain had kept the crowds away. Only a few die-hards, old men with beer guts stretching the seams of their cheap local T-shirts, ventured out into the downpour. They meandered through the rivers of filthy water that rushed down either side of the street, occasionally stopping to haggle with bored-looking bar girls. Despite the lack of customers, the girls looked like they would rather go back to painting their nails.

The atmosphere in Ruby's Club, a beer bar toward the end of the street, mirrored the gloomy weather outside. Music blasted from the bar's speakers, but it seemed unable to drown out the sound of the falling rain. A beautiful bar girl dressed in a sexy school uniform danced on the center stage, spinning around a gleaming chrome pole, but the motley assortment of locals and regular customers paid her no attention.

The few customers in the place sipped lukewarm glasses of beer from the front patio bar and watched the rain falling into the street with quiet, detached reflection.

The sole exception was a lone man standing toward the center of the patio bar. He was average height, but his arms and back rippled with muscle beneath his slim-fitting, black linen shirt. Everything about him seemed hard and angular. His hair was buzzed military short and worn in a Caesar cut. His nose was slim and hawk-like. His eyebrows were two dark slashes cutting across his forehead. The only soft thing about his face were his eyes. They were large and almond-shaped. Delicate black lashes blinked, revealing bright, baby blue irises. His left eye had a lazy tic and seemed to dart and roll toward the edge of his face.

He slammed his empty glass down on the counter. The noise echoed through the bar like a gunshot. A few of the regulars looked up in annoyance, but they glanced away after meeting the man's gaze. There was something unnerving about those strange, beautiful eyes set in such a hard face.

'*Bolshe!* More vodka! And no more of this cheap *mochá*! I want top shelf! Beluga, bitch!'

The bartender was a stocky, pretty girl whose dark skin and silky black hair were typical of girls from the northwestern Isaan region. She hurried over and set another glass down on the counter.

'No Beluga, sir,' she said with her brightest forced smile. 'Stoli OK? Good Russian Vodka!'

'Bah, Stoli is also *mochá*! All you have is piss here!'

The bartender's smile flickered. 'Stoli OK, sir?' she repeated.

The man nodded and looked away as she poured his drink. He turned to another man, who was sipping beer from a tall, frosted glass a couple chairs down at the bar. He was wearing a white T-shirt, olive green pants, and battered suede desert boots. He was taller and lankier than the Russian, and his body had the lean, taut look of a natural athlete.

'What is with this bar, eh?' the Russian grunted. 'They call this vodka? Swedish *mochá*, Finnish *mochá*, even Russian *mochá*! All piss, I say.'

The man down the bar gave no response. He did not look up from his beer.

A tall, lighter-skinned bar girl with thick, wavy brown hair sat down on the stool next to the Russian. She wore black hot pants, a black bustier top, and scarlet high heels. She leaned toward the Russian and spoke into his ear, arching her back and making sure to give him a good view of her cleavage in the process. 'Hey, mister, you have nice eyes. Buy me drink?'

She was stunningly beautiful, and her sudden appearance seemed to improve the Russian's mood. His wide blue eyes drank her in, and she leaned back as his unnerving stare traversed her body. 'Sure, baby, I buy you a drink. What's your name?'

'I'm Naiyana. What your name, mister?'

'I am Alexi. Alexi Rudov. Delighted to meet you.'

He took her hand in his. She let him caress it for a moment, then tried to pull it back. He gripped it tight in his fist. The muscles in his arms bulged. She giggled and tried to play it off. 'You strong, baby. Big, strong man.'

The bartender set down a drink in front of the girl, without asking. It was a lady drink, a tiny bit of alcohol mixed with fruit juice and club soda. Despite its low alcohol content, it cost 150 baht, about twice the cost of a normal drink.

Alexi nodded his approval and the bartender drifted away again.

'You have pretty hands,' he said, his large, meaty paw engulfing her tiny fingers. She laughed as she sipped her drink with her free hand.

'You like?' she asked. 'Come upstairs with me. I treat you good. 2000 baht.'

Alexi twisted his lips into a smile. He threw back his head and laughed. '*Da, da,* I fucking love Thailand. Drink up, my lovely. I take you back to my hotel room. Long time, 4000 baht. I want to take my time with a piece of ass this fine.'

The girl sipped her drink and smiled, but her brow furrowed in concern. Maybe it was the way he gripped her hand, or the unnerving stare, and that lazy, floating eye. Something about the man led her to shake her head. 'No, baby, I only do short time. 2000 baht, we go upstairs, right now. I make you feel so good.'

'Short time' was bar girl slang for a quickie. A brief shower upstairs, then sex in a somewhat private room that contained little more than a bed, a nightstand, and a box of condoms. Once the client finished, they would go back downstairs, and that was that. 'Long time' would mean an all-night affair, usually at the client's hotel room.

Alexi jerked up on her arm, and she gasped as he pulled her to a standing position. Her glass tipped and rolled off the bar. It shattered on the ground, as its sweet, sticky contents spilled across the counter.

'I'm not spending a thousand dollars a night for a suite at the Hilton so I can fuck in some flea-infested shithole. You come with me. I want to enjoy my time with you.'

The girl struggled to free her hand from his grasp. She no longer bothered faking a smile, and her eyes were wide with fear. 'No, baby, short time, OK? I only do short time!'

Alexi raised his free hand back, and the other patrons in the bar looked away. There was no mistaking the gesture. Everyone knew that whatever happened next, it would be safer not to get involved in yet another drunken brawl over a bar girl.

Alexi swung his arm forward in an open-handed

slap but jerked to a stop midway. Someone was holding his arm in a firm grip.

It was the man from the end of the bar. The few patrons fished crumpled baht notes from their pockets and meandered away into the rain. A couple slid inside the dark interior of the bar, to enjoy the striptease show.

Alexi found himself staring into the man's un-blinking eyes. They were emerald green, and as cold and hard as the gemstones they resembled. His face had the tan skin and dark stubble of a local, an expat who could no longer bother to shave or slather on sunscreen on a daily basis. There was a slight hol-lowness to his features, a haunted shadow that hung over his face, beneath his short, swept-back brown hair.

'You heard the lady – short time only,' the man said. His voice was low, but it cut through the noise of the rain like a steel blade. 'There are hundreds of girls working the street, and in weather like this, I'm sure you can have your pick.'

Alexi stared at the man for a second. 'Take your hand off me,' he said, enunciating each word.

The man removed his hand. Alexi squinted at him. 'Who the hell are you? Have we met?'

The man looked Alexi in the eye and shook his head. 'No. You don't know me.'

Alexi glared at the man and looked him up and down.

The man was known by many names throughout town. Few knew his true identity. In Pattaya, most knew him as Mark Waters, a shady *farang* expat with a questionable source of income and an intimidating stare that tended to silence unwanted questions.

His real name was Thomas Caine.

'Let's drink,' Caine said. 'This day is shitty enough as it is.' He gestured to the bartender, and she hurriedly prepared two vodkas on ice.

Alexi let go of Naiyana. She took a few steps back, but did not leave the bar.

'Something about you looks familiar,' Alexi said.

Caine shook his head. 'I said you don't know me. I don't know who you are either, and I don't really care. Do you want a drink or not?'

'Come on, baby,' Naiyana pleaded with Alexi. 'Let's go upstairs. We have good time. I lots of fun, you see!' He ignored her.

A shadow crossed the bar. Caine looked up and saw a second man step up behind the Russian. He was taller, and his arms and shoulders bulged with thick ropes of muscles beneath a skin-tight black T-shirt.

Caine sighed.

'Who I am is not so important, I guess,' Alexi said. 'But please, meet Gregor. Gregor is happy to make your acquaintance. And you will see, he is very important man.'

The bartender slid the two drinks over to Caine and Alexi. Alexi ignored his. Caine picked up his and took a long sip. 'Funny, he doesn't look it.'

Alexi laughed. Gregor took a step forward. 'Well, my friend, when the police fish you out of the gutter with a face full of broken teeth, maybe you will change your mind.'

Alexi threw some bills on the counter. 'But, please, first enjoy your drink. It's on me.'

He stormed out of the bar, leaving Gregor behind. The big man cracked his knuckles and stepped toward Caine.

3

As Gregor moved in to strike, Caine held the base of his glass in his right hand and swung it against the bar. The glass shattered, leaving a pair of jagged, glittering shards attached to the base.

Gregor was huge, but he moved like a diesel truck. Caine watched the muscles in his assailant's shoulders compress as the man wound back for a punch. Like a tree felled by a lumberjack, Gregor's massive right arm swung through the air in a powerful blow, but he had telegraphed the direction of the attack.

Using a small, lightning-fast movement, Caine slid left and stepped inward, closing the gap. The punch sailed past the right side of his head, just missing his face. He kept his right arm up tight against his face as a guard.

As Gregor's momentum carried him forward, Caine struck with his left fist, landing two quick rabbit punches to the man's right side. *With any luck*, he thought, *I'll bruise the bastard's liver and end the fight quickly.*

The big man struggled to regain his balance. Caine pivoted and lashed out with the broken glass. The weapon sliced across Gregor's forehead. Naiyana, still watching from the sidelines, screamed as a curtain of red blood spilled down the big man's face.

Gregor roared in fury. He charged forward, lashing out wildly with his powerful arms, but the blood in his eyes blinded him. Caine ducked under the wild swings, throwing the broken bottle aside. He waited... waited... At last, Gregor paused, panting from exertion. Caine saw his opening and struck.

He punched straight out with his left hand. The jab struck Gregor's chin. Caine winced as he felt the crushing blow against his knuckles, but he didn't slow his assault. He leaped forward, following the punch with a swift right elbow strike. Gregor stumbled backward. He reached up, wiping the blood from his face. His eyes were clear now, and they gleamed at Caine with a hateful stare.

Caine threw a right hook, but this time Gregor was ready for him. He blocked the punch with an outside left hand and hooked it around Caine's arm in the process. As Caine struggled to free his arm, the big man sliced in with his elbow, knocking Caine's face left, then right.

The power of the two blows was immense. Caine stumbled back as Gregor let go of his arm. The force of the second elbow strike had spun him around. He fought to clear the haze in his mind as he felt two strong arms wrap around his chest.

The grip tightened, and he was heaved into the air. He gasped and coughed as his breath was driven from his lungs. The grip tightened even more, and a red haze fell over his vision. He kicked his feet backward, but they dangled uselessly in the air. He couldn't make contact with Gregor's knees or shins – and even if he could, he doubted he could strike with enough force to make the beast of a man release his hold.

Gregor grunted again and ratcheted his arms tighter together. Caine felt the pressure compress his ribs and knew they would crack if the man heaved him up into the air again.

He reached out with his arms, struggling to grab something, anything he could use as a weapon against Gregor. His flailing hand felt cold glass and liquid: Alexi's drink. The man had refused to touch it before he had slinked away. Caine grabbed the glass and swung over his shoulder, striking Gregor's wounded face.

Gregor roared in pain. The vodka washed across the bloody gash in his forehead, sending a spasm of stinging pain through the huge man's face.

He did not release his grip, but his arms involuntarily flexed as the pain ran through his body. Caine slid down a few inches, and he felt his feet touch the floor.

He swung his head backward, and the top of his skull smashed into Gregor's nose. The man uttered something between a groan and a sneeze and dropped Caine. As Caine hit the ground, Gregor stumbled backward a few steps, cradling his broken nose. Rivulets of blood streamed between his fingers.

Caine sucked a lungful of breath and spun around, wasting no time in pressing the attack. With Gregor's hands occupied, Caine leaped to his feet and swung his left leg forward in a savage kick to the man's solar plexus. Gregor bent forward, grunting as the kick knocked the wind out of him.

Standing over Gregor, Caine grabbed a beer bottle off the bar counter. He swung it straight down, smashing it onto Gregor's skull. The glass exploded, lacerating his fingers and burying tiny sparkling fragments into Gregor's head.

Gregor collapsed to the ground like a rag doll.

A low groan escaped his lips, and then he was silent. Unmoving.

Caine stood where he was, panting. *I've gotten sloppy*, he thought. *Stupid*. There was no reason for the fight to have gone on as long as it had. No reason for it to have started in the first place. He could have handled it a million different ways. Why had he chosen violence?

No, he thought. *Don't lie to yourself. This is who you are. This is why you can't go home.*

This is why you had to leave her. Rebecca...

'He dead?' Naiyana asked in a quiet voice, interrupting Caine's thoughts.

He looked at Gregor's body and shook his head.

'I don't know. But if he's not, he's gonna be pissing blood when he wakes up.'

A stream of Thai profanity erupted from the beautiful girl's mouth. Caine couldn't understand most of it, but obviously she was upset.

'Hey, Naiyana, just calm down. It will be...' He

held up his hands and noticed the blood streaming from the gashes left by the shattered glass.

Sirens howled in the distance. Their mournful wailing grew closer. Caine knew what that meant. The Royal Police were on their way. He had bribed the police in the past – payoffs to look the other way when he smuggled shipments of counterfeit hand-bags or stolen iPhones. But a body, a violent altercation, blood... He couldn't take the chance that they might arrest him, even temporarily, and run his prints.

'Come, come, follow me,' Naiyana said. 'We go out the back!'

Caine followed her into the bar. She grabbed a clean towel from the kitchen as she herded him toward the rear service door. 'Here, wrap your hand.'

Caine nodded and wound the white cloth around the gashes in his hand. The towel was quickly stained a mottled shade of pink as his blood soaked through the rag.

'What wrong with you? You crazy?' Naiyana muttered.

'Something was off about that guy,' Caine said. 'You saw it yourself. That's why you wouldn't go back to his hotel room.'

The beautiful girl nodded as they turned the

corner in the small corridor that led behind the kitchen. 'He bad man I think, but I talk him into short time. We bang; he leave. Now instead, big mess. And where I find another guy in this weather? I got kid to feed, you know!'

'I know, Naiyana. I'm sorry. I was just worried for you.'

Naiyana opened the rear door, and the thick, hot air from outside exploded into the corridor. Caine squinted out into the alley that ran behind the bar. It was as devoid of life as the flooded streets out front.

Naiyana put her hand on his face, and her expression softened. 'You are good man, I know.'

Caine shook his head. 'No, Naiyana. I'm not a good man.'

'You good to me. You look out for me, other girls, too. But sometimes, when I look in your eyes...' She hesitated. 'Sometimes, I see something inside you, looking back at me. Something scary.'

The sirens outside grew louder. The beautiful girl leaned in close, and her skin smelled of baby oil and jasmine. She kissed his cheek. 'You go now. Take care of hand. Stay low for while. I come see you later, OK?'

Caine nodded. 'Right.'

He headed out into the rain.

'Hey!' Naiyana called after him.

He turned and saw her leaning in the doorway. Her smile was radiant, and for a second, he felt as if the sun had managed to pierce the clouds above with its dazzling rays. 'Thank you,' she said. 'You good friend to me.'

He waved and started away, quickening his pace. Within a few minutes, the bar, the blood, and the body of the big Russian man were all left in the gloom behind him.

4

Caine stared out the window of his small, sparse apartment. The place was clean, to the point of being sterile. No art hung on the walls; no pictures of family or loved ones sat on his desk. He never knew if he would have to leave in a hurry, so he kept his furniture and belongings to a minimum. The place felt empty.

The building was far enough away from the pedestrian street that the noise of the crowds was usually a distant murmur. But tonight, the only sound he heard was rain pelting the windows and the muddy streets below.

He watched the sheets of water run down the

cracked pane of glass. The streetlights reflected a halo of red and green circles in the droplets on the window. He thought about what had happened earlier in the day. The fight. The blood.

Naiyana had said he was a good friend. Caine wasn't sure that was true. He looked back over his past, the things he had done. The lives he had taken. All in the interest of preserving democracy.

He suppressed a grim laugh. The interests he had been preserving were those of his handler, a high-level case officer in the CIA. Him, and other men like him. They claimed they were acting for the greater good, and Caine had believed them. Over the years, he had seen the cost their vision of the future claimed in blood, a cost they relied on others to pay. Caine had begun to wonder if the price was too high.

It had been Rebecca, a woman he had worked with briefly in the CIA, who had awoken something in him... the ability to feel again, the desire to see more in himself. To be more than just a weapon, a blunt instrument sent out to murder.

Their affair was brief, but in their time together she had touched him. Changed him. But it was that love, that desire to change, that forced him to remove her from his life.

Caine was betrayed.

To cover up an unsanctioned black op, his handler arranged to have Caine and his partner disappear.

Caine saw his partner murdered in cold blood, gunned down by the targets they were sent to eliminate. Caine managed to survive the attack but suffered through a period of brutal captivity and torture. And when he finally escaped and returned home, he discovered the ultimate betrayal. His country believed that he was the traitor responsible for his partner's murder.

He knew that any further contact with Rebecca would only put her in danger. He had brought death to her doorstep. The only way to keep her safe was to allow others to believe him dead. So he disappeared.

Caine knew how to survive off the grid. He used his contacts and criminal connections to make a meager living on the outskirts of society. He had been trained to operate invisibly, leaving as little sign of his presence as possible. It wasn't a fulfilling life, but it kept him and those he cared about safe.

Deep down, he feared that all the bloodshed, all the pain and suffering he had caused, was a curse. He could never escape it. No matter how far he ran,

violence and death were always just a few steps behind him.

Now, violence had followed him to Naiyana.

There was a knock on the door.

Caine paced across the studio apartment. He
peeled back a small piece of tape that covered the
peephole in the door. The tape was a security precaution. It kept people outside from being able to
look through and track his movements, watching for
him to block the light.

Looking through the tiny fisheye lens, he saw
Naiyana standing in the dark hallway. She cradled a
bag of groceries in her arms. He opened the door.

'Naiyana, you know you don't have to—'

The beautiful girl rolled her eyes. '*Kho phak kon*,
just let me in.' Caine smiled as she pushed past him
and entered the apartment.

'Cops give you a hard time?' he asked as he shut
the door behind her. 'Did the Russians come back?'

'Cops come, ask questions. I flirt, they leave, just
like always. And you know how many Russians we
get in bar? They all the same, think their money
make them kings. I can handle them.' She set the
groceries down on the counter and surveyed the
room. 'You been living here how long? Place always
look empty. You need a plant!'

Caine laughed. 'Trust me, plants aren't my specialty.'

Naiyana gave him a hug, and Caine winced as her arms brushed against his ribs. She looked him over with concern and wrinkled her nose. 'Still sore, huh? You smell like *khîi*. You take hot shower. I cook.'

Caine didn't speak much Thai, but he knew the word '*khîi*.' It meant excrement. He locked the door, replaced the tape, and trudged toward the bathroom.

'You hungry tonight?' Naiyana called from the kitchen.

'Starving!' Caine shouted back as he stripped off his sweaty shirt and turned on the shower.

'Good. I cook lots. Keep you healthy for next time you fight.'

Caine stuck his head out the door as he waited for the shower to warm up. 'What makes you think there's a next time?'

He heard pots and pans clattering in the kitchen. Naiyana leaned out and smiled at him. 'Men like you, always a fight.'

Caine shook his head, closed the bathroom door, and stepped under the scalding hot water.

A few minutes later, he was showered and seated at a tiny folding table they set up near the kitchen. Naiyana had cooked a simple green curry, and the smells of cumin, ginger, and chicken wafted through the apartment. Somehow, the smells of Naiyana's cooking transformed the small, spartan space into something else. To Caine, for the couple of hours she was there, the empty apartment became a home.

Caine lifted his chopsticks to his mouth and devoured another bite of the spicy dish. He washed it down with a sip of cold beer from a frosted glass. 'How's your brother doing?' he asked.

Naiyana made a clicking sound with her tongue. 'Oh, Taavi? So much trouble, that one. He get into a fight today, too. Black eye.' A look of concern flashed across Caine's face, but Naiyana smiled and shook her head. 'Don't worry, nothing serious. Just boys being boys.'

Caine looked up at her as he shoveled more food in his mouth. 'If you say so. Just make sure he keeps away from the street gangs.'

Naiyana took a sip of beer and pushed at the food on her plate with her chopsticks. 'He crazy, but not stupid. I tell him you won't be there to save him next time.'

'I didn't save him,' Caine said. 'I just talked to some people. Made them see it was in their best interest to leave him alone.' Caine smiled, but a dark glint flashed in his green eyes.

Naiyana smacked his hand. 'Don't be so modest! You save his life. I owe you.'

Taavi was Naiyana's younger brother, a street thief who sold tourists cheap trinkets, and sometimes lifted their wallets in the process. He had run into trouble with the organized crime gangs that ran the area. Caine had used his connections – and a few well-placed threats – to straighten things out.

After that, Naiyana showed up at his door, offering to reward him the only way she knew how. He turned her down. He was lonely, and she was beautiful, but it just didn't feel right. The next day, she showed up with a basket of fresh chicken and vegetables from the market. Again, he tried to turn her away, but without saying a word, she brushed past him into his tiny, dismal apartment. She found her way to the kitchen and cooked him dinner.

She had repeated this simple act of kindness once a week, every week since. Now, he looked forward to Naiyana's home-cooked meals and their conversation afterwards. Somehow, she had become his closest friend, despite the fact that she knew nothing about him or his past.

When Caine's plate was clean, Naiyana poured him another beer and cleared the table. She turned from the sink and watched as Caine sat down on the small bed, wincing in pain.

Naiyana walked over and sat next to him, her face filled with concern. 'Hey, you hurt bad, huh?'

'I'm fine,' Caine said. 'Just need some rest.'

Naiyana shook her head. 'Let me see. Shirt off, now.'

'Naiyana, I—'

'No buts,' she snapped. 'Shirt off, lie down. Now!'

Caine sighed but did as she said. Naiyana whistled as her eyes danced over Caine's toned, muscular abdomen. The skin above his ribs was mottled with ugly purple bruises.

'Big, strong man, huh? That other guy bigger, though. He mess you up. Wait here.'

Naiyana got up and rummaged through her purse. She grabbed a tube of ointment and sat back down, straddling Caine's body. Caine shifted, trying to push her off.

'Naiyana, come on.'

The beautiful girl laughed and pointed her finger at him. 'Hey, don't get any funny ideas. Serious business here!' She began to rub the ointment on his bruises. Caine gritted his teeth as her fingers pressed into the sore, tender flesh.

'My mother use this ointment on my father, after

tree fall on him,' Naiyana said. 'Now, I use it when I dance. Good stuff, it help.'

'Thank you, I appreciate it.'

She shook her head. 'I keep telling you, it nothing. You help me; I help you.'

Naiyana's finger traced the small white scar that sat just above his chest, near his shoulder. 'What happen here?'

Caine sat up, and Naiyana shifted her weight off of him. She sat next to him on the bed.

'That happened a long time ago. In Japan.'

Naiyana picked her beer up from the floor and took a sip. 'Another fight?'

Caine ran his fingers through his hair. 'Not exactly. I tried to help someone. Things got complicated.'

'But you did help them?'

'Yeah. I did.'

'You save their life, too, I bet. I told you. You good man; you do good things.'

Caine exhaled. 'Listen, it's getting late, and I'm exhausted. You should go. Make sure your brother gets home safe.'

Naiyana met his gaze. Her deep brown eyes were warm and seemed to smile with a life of their own.

'Why do you fight for me?' she asked in a soft

voice. 'Other guys, they want this, or they want that. You don't want anything. You help me, look out for me, look out for my brother. All I do is cook you dinner.'

Caine stood up and put on his shirt. 'Today, you said you saw something in me, something scary?'

Naiyana nodded. 'Sometimes. But that not all I see.'

Caine sighed. 'At night, I have dreams. Nightmares, terrible things. Things I've done.' Caine touched the scar on his shoulder. 'That person I told you about, the one I helped?'

Naiyana nodded.

'Used to be, that memory was enough to keep the nightmares away. Not anymore. But when you come here, somehow I feel at peace...'

'No nightmares,' Naiyana said.

Caine nodded. 'You're a good friend to me, too, Naiyana.'

'I'm glad,' she said as she stood up and slung her purse over her shoulder. She kissed Caine on the cheek. 'Remember, good and bad in all of us. Yin and yang. People look at me; they see bad things, too. But I see more. You need to see more in you.'

Caine called her a cab, and she left his apartment, smiling at him one last time as he shut the door behind her.

That night, the sound of the rain and the throbbing pain in his muscles kept him awake for several hours. But when he finally drifted to sleep, he was at peace.

He did not dream. He slept like the dead.

5

The rain continued to drench Pattaya the following day. That afternoon, Caine met with a contact at a beer bar just off the walking street to discuss a possible business opportunity. His contact was a small, unassuming man who wore round glasses and a white linen suit. His name was Eugene Lee, and he owned a factory in Taiwan that was churning out replica Rolex watches.

With a flourish of his hands, Lee set a sample of his wares on the bar counter. He beamed with pride. 'Real one made in Switzerland, cost many, many baht. This one use Japanese movement, only 100 baht!'

Caine sipped his drink and looked around to

make sure they were unobserved. The place was dead, the rain continuing to drive away customers. He hefted the watch in his hands. The workmanship looked good. The second hand moved in a smooth, continuous sweep, rather than the choppy ticking motion of the cheaper counterfeits.

He set the sample back down on the bar. 'Save the sales pitch. My job is to get them into the country. Selling them is your problem.'

Caine threw some cash down on the counter. 'That's for the drinks. Let me know when you have enough merchandise to move. Oh, and some free advice? There's only one "x" in Rolex.'

After he left the meeting, Caine walked down a series of back alleys and side streets. He kept away from the main drag just in case the Royal Police were still looking for him. He doubted they would bother to keep looking for a *farang* who had beaten another *farang* in what would surely be reported as a bar fight over a girl. And Caine had some pull with the Pattaya cops, since he was giving Police Chief Battang a cut of his smuggling revenue. Still, he saw no point in taking chances.

As he walked through the rain-drenched streets, Caine felt a familiar sensation, one he knew intimately. A tingling on the back of his neck, a feeling that something was wrong. A half-heard sound, a barely glimpsed shadow, something observed on the edge of his sensory awareness told him he was not alone. He was being followed.

Caine continued walking at the same pace, giving no indication to his tail that he knew anything was wrong. He turned a corner and exploded into motion, leaping over a fence made of rusted chicken wire and wooden rods. He found himself in the backyard of a tiny apartment complex. Rows of colorful sarongs and other laundry hung from a line, now soaked by the rain. Caine wondered why the owner had not brought them in once the rain had started. An empty chicken coop took up the far corner of the muddy yard, and deep puddles of murky water dotted the ground.

The place seemed to be abandoned. Caine was silent as he moved around the puddles and wedged himself in a dark, tiny space behind the chicken coop. The wood of the coop was cracked and weathered. By looking through a hole in one of the side planks, he could see through the fence and observe the alley path. He doubted whoever was following him would be able to spot him.

A few seconds later, Caine heard the splashing of footsteps making their way down the alley. A lone figure stood across from the abandoned apartment building, looking left and right, as if trying to determine which way Caine had gone.

Caine didn't recognize the man. He was a local, with black hair and a young but tempered face. He looked over average height, and he was wearing a black waxed jacket over jeans. His clothes were soaked from the falling rain.

After a few minutes, the man gave up and walked further down the alley. Caine waited a moment, then leaped back over the fence. Dropping into a crouch, he stalked down the alley until he caught sight of the man. Caine had a strong aversion to people following him, and he found himself consumed by a paranoid flame of anger. Who was this man? What did he want with him? Was he another of the Russian's goons? The Royal Police? Or had the CIA finally caught up with him? Which of his many enemies had chosen to take action against him?

There was only one way to be sure.

Caine closed the distance between him and the Thai man. The alley was ending up ahead, and he had only a few seconds to make his move before they would exit onto a main street. As he moved, Caine's foot slipped on a patch of mud and dropped into a shallow puddle with an audible splash.

Caine muttered a silent curse.

The man spun around, his arm dropping to his rear waistband. But Caine was already moving. He slid to the man's side and slapped his reaching arm down and away. At the same time, he pivoted forward, driving a straight punch to the man's face. As his target staggered backward, Caine slammed his forearm against the man's throat and pushed him into a tiny alcove between two buildings, out of view of the street. His target grunted in pain as his back slammed against a brick wall.

Whoever the man was, he had good training. He threw up his left arm and twisted to the side, trying to break free of the pressure Caine's arm was exerting on his throat. Caine kept him pinned against the wall and drove his knee up, striking into the man's solar plexus and forcing the air from his lungs in a gasp of pain.

Caine spun the man around and slammed his arm down on the back of his neck. Using his free hand, he did a quick frisk of the target's waistband and removed a Glock 19 9mm. He scanned the alley again to confirm they were alone, then pressed the gun's barrel against the man's spine.

'You have something you want to say to me?' Caine hissed. 'Spit it out.'

The man coughed and sputtered as Caine increased the pressure against his neck. 'You Mark Waters, right? My name Satra, Satra Watana. Detective Watana. Chief Battang told me look for you.'

Caine pressed harder, slamming the man's face against the brick wall. 'Bullshit!'

'It's true,' Satra gasped. 'Check ID. Jacket pocket.'

Caine slipped the pistol into his waistband and used his free hand to frisk the man's jacket. Sure enough, his fingers touched a slim leather badge case. He pulled it out, flipped it open, and found himself staring at a shiny metal badge, engraved with the symbol of the Royal Police.

He tossed the badge onto the sodden ground. 'Fine. Tell Battang I pay him and I pay him well. His cut's not getting any bigger, no matter how many dirty cops he sends my way.'

The man shook his head, sending a spray of rain droplets through the air. 'No, not like that. I'm clean, dammit. Good cop! Battang said you have skills, training. You outsider. You can help me.'

'Help you do what?'

'Girls missing. Kidnapped. You can help me find them.'

'What girls?' Caine growled.

'Bar girls. Girls no one miss.'

Caine eased up the pressure on his throat. 'Battang said to find me? Why? Why would I help you?'

The man coughed. 'He say you strange man. Maybe you will help; maybe you won't. Police can't do anything. But I watch you. I see you fight for that girl other day. I see you keep an eye on her. You protect her. These girls... no one looking out for them. Just me.'

Caine dropped his arm and stepped back. 'If you're lying to me, I swear...'

The man fell to the muddy ground, spitting and gasping for breath. He looked up at Caine, and his dark brown eyes burned hot with anger. Then the anger faded into a calm, determined stare. He took a deep breath, stood up, and looked Caine in the eye. 'No lie. Follow me. We talk. I buy you beer.'

Caine sighed and gestured to the street. 'Fine. Let's go.'

They stepped out of the alley. Satra groaned as he raised his arm to hail a taxi.

'You want my advice?' Caine asked. 'Next time lead with the free beer.'

6

Satra took them to a local bar on the outskirts of the city. If the place had a name, Caine didn't know it. There was no sign outside, and no writing on the old, peeling door.

Inside, it was little more than a shack, filled with long, splintering wood tables and round stools. An old tube television was mounted in the far corner, and a Muay Thai kickboxing match was playing on the blurry screen. The excited cheers of the audience pierced the quiet mumbling of the locals who sat at the bar. The only other sounds were the rain outside and the clinking of liquor bottles tipping into glasses.

Caine walked ahead of Satra and chose a stool

that faced the entrance. The bartender, a middle-aged man with a copper-tanned face and skin like leather, shouted for their order from behind the counter. Caine ordered a Singha beer, and Satra asked for a glass of Mekong spirit – a sort of Thai whisky – on the rocks.

A fresh-faced teenage girl wearing jeans and a T-shirt brought them their drinks. Satra spoke to her in rapid-fire Thai. She nodded, memorizing his order.

As she rushed back to the kitchen, Satra turned to Caine. 'You like bar food? I order *gap klaem*, small plates. We eat, then we talk.'

Caine nodded and scanned the bar. He saw no sign of danger, so he watched the kickboxing match as he sipped his cold beer.

The food arrived quickly. *Gap klaem*, or 'drinking snacks', consisted of a variety of small dishes that were almost always served alongside alcohol in bars. The girl set down several plates, and Caine and Satra began snacking on bites of *yam khai kem*, a cold salad of pickled hardboiled eggs. A few minutes later, Caine's throat was burning from the spicy heat of *pu pad prik pao*, crab cakes fried with egg and a hot pepper paste.

Caine cooled his fiery tongue with a long sip of

beer, then set the bottle on the table. 'I appreciate the meal, but I don't like being followed. What's this all about?'

Satra was silent for a moment. Then he took a long drink of his spirit before pulling out his cell phone.

'Here, look at this.' He swiped through a series of photos. They were pictures of Thai girls, bar girls from the looks of them. All the photos appeared to be from some kind of dating site. The site's name, Thai Angels, was written in gold letters at the top of the page. Beneath each girl's photo was a heart symbol, and next to the heart was a number.

'I was investigating a missing person case. Bar girl, just twenty years old, didn't show up for work one day. Her roommate call the police when landlord complain that missing girl no pay her share of rent.'

Caine leaned back in his chair. 'Satra, come on, you're a cop. You know as well as I do these girls take off all the time. Maybe she went back home, or she's on vacation with a boyfriend.'

Satra shook his head. His dark eyes looked earnest and concerned, and he furrowed his brow. 'I think that, too, but then our technical investigation turn up this website. These are just screen captures, real website vanish, get taken down weeks ago.'

Caine looked at the pictures on the phone. 'Is one of these your missing girl?'

Satra set the phone on the table. 'This her.' He swiped to a candid shot of a beautiful Thai girl. She was standing outside a bar, smiling at tourists in the streets. She was dressed in a skin-tight red baby tee and black patent leather hot shorts.

'Look here.' Satra pointed to the heart symbol beneath her picture. The number next to the heart was 150. 'On real site, you could vote for how much you like a girl's picture. If you like how she look, you give her hearts.'

'So your girl was popular. She's pretty, no big mystery there.'

Satra nodded. He swiped through more photos. 'All these girls on same site. This girl missing.' He swiped to another photo. 'This girl missing, too. And this one...' He continued swiping through a series of eight pictures. All the girls were beautiful, young, and dressed for work. Caine didn't recognize any of them, but he noticed that all the photos were candid shots, taken with a telephoto lens.

'All pretty, all bar girls, all missing. And look at

hearts.' Caine saw that the heart count beneath each missing girl was high. 155, 129, 140...

'Every girl with hearts over one hundred is missing,' Satra said. 'This no coincidence. Thai Angels is no dating site. These girls are being targeted.'

'Targeted by who?' Caine asked.

Satra's eyes darted around the bar, and he lowered his voice. 'I don't know. Website go down soon after we find it. I start talking to girls, asking around. Putting pressure on dealers, street punks, anyone with links to *chao pho* families. You pay them off as well, yes?'

Caine nodded. The *chao pho* families were a loose collection of patron-run crime cartels. They were the de facto controllers of organized crime in the cities of Thailand, and anyone operating a business, legitimate or otherwise, was almost certainly paying a cut to the family that controlled their territory.

'You think the *chao pho* put up this website?' Caine asked. 'I know some of the families are involved in human trafficking, but this doesn't really seem their style. Too high profile. Too much risk.'

Satra nodded. 'Maybe you right. But soon after I start questioning, the investigation is stopped. I ordered to drop case.'

Caine squinted as he sipped his beer. 'Dropped? Why?'

'You remember the bombing, couple weeks ago?'

'Yeah. Muslim extremists, according to your National Police Chief. He paid the entire department a reward out of his own pocket, right? I thought you had the suspect in custody.'

'Yes, he pay reward to himself and other officers. Sugar to ease bad taste of medicine. He make big announcement, say case solved, everything OK. But that was all lie.'

Satra took another sip of his drink. 'The day of explosion, police received a note. Says to lay off the *chao pho* investigation. Stop searching for girls, or there will be more bombs. More explosions. Note was written in blood of a policeman, man working with me. Man asking questions. Good man. He missing now, too.'

'So why aren't the Royal Police going after whoever is responsible? You'd think they'd be even more driven to catch these guys now.'

Satra shook his head. 'In Thailand, tourist industry is everything. Justice, the law, lives of few bar girls... these mean nothing compared to the millions of dollars tourism bring here. If more bombs explode in city, more tourists are killed... tourists go away. Money go away.'

He sighed, then clenched his hand in a fist. 'I know you don't trust cops. Many cops here are bad, dirty. They are poor, their salary is very little, not enough to raise a family. So they take money, look the other way. But not me. My father was police officer. And his father before him. I cannot just let this go. This in my blood.'

He leaned across the table. 'But I am only one man. Chief Battang refuse to let me use police resources to find these girls. He afraid if I caught, it look like police support investigation again. But you... you have skills, training. I see you fight that man. You have connections to *chao pho*. You can help me. You can help these girls.'

Caine was silent. He finished his beer and quietly set the bottle down on the table. He stared at Satra, then looked away. 'Satra, I can't get involved in something like this. And believe me, I'd only make it worse if I did.'

Satra stared at Caine. 'And what about the missing girls? If they leave Thailand, no one see them again.'

Caine stood up. 'Satra, you seem like a good guy,

so take my advice. Listen to your chief, drop this case, and stop playing hero.'

'You can give up so easily? You can just walk away?'

'I heard you out. I gave you an answer. The answer is no. Don't follow me again.'

Caine fished a few crumpled baht notes from his pocket and dropped them on the table.

'Here. Drinks are on me.'

He turned and walked out of the bar, back into the muggy, hot air, the gray skies, and the falling rain. He walked a few blocks, letting the droplets of water soak through his hair and clothes. He forced himself to forget Satra's words, and the images of the missing girls. He did not look over his shoulder as he walked through the wet, muddy streets. He knew Satra would not follow. It had all been a silly mistake.

In his heart, he knew he was not the man Satra was looking for. Now, Satra knew it as well.

7

A few days later, the rain stopped, and Pattaya sprang back to life. That night, the neon lights blazed above the heads of the tourist crowd as they meandered up and down Soi Six and the other walking streets in the area. Each and every soul wandering beneath that explosion of color and light was seeking something in the hot, humid night air: cheap beer, cheap food, cheap sex.

For those seeking all of the above, Ruby's Club did not disappoint. Now that the rain had stopped, Ruby's was going out of its way to make up for lost time. Beer and drink specials were advertised all night, and the club bussed in girls from other bars to work extra shifts.

Naiyana smiled as she spun around the chrome pole above the main stage. She was naked, with her neon bikini top and briefs scattered on the stage below her. As she twirled around, she saw a kaleidoscope of colorful lights and faces, laughing and cheering in the shadows. The applause and music were deafening. The spinning lights danced across her body, reflecting bursts of color in the sweat, oil, and glitter that covered her skin.

Sometimes she found herself overcome with the energy and excitement of the crowd. The men, the girls, the lust and decadence in the air... sometimes she could feed off it, drawing strength from the wild, chaotic currents of energy. Other times, that same chaos seemed to feed off her instead, devouring her piece by piece.

But tonight was a good night. She felt alive, happy. With so many men in the bar, the odds were good that a few would be young, good-looking *farang*. Men with kind smiles and fat wallets that would be more than satisfied to pay for an hour of her time. The money meant little to them, but for her and her family, it was all that kept them going. It was food for her daughter, a roof over her mother's head, medicine for her father. Her family never asked her how she provided all these things for them. They already knew, for there was only one possible answer. To speak of it would be rude and shameful.

Naiyana shimmied to the top of the pole and flipped upside down, hanging on with her strong, tan legs. She closed her eyes, feeling the pulse of bass vibrate over her hot, naked skin. Her thick, dark mane of hair swung through the air below her. She flexed her thighs, allowing her body to slide down the pole, slowly spiraling around it as she fell. When her hands touched the ground, she did a quick flip off the pole. She smiled, bent over, and gathered her clothes and a few crumpled baht notes from the stage. The music skipped to a new song, signaling that another girl's show was about to start.

Naiyana left the stage and headed for the bar. She slipped back into her bikini as she pushed through the crowd. She felt men touching her, grabbing at her, but she ignored their groping hands and kept a wide smile plastered on her face.

She took a seat at the corner of the bar, and the bartender set a glass of club soda down in front of her. She sipped the cool liquid as she surveyed the crowd. After weeks of slow nights, she was anxious to book some short time. A handsome, young *farang* would be nice, but right now anyone would do.

'You breaking my heart,' a deep voice shouted into her ear. 'Beautiful woman like you should not sit alone.'

She glanced back and found herself staring into a pair of large blue eyes, set in a harsh, angular face. It took her a moment to recognize the man. It was the Russian, the one from the other day. Her friend had beaten the man's hired thug to a bloody pulp. She smiled, but her eyes darted around the bar, searching the crowd for the two large bouncers that were working that night.

The Russian saw her anxious eyes and smiled. 'Please, let me buy you drink. I wish to apologize. My behavior the other night... I was not exactly the gentleman, yes? Too much cheap vodka, I'm afraid.'

Naiyana looked sideways at the Russian as she sipped her club soda. He seemed calmer than before, but something in his gaze still set her nerves on edge. *It's not the lazy eye*, she thought. It was the intensity of his stare, the hunger behind those bright blue orbs set in such a dark, hard face. They reminded her of a wild dog in the street, eyeing a hunk of meat.

Alexi snapped his fingers and held up a thick wad of baht notes. Naiyana eyed the stack of cash with an equally hungry gaze. The bartender took notice; within a few minutes, a vodka on ice and another lady drink for Naiyana were set down in front of them.

Drink in hand, Naiyana spun on her stool to meet Alexi's intense stare head-on.

'Your friend OK?' she asked.

Alexi laughed as he nodded. 'Gregor? Yes, yes, he's fine. He has a few new scars, but he deserved it, no? He's a bit over-protective of me, I'm afraid. His father and mine are old friends, so we are like brothers.'

She sipped her drink again, turning everything over in her mind. The bar was full; there were plenty of potential customers. But this man had money. And he desired her. He seemed to think himself important, and in her experience self-important men tended not to last long in bed. She would be back downstairs in twenty minutes or less, with plenty of time to approach more men.

She smiled and drank, pretending to listen to Alexi as he boasted of his family's heritage back in Russia. Her mind was far away, doing a series of mental calculations. And the final equation was the same as it always was. She didn't like this man – but that didn't matter in the slightest.

She leaned over and let her hair graze the side of

Alexi's face. She rested her hand lightly on his thigh, curling her fingers between his legs. 'You handsome man. I like you. You want go upstairs, short time?'

Alexi blinked. His eyes no longer looked hungry. They looked cold and distant. But he stood up and wrapped his thick, muscular arm around her waist. He looked down at her and smiled. '*Da*. I thought you'd never ask.'

8

Caine pounded on the apartment door. Chips of red paint cracked and flaked off from the force of his blows. 'Satra, it's me. Get up!'

Caine looked left and right as he knocked on the door again. The dark, narrow hallway of the apartment complex was silent and empty. If anyone was awake, they didn't seem inclined to poke their head out to investigate the noise he was making. *In this part of town, that's probably a smart call*, Caine thought.

He raised his hand to knock again but stopped when he heard footsteps from inside. The sound of creaking wood grew louder as they approached the door. He heard the rattle of a deadbolt turning, then the door cracked open. A chain kept the door from swinging open all the way. Satra's face hovered into view behind the door. His eyes were half-closed, and his hair was mussed and disheveled.

'Waters? What the hell, man? You know what time it is?'

Caine slid his foot into the doorframe. 'We need to talk. Let me in.'

Satra blinked, rubbing his eyes. He squinted at Caine. 'Why? Thought you not interested in helping?'

'It's Naiyana. She's missing.'

'Who?'

'The girl at the bar. My friend. She's missing. She cooks me dinner every week, but this time she didn't show. The bartender where she works saw her go off with that Russian, Alexi. No one's seen her since.'

Satra sighed. He slid aside the security chain on the door and opened it wide enough for Caine to enter.

Caine scanned the hall one more time to make sure they were alone. A nagging voice inside his head screamed at him that this was a mistake. Cops, secret investigations, some kind of half-assed rescue... all of this was madness. He was in Thailand to lie low, not to court more death and violence.

Then he remembered Naiyana, smiling at him in the rain. '*You good friend to me*,' she had said.

Caine bit his lip to silence the voices in his head. He made his decision.

He was operational now. There was no more room for doubt. He stepped across the threshold into Satra's tiny apartment.

The Thai cop rubbed the sleep from his eyes and shut the door behind him. 'Welcome to my office, partner.'

* * *

A couple hours later, Caine paced back and forth inside the tiny apartment, sipping coffee from a stained yellow mug. There wasn't much room to walk, as the apartment was only a single room with a small adjoining kitchen. The windows were open, but no breeze stirred the threadbare curtains that hung over the sink. The place smelled like old take-out food and sweat.

Satra sat in front of a sagging table that he had converted into a makeshift desk. Its surface was covered with cardboard boxes and manila folders, all containing files related to the case. He had told

Caine that he had 'borrowed' them from HQ, without Chief Battang's knowledge.

Satra spoke a rapid stream of Thai into his cell phone. He listened for a second, nodding, then stood up and paced along with Caine. When he ended the call, he dropped down to a sitting position on the futon mattress that served as a bed in the tiny room.

'Anything?' Caine asked.

Satra rubbed his face briskly with his hands, then ran them through his hair. 'Word on street is new Russian Mafia family in town, looking to build pipeline to smuggle girls to the West. I believe you know one of them.'

'Alexi Rudov,' Caine snarled.

Satra nodded. 'If he buy these girls, they will leave Thailand in few days. No one has seen Alexi or Russians since they leave Ruby Club.'

'We have to find him.'

'I just talk to my contacts. Street people, hustlers, they tell me the truth. They see Rudov leave bar alone. No girl, no men.'

Caine nodded. 'Same story at the Hilton. He checked out a couple hours before he was spotted at Ruby's. None of my sources place him or the other men he was with at any new hotels in the last twenty-four hours.'

'Maybe she left club on her own? Like you said, bar girls disappear all the time.'

Caine shook his head. 'Not this one. She and I... We're close.'

Satra looked at Caine and raised an eyebrow. Caine shot him an angry glare.

'Not like that,' he said. 'We're friends. I helped her out once. That's all.'

'But you risk your life in bar fights, and now you help me in illegal investigation? All for this friend? Battang was right. You are strange.'

Caine set down the cup of coffee on Satra's desk and picked up a file folder. 'I was betrayed once. Betrayed by someone I trusted. Took me a long time to trust someone again.'

'And you trust her?'

Caine looked up and his green eyes glittered in the dim light. 'I said she's my friend. Now drop it.'

Satra nodded. 'OK, well, I thank you for helping. But it look like our lead goes cold.'

Caine flipped open the folder. It contained a series of photographs taken at the bombed floating market. Incinerated wood beams, black with soot, had collapsed into the muddy canal. The beautiful, long tail boats that once darted across the canal's surface like dragonflies were now torn, mangled shreds of flotsam and jetsam. The river water was stained black by ash.

And the bodies... They were burned and mangled almost beyond recognition. But to one who had seen such horrors before, their twisted, charred forms were instantly recognizable.

One by one, he flipped through the images of death and destruction. He coldly processed the information each picture contained.

'The lead may be cold, but not the case. If we can't find the Russians, then we work the other side. You said the Russians are here to take delivery of human cargo. So who is the trafficker?'

Satra looked up at him thoughtfully. 'We've never seen anything like this website before. But the most likely culprit would be a *chao pho* crime family.'

'Then it stands to reason they were behind the bombings.'

'Makes sense, sure. But which family? And where are they holding girls?'

Caine held up a picture. 'When you investigate a crime scene, you dust for fingerprints, right? Well, explosives leave their own kind of fingerprints. See all these black burn marks on the wood? That's excess carbon that didn't burn up in the explosion. Characteristic of trinitrotoluene.'

Satra sighed and glared at Caine. 'Also called TNT, yes? Our forensic lab is not backward, Mr. Waters. We already investigated that angle. TNT is very common industrial explosive. Many companies use it here in Thailand. Mining companies, chemical companies... Could have come from anywhere.'

Caine continued to flip through the pictures. He stopped at one that showed a mangled, twisted scrap of aluminum, with wires and electronics protruding like black, burned tendrils. He held up the picture for Satra to see. 'This is the detonator, isn't it?'

'We think so. Too damaged to say for sure, but it was found near center of blast. Not much left of it to go on.'

Caine nodded. 'It's badly damaged but look at this... See this scrap of tubing here? That's fiber optic cable. It used a laser pulse to detonate the explosive package. Highly reliable. Whoever set this off probably used a remote signal keyed from a cell phone. The signal triggers the laser, and detonation takes less than a millisecond.'

Satra stood and took the picture from Caine's hand. He examined it closely. 'We didn't catch that. How you be so sure? This just a picture of some scrap.'

Caine looked Satra in the eye. 'I've seen these devices before. Up close. Trust me, I know.'

'OK, so fancy detonator. Hard to find. Not many people that sell this stuff here in Thailand.'

Caine shook his head. 'No, not many at all. In fact, only one that I know of. I'll take the detonator lead. You keep looking for Alexi. I'll need a weapon.'

Satra opened a file box on his desk and removed a few dusty folders and stacks of paper. Underneath was a slim wood case. He lifted the lid and pulled out a battered old pistol, a Colt M1911. He handed the heavy gun to Caine. Caine gripped it and turned it side to side, hefting its weight.

'This my father's gun. He carrying it when he killed in line of duty.'

Caine tested the magazine eject button and slide. The gun was old and battered, but its mechanisms were smooth and well-maintained. The magazine slid out with a precise, metallic click. He nodded his approval. 'You've taken good care of it. Thank you.'

'We need understanding between us, Mr. Waters. I desperate; I come to you for help. I see you have skills. I see in your eyes, you dangerous. That good, we face dangerous men. But we face them and bring them in for justice. Not for revenge. We good?'

Caine slapped the magazine back into the pistol.

He thumbed the slide release lever and it slammed closed, readying the gun to fire. He slid the gun into his waistband and looked back at Satra.

'I'm not after justice or revenge, Satra. I'm just trying to help a friend. If you want my help, that will have to be good enough. Otherwise, I do this on my own. I'll call you if I find anything.'

Caine walked out of Satra's apartment, shutting the door behind him.

As he strolled down the dark, quiet corridor outside, he wondered if his words had been true. Finding Naiyana was his priority. But if those who had taken her had hurt her in any way...

He thought of the devastation he had seen in the pictures, of the innocent lives these men had already taken, and the new lives they were about to destroy. Caine knew that, when he found them, he would make them pay a price for the suffering they had caused. The price would be paid in blood and pain. But was that justice? Or revenge? Caine wasn't sure what to call it. He only knew it was a certainty.

That was good enough for him.

9

Eddy Ashikaga sighed as the beautiful young Thai girl standing above him pressed her fists into the knotted muscles on his back. He grunted as she began to knead the tight, sore flesh. 'You know, you're stronger than you look,' Eddy said, turning his head to smile at her.

The room was dark, and he could barely see the girl in the dim light. She was wearing a tight pink T-shirt with an anime cat on the front and skin-tight spandex shorts. The cat on the shirt was winking. 'I like your shirt,' he said.

She giggled and stopped the deep, kneading motion. Her fingers began to lightly dance over his tan skin. 'Thank you. You strong man. Sexy body,' she said in a high-pitched voice.

Eddy laughed. His scrawny, middle-aged body was not his or anyone else's definition of sexy. At forty-five, his jet-black hair had developed a generous dusting of white, and the bald spot in the center of his head was growing larger every year. The only other part of him that was growing was his gut.

But here, in a dark massage room, lying face down with a towel over his ass, he found himself inclined to believe the girl's sweet lies.

The girl's fingers brushed over his right arm, tracing the intricate lines of the dragon tattoo that curled around his bicep. 'Nice tattoo. Very sexy. You gangsta man?' she asked.

'Sure,' he yawned. 'Yakuza, you know? Japanese gangster. I'm a bad man.'

The girl began pushing down the towel. Her fingers drifted lower and lower. The soft, brushing touch moved down between his legs. 'You want special massage? 500 baht only.'

'Ah, *kimochii*,' Eddy said in Japanese. 'I like. Why else would I be here?'

The girl giggled again and removed the towel. 'OK, please turn over.'

A man's voice called out from the darkness. 'For

the love of God, please don't. Stay where you are, Eddy.'

The girl gasped. Eddy looked up, but the room was cloaked in shadows. 'What the...? Who the hell is that?'

With a click, light bathed the room. Caine sat on top of a stool next to the small table that held the girl's massage oil and other supplies. His back was against the wall, next to a curtain that led into a back room.

He was pointing a gun at Eddy's head.

'Ehhhh, wait, I know you,' Eddy said, pulling the towel back around his waist. 'Waters-san. Mark Waters, the Yoshizawa family's *gaijin* pet.'

The massage girl looked confused. Caine smiled at her, but his eyes were cold and focused on Eddy. 'He told you he was yakuza, right? That's only part of the story. Show her, Eddy.'

'Look, what is this—?' Eddy was cut off by the metallic click of Caine cocking his pistol.

'Show her,' Caine repeated.

Eddy sighed and pulled his right arm from under the towel. The girl gasped. Both his pinky and ring fingers were missing, severed at the first joint.

'You see,' Caine continued, 'it's true that Eddy here used to be a member of the yakuza. But they kicked him out years ago. He moved here and set up a nice little arms smuggling business for himself. Now, I've heard two conflicting stories about the missing fingers.'

'Come on, man. What the fu—'

'Version one is, Eddy sold the Yoshizawa family some explosives for a bank vault job, back in Japan. But the detonator was faulty and the charges didn't go off. The cops showed up, and Isato Yoshizawa's handpicked group of thieves, including his brother-in-law, got arrested and did hard time. Isato was so furious that he demanded two of poor Eddy's fingers as compensation, rather than just one.'

The girl began inching toward the door. 'I not know him. Please, I go now.'

'No,' Caine said in a loud, sharp voice. The girl froze. Caine's eyes softened, and he lowered his voice. 'I'm sorry. I promise I won't hurt you. But I need a few more minutes here undisturbed. Just sit tight, and this will all be over soon.'

The girl hesitated, then nodded. Caine looked back at Eddy.

'Now, the other version of the story – and I'm partial to this one – is that Eddy was building the bomb for Isato himself. But he got cheap and took some shortcuts. He used a home brew detonator, and he rushed the wiring. And wouldn't you know it? The damn thing blew up in his hand.'

Caine shook his head, his cold green eyes glaring at Eddy. 'Doesn't really matter which version is true. Either way, you are one unlucky bastard, Eddy. And it doesn't look like your luck is going to improve today.'

Eddy glowered at him, but did not move. 'Just tell me what you want,' he said.

Caine stood up and walked to the edge of the table. He kept the gun trained on Eddy as he grabbed the man's left arm. Eddy tried to yank it back, but Caine's grip was like iron. 'No sudden moves, Eddy. Just tell me what I want to know. You sourced components for a bomb that was used in the Pattaya floating market. I want to know who you were working for.'

'I don't know what you're talking about, man. I run guns, sure, but I don't work with explosives anymore. Never had much luck with them.'

Caine twisted Eddy's hand over, so the palm faced up toward the light. The tips of his fingers were stained a yellowish orange.

'In World War Two, women who worked with TNT in munitions factories were called canaries. Do you know why?' Caine asked.

Eddy was silent.

'It's because TNT is toxic. Prolonged exposure to its chemicals affects skin pigmentation. Turns it yellow. Even short-term exposure can discolor the skin on your fingers. Takes a week or two to work through your system. So you see, I already know you're lying. Last chance, Eddy.'

Caine gripped one of Eddy's yellow-stained fingers in his fist.

'Give me a name.'

Eddy looked up at him, and his eyes were wide with a mix of anger and fear. '*Oroka na baka*,' he hissed, calling Caine a stupid idiot. 'We can't talk about this here. Let's go somewh—'

Crack!

Caine jerked the finger down and back, snapping the bone.

'Arrrrghhh!' Eddy's scream of pain was loud and high-pitched. Caine grabbed the next finger on his hand and pressed the butt of his pistol into Eddy's spine.

'Give me a name,' he repeated, his voice low and calm.

'Please, just listen. I can't—'

Crack!

Again Eddy cried out, this time a guttural, primal shriek of pain and suffering.

'Stop wasting my time. Name. Now.'

He grabbed the next finger.

'*Chotto, chotto*, OK,' Eddy screamed. 'Look, he didn't give me his name, and I didn't ask. But I met them at a house by the beach.'

Caine paused. 'What beach?'

'Na Jomtien. I can write down the address.'

Caine looked up at the girl. 'Can I borrow a pen?' he asked. She opened a small drawer in the supply table and rummaged around for a second. She pulled out a crumpled old business card and a pen. Caine took them and set them on the table next to Eddy's right hand.

'Do it,' Caine ordered Eddy.

Eddy grabbed the pen and scribbled down an address. His handwriting was almost illegible due to his missing fingers. Caine eyed the small scrap of cardboard for a second, then slid it into his shirt pocket.

'Thank you, Eddy. See how easy that was? Now, I highly recommend you leave Thailand for a while. At least a month or two. For your own safety.'

Eddy eyed him suspiciously. 'Why? What are you planning to do?'

'Let's just say, if you stay here, I doubt your luck will get better anytime soon. If these people are who I think they are, and they find out you talked, losing a couple fingers will be the least of your worries. Leave. Tonight.'

Caine made his way to the door. 'Enjoy the rest of your massage.'

He slid out the door. A few seconds later, the girl scurried out of the room. Grimacing in pain, Eddy wrapped the towel around his waist, sat up, and frantically began to throw on his clothes.

10

Sitting alone at an outdoor table at the Glass House restaurant, Caine watched as the sun sank toward the ocean. Crimson and gold reflected across the rippling water as it slipped behind the horizon.

The Glass House was a beautiful, romantic spot, with a glass-enclosed gazebo for indoor dining. The outdoor patio was perched on a tree-lined cliff and looked out over the water, giving diners an unparalleled view of the ocean.

Caine once again felt the pangs of loneliness. He realized it was foolish of him to have chosen this spot for dinner. This was a place for couples. And Caine was, as usual, alone.

A pretty waitress came and took his check and

payment with a bow. Caine sipped the remains of his beer, then stood up and walked toward the edge of the patio. He peered through the trees at the ocean and the sandy beach that lay below.

To his left, a fair distance down the beach, he could just make out the gleaming white house at the address Eddy had given him. Satra had not managed to track down the Russian's whereabouts yet, but he had been able to run a title search on the address. The house was owned by a local entertainment company and used for so-called 'corporate housing' purposes. But, as Caine had suspected, that was only the first link in the chain. Like a spider working in reverse, Satra had untangled a web of holding companies and dummy corporations until he was left with a single thread. The final link in the chain led to a family with known *chao pho* ties, based out of the Chonburi province.

Caine had done surveillance runs of the house earlier in the day, posing as a jogger or a tourist walking along the beach. He had spotted several men patrolling the grounds. They dressed in muscle shirts and shorts and looked like low-level thugs. An older man with a round, pockmarked face and thinning black hair had paced outside more than once, yelling into a cell phone. Caine took him to be middle management.

Caine had seen men like these before. He noted their watchful eyes, the bulges under their armpits, the flashes of a pistol butt hanging above their waistbands. Everything he saw confirmed his suspicions. Whoever owned this house, they were definitely connected to organized crime of some sort.

Caine considered several ways to approach the house, including swimming in from the ocean. But with so little intel to go on, he felt the risk was too great. He had no idea how many men might be in the house. If a guard or sniper spotted him before he made it to shore, he would be an easy target.

No, he thought, *I need a different plan. Something unexpected.*

Caine pulled out his burner cell phone and dialed the number of a local escort service. 'Devil's Den,' a woman's voice said on the other end. She spoke English, but with a heavy accent.

'Yes, I'd like to order some girls for the evening. I'll need six. No preferences, whomever you have available.'

'What hotel you at, honey?' the voice asked.

'No hotel,' Caine answered. 'Send them in a limo,

with a driver, please. You can pick me up at the Glass House.'

'Six girls plus limo, very expensive date, sir. I give you special deal. Twenty-thousand baht for night. You pay advance?'

Caine smiled. 'But of course.'

* * *

Caine sat in uncomfortable silence as the limo drove down the winding beach road. Surrounding him were the six escorts he had ordered. They were all wearing tight dresses, miniskirts, and a variety of other provocative outfits. One of the girls, a young minx with a short bob haircut dyed bright pink, leaned against him. 'Why you so stiff, huh?' she murmured into his ear. 'This a party!' She pulled out a small glass vial from her purse and offered it to Caine. 'You want?'

'No, thank you,' Caine said, removing her hand from his chest. He leaned forward past a pair of giggling girls who were locked in a sensual embrace. They were most likely high on a combination of ecstasy and speed. These girls were all sourced from the local bars, and would have to go back to work, or entertain clients like he was pretending to be, for the rest of the night. They used a combination of drugs and alcohol to stay awake.

He knocked on the smoked glass divider that cut off the back of the limo from the driver's section. With a mechanical hiss, the glass slid down. The driver looked back at him.

'Yes, sir?'

'When we get there, just let me do the talking. My friend is a heavy sleeper, so lean on the horn. And turn up the music, OK?'

The driver smiled. 'Sure, boss, anything you say.' He turned a knob on the stereo, and Caine felt his eardrums pulse as the heavy bass of electronic dance music thumped through the cabin.

Caine smiled and gave the driver a thumbs up, which he enthusiastically returned. With a hiss, the glass divider raised back up.

The limo pulled up to the gates of the white beach house. Caine opened the door. 'We're here! Everybody out.'

As the girls piled out of the limo, laughing and chattering, the limo driver began pressing the horn. Its bleating honk filled the night air, cutting through the thumping bass of the stereo speakers. The girl with the pink hair bent over the trunk of the limo and began setting up a line of white powder on a small mirror. One of the other girls squealed with excitement and ran over to join her.

Another girl, wearing a skin-tight black dress and six-inch heels, slinked over to Caine and grabbed his arm. 'Wow, this your house, mister? You big shot, huh?'

'No, this isn't my house. My friend lives here. He's the one paying for the party.'

'You must have important friends, huh?'

'Let's find out,' Caine said. He walked up to the gate. Its iron bars were gleaming white, like the rest of the house, and a small intercom box was mounted on a pole a few feet away. Caine pressed the intercom button. 'Hey!' he shouted into the microphone. 'I'm here with the girls.'

The intercom crackled to life. A stream of rapid-fire Thai spat out of the speaker.

The girl raised her hand to cover her mouth. 'Your friend, he is very angry!'

'Well, he's about to get angrier,' Caine said. He pressed the button again. 'Hey, come on, the boss ordered six girls and a limo. I'm here with six girls and a limo. Let's do this.'

The intercom crackled to life again. This time the voice spoke in English. 'We no order girls. Wrong house. You go away now!'

Caine turned back to the driver and gave him the thumbs up. The driver smiled and turned the music up louder. The windows of the limo rattled as deep beats pumped through the air.

Caine pressed the talk button again. 'Look, man, we got drugs, we got booze, and we're not going anywhere till I get paid. So get that short, pudgy little guy down here, and let's take care of business!'

The girl leaned over Caine's shoulder and shouted into the intercom. 'Yeah, we bring the party bitches!'

'You tell him,' Caine said.

He looked back at the limo and smiled. Whatever was going on in the house, he was sure the last thing the occupants wanted was to draw attention to themselves. And a limo full of hookers, drugs, and blasting loud music tended to draw exactly the wrong kind of attention.

A few minutes later, he saw the front door of the house open. The man with the pockmarked face and balding head, the one Caine had pegged as a manager, came storming out. He was accompanied by one of the muscle-bound thugs. The manager shook his fist and shouted at Caine in Thai.

Caine adopted a relaxed pose and gave the men

his best smile. 'Hey, boss! Look at these girls. Beautiful, right?'

The girl with pink hair looked up and rubbed white powder off her nose. The other girls laughed. 'Come on, baby, let's go for a ride,' she said. 'We show you good time, boss man!'

The thug pushed a button on a small remote control that hung from his belt. The gate swung open. Caine raised his arms and turned his smile up a few watts. 'See, I told you this guy likes to party.'

The thug walked toward him at a steady pace. He raised his arm. He was holding a pistol, aimed at Caine's head. His grip was typical 'gangsta' style, with the barrel of the pistol pointed down and the butt tilted sideways.

Amateur, Caine thought.

The girls screamed and huddled behind the trunk of the limo. The manager walked up to the driver's side window and pounded on the glass. The window lowered. He screamed in at the driver in Thai.

A look of fear flashed over the driver's face, and he turned down the music. Only the low chugging of the limo's engine could now be heard over the night breeze. In the distance, waves crashed on the beach, and a seagull cried from overhead.

The manager turned and glared at Caine.

'You make mistake. People in this house, they want privacy. No girls, no noise, no cops, understand? You stupid man. Leave now, or we clean up mistake. We clean up you, *farang*. Got it?'

The man with the gun continued walking toward Caine. His eyes were covered by cheap mirrored sunglasses, but there was no mistaking his twisted, leering smile. Caine knew a killer when he saw one. He could see his reflection in the thug's glasses.

Caine kept up his relaxed, friendly posture, but instead of backing away, he took a step toward the gunman. He raised his hands slightly, as if to signal surrender. 'Hey, boss, all good. Ladies, party's off – let's get back in the limo.'

The girls muttered to one another in scared voices as they opened the door and piled into the back of the long black vehicle. Caine took another step forward. The gun was only a couple feet from his head. He saw the gunman sneak a sideways glance at one of the girls as she bent over to climb into the car. It was just a fraction of a second, but it was enough.

Caine's left arm shot forward and pushed the gun sideways, toward his right side. His fingers wrapped around the barrel, and he punched downwards, driving the gunman's hand down to his waist. The gun was now pointing ninety degrees to Caine's right, aimed toward the limo. He knew he had to act fast, or the gunman might squeeze off a shot and injure one of the girls in the car.

Even as the gun moved downwards, his right hand was winding back. He snapped it forward, punching the thug in the face. As the man stumbled backward, Caine let the momentum from the punch carry his arm forward, sliding along the man's arm until he felt the cold metal of the pistol. Now, both his hands held the gun in a firm grip.

With a powerful twist, Caine yanked the barrel of the gun, straight up. There was a loud crack as the bones in the thug's trigger finger snapped. The man screamed, and he loosened his grip on the pistol. Caine yanked the weapon away and took a step back.

The thug bent over, cradling his broken finger. Caine swung the pistol butt down on the back of the man's head. He grunted in surprise and fell to the ground. Caine kneeled, clubbing him on the head once again. The man would not be getting up anytime soon.

Panting, he turned and pointed the gun at the manager. 'You... take out your wallet.'

The manager froze, barely able to comprehend

the sudden explosion of violence he had witnessed. His beady eyes glared at Caine with surprise and fear. 'You crazy? You try to rob this house?'

'Do it.'

The man fumbled for his wallet and held it out to Caine. Not moving, Caine kept his gun aimed at the manager. 'All your cash. Give it to the girls. They deserve a tip.'

The man did as he was told, taking several thousand baht notes from his wallet and holding it out toward the limo. The rear window rolled down, and the girl with the pink hair grabbed the cash. The limo roared to life, kicking up dust as it drove in a circle around them and then tore off down the beach road. Its red taillights disappeared over a hill. Caine was alone with the man in front of the house.

He walked over to the short, pudgy man, spun him around, and frisked him. The man was unarmed. Caine took a step back. 'What's your name?'

The man was silent for a moment, but then spat out, 'Lau. Lau Somchai.'

Caine pushed his shoulder with the barrel of the gun. The man stumbled forward. 'OK, Lau,' Caine said. 'I want to talk to your boss.'

11

Caine clenched the fabric of Lau's shirt in his right hand and the gun in his left as he followed behind the shorter man. He pivoted left and right, keeping Lau between himself and the other thugs that stared at them as they made their way through the house.

It was dark outside now, and the interior was dim, lit only by an occasional lamp or flickering TV. The house was modern contemporary in style and decorated almost entirely in white. The hired muscle, in their cheap shirts and knock-off jeans, looked out of place in the gleaming, pristine surroundings.

Lau led him out a set of sliding glass doors and down a staircase to a blue-tiled patio. The sound of the waves was louder now. The beach was somewhere out in the darkness. Turning left, they walked down another flight of stairs. At last, they emerged beside a shimmering, rectangular swimming pool. The lights from the pool reflected across the water, casting a rippling glow over the patio.

A figure was hunched in a white plastic chair. A few other chairs were set up around an outdoor patio table. The figure was facing a large, flat-screen TV that had been set up on a stand. A dirty orange extension cord ran from the TV into the house, powering the Thai soap opera that flickered on the enormous screen.

'You one crazy *farang*,' Lau whispered, as they walked toward the dark figure. 'You get in here, no problem. But you never get out. You die here.'

'Just introduce me,' Caine muttered.

He spotted several gunmen perched on the balcony above them, training their weapons on him. He realized Lau might be correct. If things did not go well, it was unlikely he would leave this house alive.

As they reached the table, Lau dropped to his knees. The pudgy little man bowed, touching his head to the ground. '*Chao Mae*, forgive me. I fail you!'

The figure in the chair turned to face them. Caine was surprised to see an elderly woman's face eying him with dark, sunken eyes. She was dressed in a pink robe over her fluffy white slippers. A silk scarf held back her stark white hair, although a single gray curl flopped across her wrinkled forehead.

'Yes, you have failed me, Lau,' the woman said. 'How many times have I told you, never interrupt my dramas?' Her voice was low and raspy. Caine could hear years of smoking and drinking in the harsh, scratchy tone. Her eyes darted back and forth over his face, like a serpent's tongue. 'Who the hell are you?'

Caine eyed the old woman, but kept his gun trained on Lau. 'My name is Mark Waters.'

The woman turned away and poured herself some tea from a metal pot on the table. 'Huh. I'm old enough to know a lie when I hear one. But what do I care? None of my business what you write on your tombstone. You can call me Anna. Sit and have some tea, while things are still civil.'

Caine watched as several gunmen moved down to the pool. They hung just out of the light, keeping their weapons aimed at him from a distance. He shrugged and walked over to the table. Whoever this woman was, the men seemed to be protecting her. His best chance to survive was to stay close to her. She made a waving motion with her hand, and Lau

stood up. He glared at Caine, then turned and shuffled back into the house.

Caine sat down in one of the patio chairs and
placed the gun on the table, making sure to keep it
out of the old woman's reach. Anna sat to his right.
Across the table from him, sitting in the free chair,
was a small doll.

The doll was exactly the same size as a young
human girl. Its porcelain skin had a pink glossy
sheen to it. Thick black hair fell to its shoulders, and
Caine was certain the strands were real human hair.
Its plastic eyes sparkled, reflecting the rippling glow
of the pool. The thing almost looked alive in the
dim, shifting light, and Caine found the effect unnerving.

The doll was dressed in expensive, designer
clothes. A plate of real food sat on the table before it.

Anna flashed him a toothy smile and poured him
a cup of tea. She poured another cup and set it before the inanimate figure. 'This is my *luk thep*. Her
name is Tia. Say hello to Tia, Mr. Waters.'

Caine turned his gaze from the doll to the old
woman. 'It's a doll.'

'It's not a doll; it's a *luk thep*. Do you know what
that means?'

Caine shook his head.

'It means "child angel",' the woman rasped. 'She was blessed by a Buddhist priest. She's not a toy; she's a talisman. Now say hello, or I'll have my men flay you alive.'

Caine turned to the doll. 'Hello, Tia. Pleased to meet you.' He spoke as if he were talking to a small child.

The woman smiled and turned back to the TV. 'Damn, now I'm lost. You picked an inconvenient time to disturb me, Mr. Waters.'

Caine took a sip of tea. *The woman is deranged*, he thought. He would have to proceed carefully. 'I was expecting to find a *chao pho* godfather in this house.'

She gave him a shrewd smile. 'Instead, you found a godmother. The correct term is *chao mae*. Surprised?'

Caine nodded. 'Pleasantly.'

'We'll see. I haven't decided if you get to live or not. What are you doing here?'

Caine reached into his pocket, noting the way the gunmen surrounding them tensed up. They relaxed when he pulled out his burner phone. He had saved digital copies of the pictures Satra had shown him on its memory card. He called up the pictures and slowly slid the phone over to Anna.

'This website. Thai Angels. I believe the *chao pho* are running it. These girls have been taken.'

The woman picked up the phone and flipped through the pictures. 'Your chances are getting worse, Mr. Waters. I don't see why I should care about some kidnapped bar girls.'

'I want them back. That's why I came here.'

The woman put down the phone and squinted at him. Her face was cold and still. She gave Caine the impression of a gargoyle statue: cold, lifeless, and eternal.

'Why?' she asked. 'Why do you want them back? What are they to you?'

'That doesn't matter,' Caine answered quietly.

Again, the woman uttered her raspy chuckle. 'I think you will find it matters a great deal.'

Caine leaned back in his chair. 'Anna, obviously you are a powerful woman. I don't want to make an enemy of you. I mean no disrespect, but please believe me when I say I have fought my way into and out of worse places than this.'

Anna nodded. 'Yes, yes, you've got balls, and you've got skill – I'll give you that. You're what, a con man, a smuggler? Some kind of two-bit criminal, or at least you're pretending to be. And yet you're risking your life sitting here at my table, looking for these girls. Girls are a dime a dozen in Pattaya, so I know this isn't a business transaction. Which means this is personal, isn't it? You want to save them. Save them from some horrible fate worse than death, yes? What are you, some kind of guardian angel?'

Caine stared at her but said nothing.

Anna's voice grew even more dry and raspy. 'But the way you took care of my men, fought your way into this house... I can see by the look in your eyes, you've watched men die. It leaves a mark on you. Blood always stains.'

Caine shifted in his chair. 'I'm sure you've seen your share of blood, Anna.'

The old woman nodded. 'Oh, yes. Take it from me, whatever your name is – you can be both an angel and a devil for only so long. Sooner or later, you have to choose one.'

Caine reached out to grab the phone, and Anna slammed her hand on top of his. The movement was sudden and powerful, and Caine was shocked the old woman could move so quickly. Her stare pierced him like icy nails.

'If you wait long enough, Mr. Waters, one will choose you.'

She released his hand, and he took back his phone.

'As I said, I don't want to make an enemy of you,' Caine replied, 'but I warn you not to make an enemy of me. I'm not looking to save the world. I just want these girls back. I'll do whatever it takes to get them.'

Anna nodded. She turned her attention back to the TV. 'This actress is lovely, don't you think? She plays the mother of the wealthy businessman. She's a real dragon lady, the power behind his throne, so to speak. He wants to marry the common girl from town, but the mother has already arranged for him to marry his business rival's daughter.'

As Anna rattled on about the plot of the drama, a servant emerged from the house to clear their dishes. He removed the plate of food in front of Anna's doll and replaced it with a small dish that held a colorful assortment of macaroons.

'When police tried to investigate this website, your people set off a bomb in the floating market. How many real children did you kill there?' Caine asked in a cold, flat voice.

'Oh, bullshit,' Anna snapped. Her nostrils flared with anger and indignation. 'My people didn't set off any bombs. Whoever led you here is covering their tracks. You've been played, Mr. Waters. That website isn't run by me, or any other *chao pho* family.'

'You expect me to believe the *chao pho* doesn't engage in human trafficking?' Caine asked.

'Yes, I traffic women. Poor girls from shit towns come to me, desperate for a new life, willing to do anything to make enough money to feed their families. Do I profit from their misery? Certainly. I'm not going to apologize for that to a man like you. We both know you've done far worse, and you don't have as many years behind you as I do. Am I wrong?'

Caine returned her stare, waiting for her to continue.

'I ship them all over the world, and they do what they have to. It's not pretty; survival never is. But kidnapping local girls, auctioning them off like cattle? That's not only shameful, it's bad business. Too much risk. Sends people like you to my door.'

'Why should I believe you?' Caine asked.

Anna twisted her dry, cracked lips into a smile. 'Because I can prove it to you. I can tell you who is really running the site – and, with a little luck, where to find your precious bar girls.'

Caine leaned forward in his chair. 'Where are they?'

'Not so fast,' Anna cackled. 'I'm not in the habit of giving out information for free. There's a price.

And you did say you would do whatever it takes, didn't you?'

Caine glared at the leathery old woman. 'Fine. How much do you want?'

Anna smiled again. 'Do I look like I need your money? No, no, keep your baht. You have skills, connections. You were able to find me here. I want you to put those skills to work for me. A favor, chosen by me at a later date. Nothing too far south of your moral compass, I promise. We have a deal, yes?'

Caine hesitated for a moment, then nodded. 'Deal.'

Anna spit in her hand and held it out to Caine. He shook it.

'Good.' The old woman took a deep, wheezing breath. 'Now, the people running that website are not *chao pho*. They are the Red Wa. Have you heard of them?'

Caine thought for a second. 'Drug runners. They operate in the hills, on the northern border. Refugees and immigrants from the United Wa State, an independent territory in Burma... or I guess I should say Myanmar now.'

Anna nodded. 'You're well-informed. The *chao pho* have had good relations with the Red Wa in the past. We both have Chinese ancestry in our blood. We have a partnership in the meth trade here in Thailand.'

'So why are you selling them out to me?' Caine asked.

'One of their number, a man we call Pisac, has been muscling into our territory here in Pattaya. Massage parlors, brothels, beer bars... He has over-stepped his bounds. These are *chao pho* operations. Pisac believes his contributions to our drug traf-ficking success have earned him a cut of the profits from our other operations. We do not share his belief.'

'Pisac?' Caine asked.

'It means "devil". Whatever you may think of me, I promise you, this man lives up to the name.'

'I don't believe in devils or demons, Anna.'

The old woman shrugged. 'As you like. Anyway, I used to do business with the Rudov family. They are old-school Russian mafia, a Vor family. The father, Sergei, was recently released from prison. Just before his release, Alexi Rudov, his son, cut ties with us. We believe he is now working with Pisac and the Red Wa. They set up the Thai Angels site together. Hand-picked girls. Pretty, sexy bar girls, not filthy village peasants with crooked teeth and scrawny bodies.

Girls like this, men see, men desire. Now, they can have them, with the click of a button.' Anna shook her head. 'Shameful.'

'I had a run-in with Alexi Rudov. He's disappeared.'

'He's probably gone to the Red Wa camp, to take possession of the girls. They will be locked into a cargo container and loaded onto a ship. No way out, no sunlight, pitch black darkness. Maybe they have a flashlight, so they don't piss and shit on each other. Whatever food and water Pisac provides for them, it won't be enough. Some will most likely die on their journey. Maybe they will be the lucky ones.'

'Where is the camp?' Caine asked, his eyes glowing with anger.

Anna turned her attention back to the TV. Her show had ended. On screen, the credits rolled over a still frame image, a Thai man and woman, holding each other in a passionate embrace.

'Damn, I missed the whole show. You really fucked up my night, Mr. Waters.'

'Where are the girls?' Caine asked, his voice louder than before.

Anna picked up a remote and turned the TV off. The screen went dark.

'I don't know. Let me check with my people.

Leave your contact information with Lau, inside the house. We will send you a location within twenty-four hours, and you can rush off to save your lovelies. Assuming you survive, per our agreement, you will do a favor for me. Yes?'

'That was the deal.'

Caine stood up to leave.

'Say goodbye to Tia,' Anna snapped, her voice hard as steel.

'You know, these bar girls do what they do to feed their families. And you sit in this house wasting a fortune on food and tea for a doll.'

Anna looked up at him, and a ripple of anger flashed in her black eyes. 'I told you, she's a *luk thep*. She was blessed by a priest. That means she has a soul. She is like a daughter to me.'

'The missing girls are someone's daughters, too.'

Anna's expression hardened. 'Do you have children?'

Caine shook his head. 'No. I don't.'

Anna reached out and stroked the doll's hair. 'A thankless child is sharper than a serpent's tooth. I don't have to worry about that with Tia. She is a blessing. She brings me luck. Perhaps she will bring you luck, too. You'll need it, Mr. Waters.'

Without responding, Caine walked back into the house. Behind him, Anna remained, sitting with her blessed doll while the waves lapped at the beach in the darkness.

12

Caine caught a taxi back to the walking street area of Pattaya. He walked through the crowds of pleasure-seeking tourists amid the flickering neon lights until the streets turned darker and the crowds thinned out. The gleaming clubs and go-go bars were replaced with rickety tenements and rotting apartment buildings.

This was Satra's neighborhood. Glancing around the street to make sure he was alone, Caine pulled out his cell phone and dialed the detective's number.

The phone rang twice, and Satra picked up. 'Hey, where you been?'

'I got some information on the Russians. I believe they're up north, somewhere along the Myanmar border.'

'Who tell you that?'

'I met with someone high up in the *chao pho*. It's a long story, but according to my contact, the *chao pho* aren't the ones behind the website. It's the Red Wa, and they're working with the Russian mafia.'

'You believe them?'

Caine paused. 'Not sure. But they could have killed me. Instead, they let me go. Either way, it's the best lead we have right now.'

Satra sighed. 'Well, it match what I find. Finally got line on Russians. Witness saw them charter private plane. They fly to Chiang Mai, up north. They rent vehicle there, four by four, truck. Good for dirt roads. Maybe they going into jungle?'

'That must be it,' Caine said. 'My contact said Alexi is working with a man known as Pisac. His camp is up north. They're sending me coordinates soon.'

Satra whistled. 'I have heard of this man. I thought he was just myth, fairy tale. If we can get evidence, link Pisac to this case, Chief Battang will have to investigate. He have no—'

Caine heard Satra gasp, and then there was a loud crash.

'Satra? Satra, are you there?'

The line went dead.

Caine jogged down the street faster and hit redial on the phone.

The phone rang. No one picked up.

Caine jammed the phone in his pocket and broke into a sprint. He felt the blood roaring in his ears as he drove his legs faster across the pavement. It might have been a bad connection, or it might have been a dead battery...

In his heart, Caine knew it was neither of those things. The people they were investigating had set off a bomb in a public market and killed dozens of people, simply to discourage the police from investigating them. They were ruthless and willing to act. Satra had been turning over rocks, questioning anyone he could find about them. If word had gotten back, if just one of his contacts had squealed...

Satra was in terrible danger.

Caine was panting as he raced around the corner onto Satra's block. His apartment building was just ahead, on the left side of the street. Caine ducked behind a battered red pickup truck that was parked on the side of the road. As he caught his breath, he peered around the rear corner of the truck. The street was dark and quiet. A couple of streetlights pierced the sweltering darkness with their hazy glow, but there was still more shadow than light.

Caine moved out again, walking at a normal pace. He jammed his hands in his pockets, trying to look like a lost tourist. His eyes glanced left and right, but he saw no signs of movement.

He made his way to the front of Satra's building. A few squares of light shone from apartments that faced the street, but most of the building was dark. Either it was empty, or the majority of the tenants were early sleepers. Caine scanned the premises one last time but still saw no signs of a disturbance. No movement of any kind. Walking up to the outside gate, he slipped a small lockpick from a pouch under his belt.

He had picked the lock before, the first time he had visited the detective. It did not take him long to pick it again. A few minutes later, the door creaked open on its rusty hinges.

Caine took a step forward.

The air around him ignited in a blast of heat and fire.

Boom!

The explosion was deafening. Caine felt the hot air scald his skin, as the force of the blast threw him backward.

He closed his eyes and forced his body to go limp. He hit the ground ten feet back and tumbled away from the burning building. As he rolled, he raised his hands and covered his head. Shards of wood and glass pelted the ground around him like shrapnel.

A huge chunk of burning timber slammed into the ground less than a foot from his head. The pavement crumbled beneath it as it rolled to a stop. Caine leaped up from the ground and sprinted as far from the burning rain of debris as he could.

The telltale patter of objects striking the ground subsided. Caine stopped and turned around.

Satra's building was gone. A skeletal framework still stood, but the center of the apartment complex had collapsed into crumbling rubble. Wreckage was strewn about the ground, as if the entire structure had been thrown into the air and slammed back to earth upside down.

What little remained was engulfed in fire. Thick gray clouds of smoke rose up from the flames and blotted out the stars in the night sky.

There was no way anyone inside the building could have survived. Caine had seen enough explosions to be certain of that. Whoever had planted the charges had done their work well.

Pisac's death toll had just increased.

The moaning wail of sirens rose in the distance. Caine stared at the flames. For a moment, he wondered if Satra had been dead or alive, conscious or mercifully numb when the burning, hungry flames had consumed him and everyone else around him. Was he forced to listen to the screams of the other tenants over the loud crackling of burning wood and superheated metal?

The sirens grew louder. Closer.

Caine could barely hear them over the turmoil of thoughts that raced through his head. What if he had agreed to help Satra sooner? What if he could have stopped these people before they had taken Naiyana, before they got wind of Satra's investigation?

The sirens were just around the corner now. Caine took a few steps backward, then turned and walked into the thick darkness that surrounded the burning building. Within a few seconds, he was gone, lost in the shadows.

13

Caine rolled the heavy wood door of the boathouse open and looked inside. Behind the door, darkness stared back at him. The pier had no lights of any kind, and only the moon illuminated the grounds after the sun had set. At the moment, the moon was hidden behind a thick bank of clouds, leaving the boathouse shrouded in darkness.

He had rented the boathouse under an assumed name, and he had used a cutout from one of the local street gangs to pay the owner in cash for the year. There was nothing to tie the property back to him. Still, he clicked on a small Maglite and swung the brilliant, tiny beam through the interior, checking every shadowed nook and cranny for in-truders.

The dark, musty wood shack was empty. He stepped inside, closing the door behind him. Taking a length of chain that hung from the inner wall, he looped it around the door handle and slid a heavy-duty combination lock through the chain links. He was confident no one would be able to enter without making enough noise to warn him first.

An old fishing boat sat in the center of the boathouse, upright and perched on a single-unit dry rack. It was about twenty feet long and looked to be in terrible shape. A lumpy crust of barnacles coated its hull, and years of salt corrosion and neglect had stripped away the paint. It would have cost a small fortune to refit the vessel and make her seaworthy again. But Caine didn't care about that.

He had no intention of ever putting this rotting carcass of a boat in the water.

Caine grabbed a small utility ladder and dragged it over to the edge of the boat. He climbed up the ladder and hopped onto the main deck. The floor-boards flexed and groaned under his feet, but they supported his weight.

He stepped into the small cabin at the stern of the boat. The beam from his flashlight filled the cabin with a soft, warm glow. Kneeling, he felt along the floorboards until he located the tiny pressure plate he had installed between two of the boards. He pressed the catch until he heard it click, and felt one of the floorboards lift a fraction of an inch.

Using his fingernails, he was able to pry it up, revealing a metal door hidden beneath the floor. He removed several more floorboards, each one exposing more of the metal hatch. Finally, he removed the last board, and a small numeric keypad came into view, mounted next to a thick metal handle. The object was a safe. Its door faced up toward him.

Caine typed a series of letters and numbers into the keypad. A small light next to the safe's handle turned green. Caine grabbed the handle and pulled.

The heavy metal door lifted up, revealing its contents. The glow of the halogen bulb glinted off the metal stocks and barrels of a small arsenal of modern weaponry. A variety of pistols, rifles, submachine guns, and knives were neatly arranged in the safe, along with several other bags of supplies and an assortment of ammunition.

Caine had stashed the equipment here in case his old friends at the CIA ever came looking for him. Now, he would put it to use for another purpose.

He began to select weapons and lift them from

the safe, laying them out on a small workbench that ran along one side of the cabin. After a few minutes, he stood back and surveyed the gear on the bench.

First up were a pair of SIG P226 pistols chambered in 9mm. Next to them sat an H&K MP7 submachine gun with folding forward grip and retractable shoulder stock. Several extended-capacity magazines were stacked next to the weapon. Finally, he set a Spyderco Paramilitary 2 folding knife with a blackened steel blade down on the bench, along with a sharpening stone.

He spent the next couple hours loading magazines and field stripping the weapons. Then he cleaned and oiled their firing mechanisms and reassembled them. The work was tedious, but that didn't bother him. It kept his mind off other things. The glow from the flashlight was dim, but he had trained to perform these actions blindfolded if need be. He knew every spring and switch, every curve of metal. He knew each weapon as intimately as a lover.

He had just begun grinding the knife's blade across the sharpening stone when a beep from his phone interrupted his concentration. He put the knife down to check the phone's screen. He had a text.

He opened it, finding coordinates and a file attachment for a map. There was also a message: 'My contact says the girls will be loaded onto a cargo ship in 24 hours.'

True to her word, Anna had sent him the location of Pisac's camp. Caine opened the map file and checked the coordinates. They were north of Chiang Mai, just inside the Thai border with Myanmar. That matched with the intel from Satra. Alexi Rudov was heading north. Pisac would be there to meet him.

Naiyana and the other girls would be there as well. For twenty-four hours, at least. After that...

Caine tapped the edge of the knife's blade with his thumb and felt it bite his skin. A tiny droplet of blood swelled from the cut. Caine licked his thumb clean before folding the knife closed.

OK, he thought. *Time to go to work.*

14

Caine felt his muscles cramp and ache as he lay still in the underbrush of the jungle. An uncountable number of insects, birds, and other creatures of the night chirped, squawked, and growled, creating a strange, primal symphony. Despite this background of noise, the dark foliage he was concealed in felt still and unmoving.

It had taken hours to drive from Pattaya to Chiang Mai. Once there, he had purchased some necessary clothes and supplies. After wolfing down a bowl of *khao soi* noodles and minced pork served by a street vendor, he had rented a battered, old truck. Then he had loaded his heavy black duffel bag of weapons and the newly purchased supplies into the back. He'd driven the truck roughly sixty miles north, following the coordinates Anna had given him, to the Mae Ping River. A fishing barge had taken him across the river, for a few baht coins.

Now, after countless hours of non-stop travel and movement, he lay deathly still, looking out over the dark valley. A small tributary of the larger river snaked its way west, cutting through the thick jungle canopy below. Caine had held this position for over an hour. A pair of compact night vision binoculars were pressed up against his eyes. He turned his head back and forth, scanning the dark green curve of the river.

He had spotted a series of buildings on the northern bank. They looked like shacks, hastily constructed from scrap wood and sheets of corrugated metal. A few rust-covered trucks and jeeps were parked around the camp. A small campfire burned in a clearing between the buildings, a brilliant white-hot point of light in his goggles. Glowing green figures crouched around the fire, cooking skewers of meat and boiling water in metal pots.

Anna's coordinates were correct. This had to be the Red Wa camp. He adjusted his binoculars and peered deeper into the darkness, sweeping back and forth between the buildings. He counted at least twelve men outside. Three guards were clustered around a wooden fence-like structure. Caine zoomed in closer. He could see several figures moving within the fenced-in area. A few more were lying on the ground. It was difficult to tell through the night vision lenses, but Caine was certain they were the missing girls. He was not too late. There was still time.

Caine slipped the binoculars into a pouch that hung from his waist. He was dressed in a black T-shirt and cheap black jeans he had purchased in Chiang Mai. His weapons were stored in a water-proof pack he carried on his back. He slid across the ground, making no sound as he moved. His muscles cramped, and bits of branches and rocks tore at his skin as he dragged his prone body over them. The river was his goal, and he had to move slowly to avoid detection. An inch at a time, closer and closer.

By the time he made it to the riverbank, his body was covered in muck. Bits of grass and foliage clung to his face. He lay still, letting his weight sink into the mud. He observed the camp, listening for any noise that sounded out of place, any sign that he had been spotted. But the only sound was the rhythmic rise and fall of the jungle animals, chirping and squawking as before.

He took a deep breath and shimmied forward into the cold water. A slight current stirred the river's murky surface. Caine allowed it to push him a few yards downstream, toward the western edge of the camp. Then he dove down and swam underwater. His long, powerful kicks propelled himself through the liquid darkness.

An experienced diver, Caine could hold his breath for a long time. But here, in this dark jungle river, infested with snakes and even crocodiles, he found himself rushing to reach the opposite shore. Since leaving Pattaya, he had been running on adrenaline and luck. He knew it was only a matter of time before either ran out.

When his grasping fingers scraped across mud and reeds, he knew he had reached the opposite riverbank. Caine lifted his head a fraction out of the water, just enough to take a slow, shallow breath. Then, once again, he crept forward inch by inch. He was careful to slide across the stiff reeds without snapping them as he emerged from the river.

Keeping low, he made his way to a line of trees at the edge of the camp. He could see the flicking campfire now and make out the shadowy forms of the men surrounding it. The fire would limit their vision to a few feet. So long as he stayed in the penumbra surrounding the light, he would be invisible to them.

Circling around the trees, he stalked toward the fenced-in area. It sat near the northern edge of the camp, the point farthest from the river. Caine paused behind another clump of trees and vines as he observed the area.

The fence was constructed from sharpened bamboo poles, each placed a few feet apart in the ground. Lengths of barbed wire ran between each pole, and coiled razor wire ran along the top of the fence. There was a small gate at the front of the pen, and a thick padlock kept it locked shut. Two of the men stood guard at the front, while a third was circling the pen. Caine watched as the man passed a few feet away from him, completely oblivious to his presence.

Caine let his arm drop to his side. His fingers curled around the Spyderco knife. He slid his thumb into the hole stamped into the closed blade. With a quick flick of his wrist, the knife snapped open.

The guard was a few feet ahead of his position, staring into the pen, watching the girls. Caine accelerated, taking short, rapid steps to muffle the sound of his running. As he closed in, the guard spun

around, and Caine saw him raise a battered automatic rifle. But he was too late.

Caine knocked the barrel aside and drove the
blade of the knife up and into the man's throat. The
guard's eyes bulged, and blood spurted from his
neck. Caine slid behind him and clamped a hand
over the man's mouth, muffling his cries.

Dropping low, he dragged the man back into the
underbrush. As he moved, he twisted the knife, rip-
ping open the wound more, allowing the blood to
rush out faster. Caine waited until the man's strug-
gles began to die down. After a few minutes, the
guard stopped kicking and thrashing and lay still.
Caine grabbed the fallen man's rifle, removed the
clip, and tossed them both into the jungle. Then he
searched the corpse. He pocketed a Leatherman
utility tool and a small metal key that hung around
the man's neck on a frayed cord. Then he covered the
body with vines and scraps of vegetation.

He made his way back to the cage. Kneeling next
to one of the bamboo poles, he tapped the blade of
the knife against the wood. The sound was barely audible above the jungle noise. He tapped again. A dark
figure crawled over to him, investigating the sound.

It was a girl. She looked about twenty. Her

clothes were filthy and tattered, and her face was streaked with dirt and blood. An ugly purple bruise surrounded her left eye.

Someone had beaten her.

Her eyes shot wide open when she saw him, and Caine realized he was covered in blood from the guard he had killed. He raised a finger to his lips in the universal gesture for silence. He nodded toward the gate and the two remaining guards, standing just out of sight in the darkness.

The girl was still for a moment, a look of fear frozen on her face, like a deer caught in headlights. She looked over her shoulder at the guards, then back at Caine. She hesitated a few more seconds, then crawled toward him.

She pressed her face against the bars. 'Who are you?' she whispered. 'You help us, get us out of here?'

Caine shushed her and whispered back, even quieter, 'Where's Naiyana?'

The girl pointed over her shoulder. Caine nodded. The girl understood. She crawled back to the group of girls. Their whispers rose to an audible chatter, and Caine cursed under his breath. The guards were sure to take notice before long.

Another face crawled toward him from the darkness.

It was Naiyana. She saw him and covered her mouth with her hands. Again, Caine raised his finger to his lips. 'It's OK,' he whispered. 'Keep quiet. I'm going to get you out of here.'

'Oh my God!' Her eyes began to tear up. 'How you find me?'

Caine shook his head. 'Later. Here.' He slid the key into her hands. 'I took this from a guard. Is this the key to the gate?' Naiyana nodded as she wrapped her hands around his and took the key.

Naiyana reached a hand through the fence and touched his face. 'I knew you would come.'

Caine removed her hand and slipped the utility tool into her fingers. 'Here, take this, too. It has a knife, just in case,' he whispered. 'I'll distract the guards. When the time comes, you have to move fast. Get across the river, hide on the other side of the valley. I'll find you. If I'm not there in thirty minutes, try to find the closest village.'

'How I know when to go?' she asked.

Caine twisted his lips into a grim smile. 'Trust me. You'll know.'

He gave Naiyana a reassuring smile, then crept back into the shadows.

15

Caine made his way through the dark shadows that hung around the perimeter of the Red Wa camp. He circled behind one of the small wood shacks and dropped prone. The shack was raised about a foot off the ground, and a small creek flowed through the muddy ground beneath it. A bucket hung from a hole in the floor of the shack. It floated in a lazy circle on the dark, still waters of the creek.

On the other side of the shack, Caine could see the rubber tires of a jeep. It was parked a few feet away from the building's entrance. The vehicle stood between him and the campfire, where several of the men crouched and chattered among themselves.

From the excitement in their voices, Caine guessed they were playing a game. Gambling of some kind.

He slid forward through the brush, making his way under the shack. The water from the creek was shallow, but he had to crawl at a snail's pace to avoid splashing. The mud was cold and sticky, a welcome relief from the oppressive heat and humidity of the jungle above.

As Caine slid past the bucket, he stopped moving and listened. The building above sounded empty, and only a dim light shone down from the hole. Ahead, beyond the parked jeep, the men continued their chatter, occupied by their game.

He slid out from under the shack. For a few seconds, he was exposed, out in the open. If any guards had been watching from the shack or walking past the area... But Caine's luck held. No one walked by. The men were still gathered around the campfire. He moved under the jeep and rolled over onto his back.

Grabbing his knife, he cut two lengths of hose from the undercarriage. Then, he pulled himself out from under the vehicle. He crept along the side of the jeep, keeping it between himself and the campfire. He unscrewed the gas cap. Working quickly, he inserted the longer hose, a thin black rubber tube he had ripped from the coolant system, into the gas tank.

Next, he inserted the shorter length, a thick red hose crusted with old grease and engine oil. Once the hoses were in place, he used his knife to cut off a scrap of his T-shirt and stuffed it between the two hoses.

When the seal around the hoses was as airtight as he could make it, Caine wrapped his lips around the shorter hose. He winced as the taste of dirt and grime filled his mouth. He blew short, rapid puffs of air into the tank. As the air pressure rose in the vehicle's gas tank, it forced the fuel out, and there was only one place for it to go. A thin trickle of gasoline began to spurt from the end of the other hose.

Caine grabbed the thin black tube. He sprayed as much of the vehicle's tires as he could with the gasoline and soaked the ground beneath the jeep with the volatile fuel.

When the tank was empty, Caine crawled back under the shack. He shimmied through the mud to the hanging bucket and used it to pull himself up through the hole in the floor.

As he surfaced, he swept the area with his pistol, peering into the shadows for any sign of movement. The small building was empty. Plastic tarps covered stacks of building materials, but no guards were present. A single lantern hung near the door, bathing the room in a soft, flickering glow.

Caine holstered his pistol and unslung the MP7 submachine gun that hung by a shoulder strap at his side. With rapid, practiced motions, he extended the stock and flipped down the front grip.

He made his way to the door, grabbed the lantern, and took a deep breath.

Then, Caine kicked open the door and tossed the lantern toward the jeep.

A gigantic fireball blasted up into the dark sky.

Caine took cover behind the doorframe. The men outside began to shout and scream. Peering around the corner, he saw shadowy figures running toward the burning jeep. He pushed away from the building and opened fire with the submachine gun.

Multiple rounds of high-velocity ammunition penetrated the lead guard, and his body danced and jerked from the impact. Caine could see splatters of blood fly from his body, lit up bright red by the brilliant glow of the burning jeep.

He ducked back behind the door as another guard opened fire with an AK-47. The powerful bullets shredded the thin walls of the shack. Caine clenched his teeth as he felt trails of hot air streak past his face, missing him by only a few millimeters.

Caine backed up, taking cover behind one of the tarp-covered stacks. His visibility was now limited to the rectangle of the doorframe. He fired blind, sending a hail of bullets out into the darkness.

He heard footsteps rushing toward him. He popped up from his cover and fired again. His burst cut down an overeager guard who had charged the entrance of the shack. The guard spun and fell face down on the floor.

Caine ducked back down and ejected the empty magazine from the MP7. As he slammed more ammo into the weapon, he heard the shattering of glass and then a *whoosh*. The crackling noise of fire filled the room. Caine turned and saw the corpse in the entrance of the shack ignite in flames. One of the men outside had thrown a Molotov cocktail into the entrance. The tiny wood building was burning.

Caine stood up and sprayed a long burst of automatic fire out the door. He saw another man drop, and the remaining guards scattered. They took cover behind other buildings in the camp.

He coughed as thick, hot smoke began to fill the tiny room. Tongues of fire snaked up the doorframe, engulfing the entrance of the shack in a wreath of flame.

Caine emptied the MP7 into the rear wall of the shack. The bullets chewed through the thin wood wall as if it were paper. He let the gun hang to his side as he began to kick the wall down. He knew he could slip back down into the creek if need be, but he didn't want to take the chance of the burning building collapsing on top of him.

It took only seconds to kick a large hole in the shredded wall. Caine leaped through, hit the ground, and rolled. Behind him, the burning shack began to sag and dip as the fire tore through its thin wood structure. Sparks and burning embers drifted up into the air, like a cloud of tiny fireflies.

He heard footsteps running toward him. Drawing his pistol, he jogged over to an outcropping of trees and took cover. The crackle of automatic weapon fire burst through the air. Muzzle flash from multiple weapons lit up the jungle. He returned fire with his pistol, sending double taps toward each firing position. He looked back into the camp toward the fenced-in cage. The gate was open; the pen was empty. Naiyana and the girls had escaped.

He moved deeper into the jungle surrounding the camp.

A cluster of bullets splintered a tree to his right, sending a fine shrapnel of wood fragments into the air. A shard struck his face, and he tasted blood. He returned fire and heard screams of pain echo from the darkness.

Caine moved again, running through the jungle. Occasionally he turned and fired into the darkness. He was just covering his retreat now, hoping to slow his pursuers. Up ahead was the river. If he could make it across, he knew he could lose them in the thick jungle valley beyond. Then he could find the girls and lead them back to safety.

But first, he had to buy them some more time, let them get farther away from the camp.

Caine fired behind him again, emptying his pistol. He tossed it aside. He slammed another magazine into the MP7 submachine gun and dropped to a kneeling position. He saw shadows moving in the jungle, backlit by the burning shack.

He opened fire, sending a rain of death toward the men that pursued him.

Then he turned and pushed his way through the reeds toward the river. He saw its dark, glossy surface up ahead. In the moonlight, its rippling water looked like the scales of an enormous black serpent. Caine took a step forward and felt the cool water slosh against his leg.

Suddenly, he felt something sharp pierce his neck.

He reached back. His fingers brushed against a hard, sharp object buried in his skin. He ripped it out and examined it in the moonlight. It was a dart, the kind that was launched from a high-powered air rifle.

Caine had participated in many kidnappings – or 'extraordinary renditions', as they were known in the trade. He knew the dart would be laced with a potent sedative. He cursed. This was the weapon of a government operative, not jungle guerrillas or human traffickers. He had not prepared for this.

He took another step forward and stumbled. The muscles in his legs went numb. He collapsed, falling face forward into the river. As his head sank into the dark water, a black mist engulfed his mind. He felt light as air, as if the faint current might sweep him away.

Naiyana is free, he thought. At least there was that.

He heard splashing footsteps surrounding him. Strong hands lifted him from the water and dragged him to shore.

'*Da*, this is the man I told you about.' The voice was deep and thick, and spoke with a Russian accent. 'He is going by the name Mark Waters. But his real name is Thomas Caine.'

Alexi Rudov gazed down at Caine with his strange, blue eyes. Another man stood next to him, his face hidden by a dark shadow. *Who are these men?* Caine thought. *How do they know my name?*

The other man tilted his head, examining Caine's face. 'Bring him,' the man said. 'I wish to talk with him.' As the effects of the drug increased, Caine's senses began to deaden. He heard the sound of the man's voice twist and distort into a deep growl.

'What is there to talk about?' Alexi asked. 'You wanted to see his face. Now you see. We kill him and be done with it.'

'Who overcomes by force, hath overcome but half his foe.'

'What the hell are you talking about?'

The man strode away. 'I said bring him. Do not question me again, Alexi.'

Then, Caine heard nothing more. He sank into the black depths of unconsciousness.

16

A thin beam of light filled Caine's vision. He realized it was his own eyelids, cracking open. His thoughts felt thick and slow, as if his mind were trapped in quicksand. He felt a slight irritation at the back of his neck and remembered the dart striking him there.

He could hear the sounds of the jungle in the distance. Dirt pressed against his cheek. He was outside. The night air was humid and oppressive, and his clothes were soaked with sweat. He groaned and rolled over. His arms and legs were cuffed together with zip ties. As his vision cleared, his surroundings came into focus. He was lying on the ground, in the dirt pen, the one that had previously held Naiyana and the other girls.

He had been captured.

Two men approached the cage. They wore frayed camouflage pants and old, worn T-shirts. One of the shirts was faded red, with a white eagle printed on the front. The other man's shirt featured a can of soda in a bright yellow circle. The design looked familiar, but all the writing was in Asian characters Caine could not read.

The men murmured to each other in a singsong patois of Chinese and Burmese. One kept an AK-47 trained on Caine, while the other opened the gate and stepped inside the pen. He flicked open a butterfly knife, slit the straps that bound Caine's legs, and hoisted him to his feet.

'You follow,' the man said in broken English. 'He want to see you now.'

Caine held up his bound wrists and smiled, but the man ignored him and gave him a shove toward the gate.

They walked Caine through the camp, past the shack he had set on fire. The building was now a pile of ash and blackened timbers that had collapsed into the creek. Caine saw little movement elsewhere in the camp. He had cut down their numbers in the gunfight, and he assumed the men that were left had dispersed into the jungle to search for the girls. He hoped he had given them enough of a head start.

He was led to the largest building in the camp, which wasn't saying much. The large shack was still constructed of scavenged scraps and rotting timbers, but it was three times the size of the other buildings. A torn red curtain hung over the entrance. Caine heard classical music drifting out from between the strips of fabric.

The men nudged him forward. Caine parted the curtain with his bound fists and ducked into the dark interior.

Inside, the room was lit by several bulbous paper lanterns that hung from the ceiling. They cast a warm glow over a low square table. Mildewed cushions were scattered across the floor. Alexi Rudov sat cross-legged on one of the cushions, his large blue eyes squinting in discomfort. A few feet away from him sat an older Asian man, one Caine had not seen before.

He looked to be in his late forties, although it was difficult to tell. His face looked drawn and tired, haggard even. But his skin was tan and soft, and had a youthful appearance. His shoulders and chest were slim and athletic. He wore his hair long, and it framed his narrow, hawkish features. The hair, like his eyes, was pure jet black. Only his goatee showed any signs of gray.

He was eating from a bowl of rice and vegetables. He lifted the food into his mouth with slow, deliberate motions of his right hand. He kept his left hand under the table.

Caine stood in silence for a moment. The music played softly in the background, but he did not recognize the piece.

The man looked up and observed him with coal-black eyes. Reaching out as if in slow motion, the man pointed to the table. 'Sit. Eat.' His voice was deep and powerful.

Caine sat down cross-legged opposite the man. He held up his fists. 'Do you mind? Hard to eat like this.'

The man smiled thinly and slowly chewed his food. 'I'm sure you will manage. Try the tea leaf salad. It's delightful.'

Caine sighed. He tried to remember when his last meal had been. Whatever was coming, it would be better to face it with a full stomach. He grabbed a small metal bowl and did his best to scoop some of the rice and vegetable concoction into it with his bound hands.

The tea salad consisted of bitter green tea leaves, mixed with sliced tomatoes, cabbage, chickpeas, and nuts. The cold dish was refreshing, and mixed well with the warm, steamed rice. Caine tipped the bowl into his mouth, ignoring the bits of food that spilled to the ground.

A young boy, just a teenager from the looks of his lanky body and oversized clothes, hurried into the room. The boy filled all their cups with water from a wooden jug. Then he bowed and rushed back out through the red curtains.

Alexi Rudov stared at Caine with his strange blue eyes. His mouth was curled into a sneer. Caine carefully lifted his water cup to his lips and took a long sip. He matched Alexi's gaze with his cold, green eyes, and the Russian looked away.

He set the cup down.

'Why am I here?' he asked.

The other man looked up. 'Alexi here says he knows you. Says you used to be a spy.'

'I don't know him,' Alexi grunted, 'but I have seen his file. Back in my days with the FSB. He is a spy, and a traitor. He's supposed to be dead.'

So that was how Rudov had recognized him. Although the United States and Russia maintained an uneasy alliance, from time to time Caine had come up against operatives of the FSB, Russia's Federal Security Service. It was the modern successor to the old Cold War beast of the KGB. It made sense they would have a file of some sort on him.

'Is that true?' the other man asked.

'Who are you?' Caine asked in return.

The man smiled. 'I am Kang Long Wei, but you know of me by another name.'

'Pisac,' Caine said.

The man nodded. 'That is a Thai word, but yes. Pisac, Naatsoe in Burmese. I am the devil. Now, please answer me. Is Alexi's story true?'

Caine turned to Alexi. 'How does the FSB feel about you, Alexi? Leaving military service to work for criminals? You don't rise up in the Russian Mafia without doing hard time, and I don't see any prison ink on you. I assume your daddy did the time?'

Alexi slammed his fist down on the table. 'I kill you for these words you speak. Enough talk!'

Kang rested a hand on Alexi's arm. The Russian seemed to calm down, but his lazy eye twitched with rage. Caine knew he had struck a nerve.

Kang placed more food in his mouth and chewed. He drank more water.

'You come into my home,' he said. 'You steal my property. Kill my men. All for what? I want to understand why you do this. I want to take a measure of you as a man.'

'Considering you kidnap girls and blow up innocent people, I don't really give a damn what you think of me,' Caine replied.

Kang nodded, his black eyes open wide. 'You don't want to say, but I think you came for these girls. They are important to you... or perhaps one of them is? I think I understand now.'

'You don't know anything about me,' Caine said.

Kang laughed. 'Oh, you are wrong, Mr. Caine. You and I are not so different. When I looked in your face, I ask myself, why is a man like this, a white man, a man supposedly without honor, here in this jungle? Why is he risking his life for these girls? Alexi calls you a traitor, but when I look in your face, I see something else.'

'Yeah? What do you see?'

'I see betrayal.'

Caine said nothing.

Kang nodded. 'My eyes see the truth. I know all about betrayal. Once you are wounded by true, deep betrayal, you are never the same. Am I right?'

'Why are we wasting time with this asshole?' Alexi asked, his voice snarling with anger. 'Our shipment leaves tomorrow. The girls are missing. We have to find them before—'

'Please do not interrupt me,' Kang said, pivoting his head to stare at Alexi. 'These are city girls you are talking about. Bar girls. How far do you think they could possibly go in this jungle? My men will find them, and all will be as it was. In the meantime, I wish to enjoy my conversation with Mr. Caine.'

Alexi stood up. 'Forgive me,' he muttered. 'I seem to have lost my appetite. I go outside and smoke.' He stormed out of the room, tossing aside the red curtains as he exited the shack.

Caine was alone with Kang. Alone with the devil, Pisac. *Maybe this is my chance...*

Kang shook his head and looked back at Caine. 'Much anger in that one. Now, as I was saying... Do you think you are the only one who has been betrayed? You were what? A soldier? An assassin? I was killing for my people by the time I was sixteen years old.'

Kang pushed his bowl of food away. He set a small metal dish on a rack above a candle. Reaching into the folds of his clothes, he removed a red tablet and set it down on the plate. Caine watched as the heat from the candle began to melt the tablet.

Droplets of crimson liquid sizzled and burned on the plate.

Yaba. Caine was familiar with the drug. Its effects included sudden bursts of energy, euphoria, and feelings of invincibility.

'I fought with the Burmese Communist Party, when the military junta seized control of the government. It was still called Burma then,' Kang continued, watching the pill disintegrate. 'I say fought, but that's not entirely true. We fought some, yes, but for the most part our task was murder. I was inserted behind enemy lines. My men and I targeted officers, political figures. Schools and hospitals. Our job was to spread fear. You would call me a terrorist, Mr. Caine, but the Communist Party of Burma called me a revolutionary. They financed our war with opium money and Chinese weapons.'

Kang shook his head. 'Communism, Chinese nationalists, civil wars... it all seems like some strange dream now. None of it makes any sense to me. I don't suppose it ever did. All I knew was that I was ordered to kill. So I did. I was good at it.'

'I don't need the history lesson,' Caine said. 'If you're going to kill me, just get on with it.'

'I most likely will. After I have tortured you.'

Caine's muscles tensed but he maintained an aura of calm. 'I have no information for you.'

'Oh, I'm sure we can think of some questions. Perhaps you sent these girls somewhere into the jungle? You have a vehicle hidden across the river? A rendezvous point?'

Caine said nothing.

Kang shrugged. 'We shall see. Either way, there will be pain. Pain brings clarity. I feel you do not yet understand the true nature of where you are. Of who you are.'

'And you think you do?'

Kang nodded. 'Yes. As I said, I know betrayal well. In 1989, the Communist Party of Burma re-formed into the United Wa State. A ceasefire was declared with the Myanmar government.'

Kang leaned over the small plate and inhaled the vapor of the burning pill deep into his lungs. He looked up, and his eyes glowed with inner fire and intensity.

'Both sides had grown weary of bloodshed. Everyone wanted peace. Concessions were made. There were secret conditions to the ceasefire, back-room deals we knew nothing about. One of these conditions was that my men and I be turned over to the military, to face justice. I'm sure you can imagine what that meant, Mr. Caine.'

'Torture,' Caine said.

'Yes. Years of pain in a dark, diseased military prison. The United Wa State Army gave the Myanmar Armed Forces the location of our camp. It was a price they were willing to pay for peace. We were betrayed. Convicted as war criminals with no trial to speak of. Most of us were killed. After years of captivity, I was able to escape. But not without a cost.'

Kang lifted his left arm from under the table. His hand was chopped off at the wrist. A metal cap sealed off the wound. A claw-like hand was screwed into the end of the arm.

'Must make using chopsticks tricky,' Caine said.

'I cut it off myself, Mr. Caine. It was the only way to free my arm from the chains that held me. I spilled much blood that day. I fought and killed and clawed my way to freedom. And – much like you, I imagine – I made my way here, hoping to disappear. Other refugees from my people had crossed the border into Thailand and formed the Red Wa. They resumed their drug trade with China. I joined them. I began killing again. It was only natural. And soon, I worked my way up to become leader of this cell.

'Now I am free. I understand the true nature of this world, and my place in it. When you have suffered betrayal, when you have screamed in pain, knowing it will never end... when you have lost all hope, then it becomes clear.'

'What becomes clear?'

Kang smiled. 'That we are in hell, Mr. Caine. You, me, all of us... we are lost, trapped here in hell until we reach the next life. And once you realize that, it takes only a short time to reach the obvious conclusion.'

'Enlighten me,' Caine said.

Kang sucked in more vapor. He coughed, and it took Caine a second to realize that, beneath his gasping for air, he was laughing. 'In hell, there are only two kinds of souls – the devils, and the damned.'

The older man used his right hand to waft the smoke up to his mouth and nostrils, his eyes closed in blissful peace. He inhaled again.

Now! The voice screamed in Caine's mind. He lurched forward over the table, the fingers of his bound hands stretched wide, grasping for Kang's throat.

Without opening his eyes, Kang shifted sideways. Caine had never seen anyone move so fast. He slammed down on the table, sending Kang's food and the platter of drugs cascading to the ground. Kang raised his right arm into the air. Caine tried to roll off the table to avoid the blow, but again the man was too fast for him.

The arm struck like lightning. Caine saw the flash of steel in the dim light. The knife struck the table like a crack of thunder. The blade pierced the collar of Caine's shirt, pinning him to the table like an insect in a museum display.

Kang looked down on him and laughed. His pupils seemed to swallow the whites of his eyes. Caine heard a pair of footsteps enter the room behind him.

He shifted his eyes and saw the two guards from earlier had come, as if somehow summoned by Kang. The older man stopped laughing and gestured to the curtain.

'Show him the iron road.'

The men grabbed him under the arms and lifted him to his feet, tearing his shirt free of the knife.

'You will see,' Kang said, his voice low and calm. 'It only takes a short time... not much time at all, to decide. Devil or damned, Mr. Caine. Devil or damned.'

The men dragged him out of the room.

17

Caine bit down on his lip so hard he tasted blood. The pain... It had started as a slight irritation, but had grown in intensity. He knew it would keep increasing, building until he would no longer be able to stop himself. He would scream. But for now, he refused to give his tormentors the satisfaction.

His heart raced. Beads of sweat dripped from his body, and his tattered clothes were already soaked. His pants were sliced at the knees, exposing his legs. His hands and feet were tied to a wooden table that stood under a thatched roof. Above him, the two guards grinned as they watched his body writhe in pain. In his head, he had named them Eagle and Soda Can, after the designs on their shirts.

'The iron rod' consisted of a long, heavy metal rod that was studded with tiny spikes. The rod was rolled up and down the flesh of a man's shins. The weight of the rod itself provided all the pressure needed; the men merely rolled the heavy length of iron up and down. The motion was almost gentle.

Soon, the spikes began to prick the skin. Dots of blood appeared; with each turn of the rod, the blood increased. The wounds grew deeper. Soon, Caine's legs were covered with blood. He knew the rod would eventually strip the flesh from his shins, until nothing was left but bone and blood.

'Where you send the girls?' Eagle asked. 'Tell us, and we stop.' They asked their questions in flat, monotone voices. They didn't care about the answers. They didn't want to stop. Caine glared at them, then spat on the ground.

He had been tortured before. Those long, dark days of pain and misery had left a mark on his soul. Kang was right. After that betrayal, after that pain, Caine knew he had never been the same. The experience had scarred him. And now, as the pain built in intensity, he felt his mind regressing, as if he were being transported back in time.

It was as if this pain was all pain; there was no

difference. One second he was here, trapped in this jungle hell, the iron rod slowly tearing through the flesh of his legs. The next, he was hanging in a dark stone room, his body twitching and swaying as savage jolts of electricity ripped through his muscles. The past, the present... All was a blur, a miasma of despair and hopelessness, linked only by pain and terror.

Devils. His soul was tormented by devils.

His heartbeat was all he could hear. It drowned out the noise of the jungle, the laughing of the men. It flooded his ears with its rapid pounding. Faster and faster it beat, until he was certain it would explode from his chest.

His mind screamed at him, cutting through the roar of blood pumping through his veins. *Get a grip! Keep control. Control is all you have! If you scream, they win.*

The rod tore at his flesh.

Caine did not scream.

Suddenly, another sound cut through the red cloud of pain and fear that surrounded his senses. A soft crack, a rapid puff of air. It was a sound he had heard before, he realized. At the river, before he lost consciousness.

It was the sound of an air rifle.

The man he knew as Soda Can jerked an arm up to his neck. 'What the hell?' he uttered.

Eagle stopped rolling the iron rod. 'What's wrong?'

Soda Can slumped to the ground. Eagle immediately backed up and raised his AK-47. He scanned the darkness. 'Who there? Come out or I shoot!'

There was another soft crack. Eagle staggered back. He pulled the trigger of his assault rifle, but nothing happened.

Click, click.

Eagle fumbled with the weapon, and Caine realized he must have left the safety on. As the drug ran through his nervous system, the man struggled to throw the safety lever to the fire position.

He failed. He fell to the ground, unconscious.

Caine turned his head and saw a figure emerging from the darkness.

It was Naiyana.

Her skin was streaked with dirt and mud, and her hair was tangled with leaves and bits of vine. A light sheen of sweat made her coffee-colored skin glisten in the flickering torchlight.

Alexi's tranquilizer rifle hung by her side.

She rushed over to him.

'Naiyana, what are you doing here?' Caine hissed. 'I told you to go!'

'I did go. The other girls, they ran. I start to run, too, but I feel ashamed. You came for me. You saved me. Now I save you.'

She patted down the unconscious body of Soda Can and removed a large survival knife from a sheath at his waist. The knife was sharp, and it took only a few strokes to slice through the bonds that held Caine's wrists.

Caine sat up and took the knife from her. Scanning the jungle for movement, he severed the ropes that held his feet. He examined his injuries. His legs were bloody, but despite the pain, the wounds were not severe.

'I appreciate it, Naiyana, I do, but it's dangerous here. You could have been caught again.'

The girl shook her head. 'The camp looks deserted. I find this rifle in jeep outside the shack where the Russian sleeps, but he not there.'

'Kang sent most of his men into the jungle, looking for you,' Caine whispered.

Naiyana smiled. 'Yes, I hear them. They make noise like wild pigs, stomping around. My family come from mountains like this. When I was little girl, my father teach me how to hunt. How to be quiet, so animals don't hear me.'

'And how to shoot, apparently,' Caine said. 'Quick, help me hide the bodies.'

They dragged the two men into the underbrush of the jungle. Caine winced from the pain in his legs, but he forced himself to ignore it.

He felt the weight of the knife in his hand. The men were laid out in front of him, unconscious. It would be a simple matter to slice their throats. He didn't know when they might wake up; it was a logical precaution. His blood still boiled with rage. The pain and fear of the torture they had subjected him to still clouded his mind.

He looked up and saw Naiyana staring at him, a curious expression on his face.

'What are you doing?' she asked. Her brown eyes looked soft and concerned. Caine felt his rage subside.

'Nothing.' He grabbed one of the men's AK-47s and slung it around his shoulder. 'Let's go.'

They made their way through the dark jungle back toward the river. True to her word, Naiyana moved silently through the dense foliage. *Kang underestimated her*, Caine thought. She could have easily avoided his patrols and fled, but instead she had come back for him. She had risked her life to save him. He had seen trained soldiers panic and abandon their comrades under similar circumstances.

Suddenly, Caine detected a familiar smell. He held up his hand and stopped moving. Naiyana froze.

'What is it?' she whispered.

'Wait here,' Caine whispered back. He crept forward into the darkness, following the scent. It was smoke, from a cigarette.

With soft, slow steps, Caine tracked the scent. Using the barrel of the AK-47, he brushed aside a branch of thick green leaves. Up ahead, in a small clearing, he saw the dark form of Alexi Rudov, pacing back and forth in the moonlight. A lit cigarette hung from his lips.

Bad habit, Caine thought. *One that could kill you...*

Caine stepped into the clearing. 'Don't move, Alexi.'

The Russian spun around to face him. 'Who is there?'

Caine took another step forward, allowing a shaft of moonlight to illuminate his face.

Alexi shook his head. 'Caine. I told him to kill you.' Alexi walked toward Caine, his hands held up in a position of surrender. Caine knew the maneuver well. The Russian was trying to close the distance between them, to improve his odds.

'Don't come any closer, Alexi. Your next step will be your last.'

Alexi froze in place.

'Where is Kang?' Caine asked.

The Russian exhaled a puff of smoke. 'I have no idea. He wanders the jungle at night; nobody knows where he goes. The man is insane, yes?'

'You should choose better business partners then.'

'*Da*. This deal of ours... It was a mistake to get involved with this man. The bombings, the dead cop, you... Trust me, if I could do it over again, I would tell him to fuck off.'

'Dead cop?' Caine asked. 'You mean Satra? What about him?'

Alexi's eyes narrowed. His lips curled up in a smile. 'He is here. His body is here, in the camp. Kang has another bomb as well. I can show you. We make deal, yes?'

Caine thought for a moment. He knew he should kill this man and get Naiyana out of the camp as soon as possible. But Satra... If he had only listened to Satra and helped him, maybe none of this would have happened. And he remembered the photographs Satra had shown him, the bodies in the market. If Kang was planning on setting off another bomb, on killing more innocents as a show of force... He knew Satra would have done anything to stop it.

Caine made his decision. 'Show me this bomb, and I'll consider it.'

'*Da*, good. It is back in camp. This way.'

'One more thing,' Caine said, not moving from his position. 'If you betray me, if you make a single move I don't like, I won't hesitate to kill you. No matter what happens to me, you die first. Understand?'

Alexi examined Caine with his lazy blue eyes. He sighed and nodded. 'I understand. I have read your file. I know who you are, I know the things you have done. I have no wish to test you.'

Caine smiled. 'Good.' He waved to Naiyana. The girl moved from her place of concealment and entered the clearing. She stared at Alexi with disgust. 'You! This pig is the one who took me!'

'I know,' Caine said, 'but there's more at stake here than just us. We have to follow this man for just a little while longer. There's something we must do in camp. Then we can leave.'

Naiyana eyed the Russian, then nodded. 'I trust you. Whatever you say.'

Caine gestured with the rifle. 'All right, Alexi... show us this bomb.'

18

Alexi Rudov led Caine and Naiyana through the jungle, back toward the camp. As Naiyana had observed, the grounds seemed to be deserted. The campfire had burned out and was now just a smoldering pile of ash and glowing embers. Caine kept Alexi a safe distance ahead of them. He saw no signs of movement in the camp.

No sign of Kang.

They stopped near another large shack. The sound of a gas-powered generator puttered in the distance, near the building. Alexi pointed through the jungle. 'There. That is where they are keeping the bomb. And your friend's body. Because you are here, Kang believes the Royal Police have reopened the investigation into the missing girls. He says they will need another demonstration. Another bomb. And another letter.'

'Satra's blood,' Caine said. 'That's why he kept the body.'

'*Da*, it is as you say. I keep my end of bargain, Caine. Now you keep yours. Let me go.'

'I said I'd consider it, Alexi. I'm still considering. Naiyana?'

Naiyana smiled as she aimed the rifle at Alexi.

'Wait! You can't leave me in this jungle. You can't—'

Naiyana fired. The dart struck Alexi in the chest, just above his heart. His face filled with rage.

'You lying bastard! I kill you, then I strangle this stupid whore!'

He took a step toward them, fists poised to strike. Caine raised his rifle, but before he could fire, Alexi fell face first onto the ground. Naiyana stood over him and spit on his back. 'Russian pig!' She kicked Alexi's unmoving body.

'Keep it down,' Caine hissed. 'We still don't know where Kang is.'

'I'm sorry; you right. What do we do now?'

'There's something I have to do, for a friend. He tried to help you, tried to help the other girls, too. But Kang had him killed.'

Naiyana's features softened. 'I'm sorry for your friend.'

'Me too. Now, I want you to get across the river. Stay out of sight. I'll come find you when I finish here. Then we'll look for the other girls.'

'No, I go with you!'

'Naiyana, please – I came all this way to make sure you were safe. This is something I have to do alone. Just wait for me. I promise I won't be long.' He handed her the AK-47. 'Here, take this. Go, quickly!'

Naiyana stared at Caine, her eyes wide with concern and fear. Then she slung the automatic weapon over her shoulder. 'All right, I go. Please hurry.'

Caine nodded. 'Believe me, I will.'

The girl turned and disappeared into the jungle.

Caine stalked toward the shack. The wounds in his legs throbbed in agony. He pushed forward.

The interior of the shack was dark. Caine paused at the entrance. A rotting stench wafted out from the darkness. He could just make out a set of work lights, perched on a small metal stand near the doorframe. He crept over to the lights and felt around for a switch. When he flicked it, the lights flared, and he blinked while his eyes adjusted to the sudden illumination.

He adjusted the lights, dialing them back to a dim glow, just enough to see by. The camp still appeared to be abandoned, but he didn't want to push his luck. He scanned the interior of the cabin.

A workbench was set up in the far corner of the room. On top of the bench was a new-looking canvas duffel bag and a variety of electronics tools. A large burlap sack hung from a hook in the ceiling. It swayed gently in the night air. It was about the size of a man.

It stank of dead flesh.

Caine made his way to the sack and reached up. Using the knife he had taken from Naiyana, he sliced a foot-long incision in the top of the bag. Satra's head rolled out. A dark gash had been cut across his throat.

Caine took a step back. Again, he felt pangs of guilt gnawing at his gut. *If I had said yes sooner, if I had helped him...* He shook his head and cleared his mind. There was still work to be done.

Satra's flesh was pale and gray. Caine ripped open the bag further, revealing that the corpse had been stripped from the waist up. Knife wounds crisscrossed the body's chest and arms. Caine examined the throat wound. The edges were swollen, and thick clots of blood lined either side of the gash. The wounds in the chest were different. Those cuts were not inflamed, and there was little to no excess blood.

They were postmortem, Caine decided. Kang's men had killed Satra by slitting his throat, then removed the body before setting off the bomb in his apartment. Satra had told him that the last public bombing was accompanied by a warning note to the police, written in a missing policeman's blood.

If Alexi was right, if a new bomb was going to be set off in a public place, then this time it would be Satra's blood on the note.

Caine clenched his fist. *No,* he thought. *There will be no bomb. No note. Not this time.*

Caine walked over to the workbench. He took a deep breath and unzipped the duffel bag. Inside, he found exactly what he expected.

Two large plastic jugs were packed with a whitish yellow powder. A small electronics package was taped to the bottles, and wires ran from the center into the powder.

It was a bomb.

Caine recognized another of Eddy Ashikaga's military-grade detonators in the center of the wires and circuits. The plastic jugs held compressed TNT. Based on the amount present, Caine judged the bomb was powerful enough to wipe out a city block.

Or, he thought, *the entire Red Wa camp.*

The detonator was attached to a cell phone. The device could be set to detonate upon receipt of the call. The call could also trigger an alarm timer in the other phone, giving more time for the bomber to make his escape. Caine was familiar with such devices. He had used them many times himself.

Caine examined the phone. The model wired up to the detonator used a push to talk system. Essentially, the phone was capable of acting as a short-range walkie-talkie. Perfect for areas with poor cell reception.

Caine searched the workbench and found another identical phone, sitting in a charging cradle behind the duffel bag. He turned on the phone and checked the battery. It was charged, and active. There was only one number programmed into the phone's memory.

Caine reached into the duffel bag and pressed a button on the detonator. A small screen blinked to life, showing some menus and options. Caine quickly navigated to the settings he was looking for. He determined that the device's timer was set to five minutes. Caine pressed another series of buttons. A red LED light began to blink on the device. It was now armed.

As he zipped up the bag, he heard the wood floor creak behind him. He felt the old, familiar tingle on his neck, that sixth sense of danger, honed by years of instinct. Caine twisted his body to the right and felt the red-hot sting of a blade cutting across the skin of his shoulder.

His sudden movement had turned what would have been a fatal stab into a painful slash instead. Still unable to see his adversary, he threw his left elbow back and felt it connect with a man's face. His attacker grunted and stumbled back as Caine whirled around. He slipped the cell phone into his pocket and held up the survival knife in a defensive pose.

He found himself facing Kang Long Wei. The dim light cast shadows over the hollows of Kang's gaunt features. Staring out from the grim, demonic face were his eyes, two burning black dots. They looked like tiny eclipsed suns, blazing with drug-induced fury.

Kang. Pisac. The devil.

In place of the metal claw he had used at dinner, a foot-long blade was now screwed into the metal cap at the end of his arm. The weapon's cutting edge was serrated with a series of savage-looking barbs.

'Nice knife,' Caine said.

'I see you have made your choice, Mr. Caine.' His voice was a deep and guttural rasp. 'Welcome to hell. Let's see just what kind of devil you are!'

19

Caine charged toward Kang and swung out with his knife in a tight slash. Rather than block the feint, Kang stepped backward, moving out of range. As the blow swung past him, he hopped forward again, thrusting with the blade that was affixed to the end of his arm.

Caine pivoted and pushed Kang's knife arm away, causing the thrust to go wide. At the same time, he transferred his blade to his other hand and stabbed upwards, aiming for the exposed pit of Kang's arm.

Kang swung his right arm down into a block before the blade touched his flesh. He slashed inwards with his knife, forcing Caine to break and step away.

The two men sized each other up and began stepping left and right, each angling for an opening. After a series of feints and blocks, neither man claimed the advantage. They continued bobbing and weaving across the floor of the shack.

The two men's fighting styles were completely different. Caine kept his attacks and blocks in a tight box pattern, roughly the width of his shoulders and from his neck to his groin. His thrusts and slashes were quick, efficient movements. They used a minimum of energy, and did not leave him exposed to an easy counterattack.

But Kang spun and whirled his blade through the air with a fluid, dancing motion. He fought as though his weapon was a natural extension of his limb. The sweeping, erratic movements were difficult to predict. They seemed to leave him wide open, a weakness that should have been easy to exploit. But time after time, Caine found his attacks blocked, or Kang spun out of the way before his blade could strike.

Caine wasn't sure if it was due to Kang's drug-fueled euphoria, or if it simply came down to a higher level of skill, but the truth was undeniable – Kang was faster than he was. And Caine knew that a knife fight in a tight, closed environment like the shack would give him no opportunity to rest. Sooner or later, Caine would grow tired.

Caine saw an opening and stabbed inwards, thrusting the tip of his blade sideways toward the right side of Kang's neck. But the older man's right arm swung up into the air like a cobra, raising to strike. His palm slapped Caine's wrist away, and his body swung sideways, leaving his left arm facing Caine. He swung out, and the blade sliced across Caine's mid-section.

Kang's right hand hooked around in a punch, and Caine felt his neck snap back as the blow connected. He stumbled backward, struggling to put some distance between himself and Kang's blade.

Kang smiled serenely. 'Perhaps I was wrong about you, Mr. Caine. You have allowed yourself to hide amongst the damned for too long. You have lost your power. But here in hell, only the powerful survive.'

Caine slashed forward again, but Kang blocked the blow with little effort and thrust with his knife. Caine dodged, but Kang diverted the thrust in midair. He slashed upwards, cutting across the flesh of Caine's knife arm. The bloody wound joined those on his abdomen and legs. Caine panted for breath.

'You are getting tired. Slow.' Kang punctuated his words with another thrust. Caine stepped forward and blocked the blow, but before he could counter strike, Kang's fingers lanced forward, driving into his throat. Caine gasped for air. His knife fell from his grasp, clattering to the floor. He raised his hand to protect his bruised throat from another blow.

'It is time,' Kang said, his lips curled into a smile. 'Time for you to leave this hell. The next one awaits you.'

Caine shuffled backward, trying to increase the space between them. He needed to buy some time, catch his breath. But suddenly, he felt a heavy weight brush up against his back. His retreat was blocked by Satra's hanging corpse. He heard the rope creak as the burlap sack pulled and spun on the hook in the ceiling.

'Maybe so, Kang,' Caine said, the words hissed from his swollen, injured throat. 'But I promise you I won't be alone.'

Kang snarled and thrust forward with all his strength.

Caine pushed backward, using the motion to spin his body around the hanging carcass. As he fell back, Kang's long knife drove forward, just missing Caine. It slashed through the burlap sack and plunged deep into Satra's corpse. The blade sunk up to its hilt.

Kang found himself staring into the gray, lifeless face of the dead policeman. Satra's eyes were unblinking, unseeing. His lifeless head dropped forward from the force of the impact. Kang cursed in Chinese and yanked his arm back to withdraw the blade.

The blade would not budge. He pulled harder, and Satra's body swung toward him. The blade was still embedded deep in the corpse's flesh, refusing to come free.

Caine stumbled to his feet. He watched Kang struggle to free his blade and realized what must have happened. He had seen it happen in knife fights before. The serrated barbs on Kang's knife had caught on the ribs of the corpse. The knife was stuck, and Kang would not be able to pull it free without cutting down the body.

Caine stepped forward, adrenaline crackling through his body. This was his chance! His fist lashed out in a kidney punch. Kang gasped as the blow struck its target. The man collapsed to the ground, his arm still trapped in the flesh of the swaying corpse.

'This isn't hell, Kang,' Caine gasped, 'but I'll see you there someday.'

Caine charged forward and ran out the door of the shack. He raced through the camp, running as fast as he could toward the river. As he ran, he pulled the cell phone out of his pocket.

He had already pressed the send button and triggered the detonator, just after Kang's attack. He had meant what he had said to Kang: he would not go to hell alone.

The screen of the phone showed a small countdown clock. There were ten seconds left.

Ten seconds to make it to safety.

Searing pain shot through his legs as he ran through the jungle camp. Leaves and branches smacked at his face. The air he sucked into his lungs felt like molten lead being poured over his raw, damaged throat.

Up ahead, he saw the black surface of the river. He pushed himself harder. *Faster, dammit*, he screamed at himself. *Run faster!*

He felt the cold water strike his legs, and the pain from his wounds flared white-hot. He dove forward into the river's dark embrace. Behind him, the world erupted in thunder and fire. The shockwave was deafening. Even underwater, he felt as if a giant had slammed his fists into both his ears. He tumbled beneath the surface, sinking deeper into the currents.

Above him, the rippling black water lit up bright orange. Even with his eyes closed, he could see the glow of the explosion. The hot jungle air ignited into a massive cloud of fire.

And then it was over. The glow receded into the darkness, and the thunder echoed into a distant murmur. Then, the only sound was the rush of water around him and the tiny bits of debris that pelted the river's surface.

Caine rose up from the murky depths and gasped for air. His legs buckled as he stepped onto the opposite riverbank. He paused for breath. He felt exhausted, as though just one more step was beyond the feeble reserves of energy he had left.

Then he saw Naiyana. She rushed down the hill toward him. He forced himself to trudge forward, one step after another, until at last he was standing on dry land.

Naiyana embraced him. As he felt her warm arms wrap around his body, he collapsed.

'Oh my God, you're hurt!' she said. She ran her hand over his abdomen, leaving streaks of warm blood across his flesh.

'I'm fine,' he gasped. 'I just need a minute.'

He sank to the ground. Naiyana cradled his head in her lap as he rested.

He was at peace.

* * *

It was just past dawn when the soldiers from Kang's camp returned, leading the other girls at gunpoint. There were six men, armed with a collection of pistols, machetes, and one AK-47. The girls looked exhausted, their bodies streaked with dirt and mud from their flight through the jungle.

As the group neared the riverbank, the men began to chatter amongst themselves in their strange mix of Chinese and Burmese. The rising sun cast its light on the remains of the camp. Blackened trees and smoldering timber were all that remained. A few plumes of smoke floated up into the purple and orange sky. The girls stared at the destruction with numb, half-opened eyes.

As the men debated what to do, Caine stepped out from behind a grove of trees. He wielded an AK-47, and he took aim on the man in the rear of the group. He pulled the trigger, firing a short burst of gunfire.

Red holes exploded across his target's back, and

the man fell. The other men spun around and found themselves facing down the barrel of Caine's rifle. The girls screamed and dropped to the ground.

'Kang is dead. Your camp is gone,' Caine shouted. 'Drop your weapons. Leave now, and you live.'

The men muttered to each other in quiet, nervous tones. Then they lowered their weapons to the ground and retreated, dispersing into the jungle. A few minutes later, they were out of sight. The only signs they had ever been there were the small pile of weapons and the single corpse that lay on the ground.

Naiyana stepped out from behind the trees. She ran over to the group, and they embraced, chatting to each other in rapid-fire Thai. Caine couldn't understand what they were saying, but after the ordeal they had been through, he was glad the girls seemed to be in good spirits.

Something nagged at the back of his mind. He thought about the operation, the Red Wa, the Russian Mafia connection, Alexi Rudov.

He realized there was still one last task to complete, to ensure the girls' safety, as well as his own. He took a deep breath and walked back to the river. When Naiyana saw him heading toward the smoking ruins of the camp, she put a hand on his shoulder.

'Where you go? We get out of here now, yes?'

Caine picked up a pistol from the ground and handed it to her. 'There's just one more thing I have to do. I promise, it won't take long. I doubt those men will come back, but just in case, take this. Keep an eye out.'

Naiyana looked uncertain, but she nodded. Caine stepped into the water.

'Hey, wait!' she called after him. He glanced back at her. Her eyes were warm and alive, and her smile felt like sunshine on his face. 'The other girls, they want to say thank you.'

Caine nodded. 'Tell them they should thank Satra. He was the man in the shack, the one... The one who died. Tell them he's the one who saved them.'

'He good man. You good man, too,' she said in a quiet voice.

Caine was quiet for a moment. 'I'll be right back,' he said. Then, once again, he strode into the water and crossed over into the blackened, dead camp.

20

A couple weeks later, Caine made his way across the outdoor patio of the Glass House restaurant. The rainy season seemed a distant memory, and the sun blazed high overhead in the azure sky. Its warm beams were refracted into a thousand pinpoints of light by the glass gazebo in the center of the grounds.

Caine spotted the table he was looking for and walked over. Anna was seated beneath an enormous white umbrella. Next to her, sitting in its own white chair, was her doll. Her *luk thep*, Caine corrected himself, Tia. A platter of food was set down in front of the doll. Caine estimated that the cost of the food on the doll's plate could feed the average Thai family for a week.

He sat down opposite Anna. He was dressed in khaki shorts and a white linen shirt, with the sleeves rolled up to his elbows. The wrinkled, leathery old woman cast a disapproving eye over his battered and bruised arms and legs.

'You look like shit. Took a beating, I see.'

'I gave as good as I got.'

Anna nodded. 'So I heard. No more Pisac. No more Thai Angels website. And no more Alexi Rudov, apparently.'

Caine stared back at her and said nothing.

Anna took a sip of water from a crystal glass and leaned back in her chair. 'Well, I hope it was worth it. How is your pretty bar girl? She make all your fantasies come true?'

Caine looked out over the water. The rolling waves reflected the sun's brilliance like a sea of liquid gold.

He turned back to Anna. 'She's gone now. Moved back to her village, to be with her family.'

Anna peered at him from under the shadow of her umbrella. 'Why don't you go visit her?'

Caine shook his head. 'No, I think she's better off now. It's for the best. I appreciated her friendship, but my situation is... complicated. She's safer this way.'

Anna nodded. 'Ah, too bad. But, as you say, maybe for the best. Well, all that remains is my payment. You owe me a favor. Would you like a drink?'

'No, thank you. I won't be staying.'

Anna looked over Caine's shoulder. 'Here he comes now. He's not much, but he's loyal to me. More loyal than my own children. I think, with the right partner, he could go far.'

Caine followed her gaze and saw Lau shuffling toward them across the patio. The pudgy man was dressed in a loud Hawaiian shirt and designer sunglasses.

'What's he doing here?' Caine asked.

'That's my favor,' Anna said. 'Your smuggling operation is small-time, but you have skills, relationships, and you've already paid off the police. Lau here has connections to suppliers, factories in Indonesia, Vietnam, Thailand. Working together, you two can increase your profits considerably. The *chao pho* will take a percentage, of course.'

Lau sat down next to Caine, beaming.

'I work alone,' Caine snapped.

Anna stared at him with cold, dark eyes. 'Not

anymore. You will work with Lau, or you won't work at all. That is my price.'

Caine leaned back in his chair. He knew the old woman could make his life difficult if she chose to. And, after recent events, the last thing he needed was another enemy.

He sighed. 'Fine. But I smuggle liquor, cigarettes, counterfeit jeans, fake purses...' He leaned forward and stared at Anna. He did not blink. 'No drugs. No guns. No people.'

Anna laughed. 'We start small then. Keep you on the side of the angels for a little while longer, Mr. Waters.'

Caine stood up. 'I don't believe in angels, or devils. I'm neither of those. Do you have a word for that?'

'Oh yes, of course. I call them *phi tai hong*.'

'Yeah? What does that mean?'

Anna stroked the hair of her *luk thep* doll. 'It is a spirit... a person who is dead but does not realize it.' She looked up at him. 'A lost soul.'

Caine nodded. 'Well, I don't believe in ghosts either.' He turned to leave. Lau stood and grabbed his shoulder.

'Hey, wait. I contact you tomorrow about shipment. Good stuff. We make lots of money! But one problem. The Russian you kill, Alexi... What if Russian Mafia trace back to us?'

Caine stared at his new partner. Lau's tiny, pig-like eyes were covered by the mirrored blank stare of his sunglasses. The man's face was hungry, eager, and his lips were curled up in a nervous smile.

'Don't worry about it,' Caine said. 'I took care of things.'

He slipped Lau's hand off his shoulder and walked away. Caine had worked with men like Lau before. Men whose hunger for money, or power, or whatever vice they craved, consumed them. It was a slippery slope. The more you worked with people like that, the more they rubbed off on you. They could infect you, like a parasite that consumed from within.

Caine wondered if he, too, would descend down that treacherous slope. How long would it be, how far would he have to fall, until one day he would wake up and not recognize his own reflection?

As he left Anna and Lau behind, Kang's words echoed in his mind.

It only takes a short time.

Not much time at all...

* * *

The limousine cruised to a stop and idled in front of the dark warehouse. The night sky was still and cloudless. The moon bathed the metal walls and chain-link fence that surrounded them in cold, harsh light. Smoke rose from the limo's exhaust as the engine rumbled in the cold air. The windows of the vehicle were fogged, and the front wipers swept back and forth, clearing away the ice crystals that formed on the windshield.

The rear door opened, and a tall, powerfully built man stepped out. His expensive suit and heavy cashmere overcoat shielded him from the harsh temperature. *The coldest month in St. Petersburg, Russia might be February*, the man thought, *but a November night was no picnic either.*

His hair was steel gray and cut military short. His eyes were large and piercing blue. His name was Sergei Rudov.

He ran one of the largest crime families of the Russian Mafia. He was Vor, a thief in law. He had done time, earned the respect of his elders, and consolidated his power as he rose through the ranks of the darkest, most hellish prisons Mother Russia could lock him away in. Every step of the ladder, every man he killed, every crime he committed, was etched in black ink across his skin. A vast tapestry of prison tattoos hid beneath his tailored suit. The ornate designs covered every inch of his flesh save for the hard, thick lines of his face.

As he walked toward the warehouse, the door slid open. The screeching sound of metal scraping against metal echoed into the still night. A slim man in a black suit rushed out to meet him.

'Mr. Rudov, please accept my condolences. I am so sorry to be the one who—'

'Show me, Antonovich. Now.' His breath was an icy cloud of mist in the cold Russian night.

'*Da*, of course, sir, this way.'

The lanky man, Ivan Antonovich, led Sergei to a shipping container that lay in the center of the empty warehouse. Several armed men stood guard around the container. The men shifted on their feet and shrank back into the dark corners of the warehouse as Sergei and Ivan marched past them.

'The shipment was intercepted by our people at the Baltic Shipyard, as always, sir. We brought it here and opened it. We had vans outside to transport the merchandise... uh, the girls, to their respective buyers. But instead...' Ivan's voice trailed off.

The metal door of the container was open. Sergei stood at the edge for a moment, then stepped inside its long, narrow confines. A single body lay on the cold floor. A piece of paper was attached to its chest by a knife, stabbed deep into the corpse's flesh. The body was burned and its clothes were torn and shredded, but Sergei was able to identify who it was.

Alexi Rudov.

His son.

Sergei ripped the dagger from the mangled corpse and held up the note. It appeared to be written in blood. The writing was Russian. He read it aloud, and his voice echoed through the container.

'Death to those who betray Pisac, the devil of the Red Wa.'

Ivan slowly approached behind him. 'Sir, it is Alexi, yes? The Red Wa has killed him?'

'Put out the word, Antonovich,' Sergei's voice rumbled. 'Any member of our organization working with the Red Wa will face death by my hand.'

He crumpled the note in his hands.

'As of now, we are at war.'

PART II

COLD KILL

SIX MONTHS LATER

21

An explosion of light and sound filled the chilly air inside the *Tsvet Sapfira* Club. Spinning beams of neon shimmered as they danced across the glistening surfaces of the bar. Every piece of furniture in the club, from the chairs and tables to the glasses lined up across the counter, was carved from clear blocks of ice. As their frozen surfaces made contact with the air, they melted, releasing tiny droplets of moisture. The resulting mist refracted the club's lights into a prismatic rainbow of colors.

At the entrance to the bar, some of the patrons draped white fur parkas over their club attire. The freezing temperatures of St. Petersburg, Russia, had not deterred the young women in the crowd from wearing as little as possible. Their short, sparkling cocktail dresses exposed their long, smooth legs as they twirled on the dance floor. Goosebumps dotted the surface of their creamy skin, but they didn't seem to mind.

A tall, broad-shouldered man cut through the crowded club. He did not wear a parka over his dark suit. His deep-set brown eyes drank in the bar and its patrons with a smoldering, hungry gaze. His tan skin seemed oblivious to the cold. A tousled mane of thick black hair swept back from his lined forehead, while one heavy curl hung down in front of his face, lending his features a wild, disheveled look.

He pushed past a trio of girls laughing on the dance floor. They looked like models, or actresses... The club's sweeping lights revealed them in quick flashes. Long blonde hair, wide blue eyes, petite bodies perched on slim, gazelle legs. One of the girls slipped her hand onto the man's chest as he passed. He stopped moving and looked down at her.

'*Privet!*' she said, her words slurred. 'You are not cold?'

The man curled his lips into a smile. His nostrils flared.

'*Nyet*, my dear. In here is a tropical paradise compared to what I know as cold. Now, if you will excuse me.'

She laughed. 'Why don't you relax? Buy me and my friends a drink?' Her hand drifted down his shirt. 'Don't you like us?'

He took her hand, gripping it in his long fingers. He leaned toward her and spoke in a deep growl. 'I am afraid I have business to conduct. Otherwise, I would like nothing better.'

His lips parted, revealing ivory white teeth. His canines were large and pronounced, almost like fangs. 'Lovelies like you and your friends... I could almost eat you alive.'

At the sight of his leering grin, the girl took a step backward. The drunken flush drained from her face, and she visibly paled. She yanked back her hand but said nothing.

The man nodded. '*Dobryy vecher...* Good evening.'

He left the women behind and continued across the dance floor. He walked past a row of sparkling ice sculptures, a series of frozen men and women intertwined in a variety of lewd positions. He ignored them and approached an unmarked door at the rear of the club. A pair of beefy men in gray suits and fur parkas flanked the door.

One of the guards stepped forward. The man in black stood his ground and lifted his arms to his sides. The guard patted him down for weapons, then took his cell phone and wallet from his pockets. Flipping open the wallet, the guard examined the man's ID. Then he cupped his hand over his ear and spoke into a slim wireless headset.

'Piotr Zasko,' he read, shouting over the music. A few seconds later, he looked up. 'Good evening, Mr. Zasko. He is expecting you downstairs.'

The man known as Zasko slipped his phone and wallet back into his pockets. He waited as the other guard opened the door for him.

Zasko stepped through the dark entrance and descended a flight of stairs. As his eyes adjusted to the dim light, he heard the clang of the metal door slamming behind him. The music upstairs became muted and distant.

The stairs led to a cavernous underground storage room. The furniture here was not made of ice, but the air still held the chill of upstairs. Rows of shelves lined the dark, shadowy room, each one lined end to end with frosted bottles of vodka.

A deep voice boomed from the far corner of the room. 'Piotr, welcome. It is good of you to come.'

Zasko turned toward a huge man marching toward him.

Sergei Rudov... head of the Rudov crime family.

The men hugged. Zasko stiffened as he felt Rudov's arms crush around him. The man was pushing seventy years old, but he was built like a Russian tank. Zasko slapped his back, then gripped his shoulders. He stared into Rudov's piercing blue eyes.

'I was sorry to hear about Alexi,' he said.

Rudov nodded but said nothing. He draped one of his muscular arms over Zasko's shoulders and led him to the back of the room.

'Alexi, Alexi...' the older man muttered, exhaling a puff of mist into the freezing air. 'He was good boy, but a fool, nonetheless. This business of his with the Red Wa syndicate, with this man, Pisac, the Devil... Foolish. He ruined our trade with the *chao pho*, and for what? Now he is dead, and he has led us into a war with this Red Wa gang. Our operations in Southeast Asia have suffered.'

'I thought you had new information?' Zasko asked, keeping his voice low. 'That his killer was not part of the Red Wa?'

'*Da, da.* Come this way. Our guest has been most cooperative.'

Rudov led him around a row of colorful, expensive-looking bottles. There, in a dark corner behind the shelves, a man sat tied in a chair. He was naked, and he shivered in the freezing air of the frigid room.

'Mr. Ashikaga,' Rudov boomed. 'I was just telling my friend here how helpful you have been. I'm sorry to have interrupted your vacation in Hawaii. This basement is a bit colder than the beach at Waikiki, eh?'

'This is the man you told me about?' Zasko asked. 'The arms dealer who was working with Alexi and the Red Wa?'

Rudov nodded. 'Eddy Ashikaga, meet Piotr Zasko.'

Two of Rudov's men loomed over the shivering man. Judging by the cuts and bruises that marred his face, they'd been working him over for hours. One of them drove a meaty fist into Eddy's stomach. The blow connected with a dull thud, and the man groaned in pain. He coughed up a mouthful of blood and spat it on the icy floor.

'T-t-t-told you ev-ev-everything, s-s-swear!' the man hissed through chattering teeth.

One of the thugs, a tall slim man in a charcoal suit, grabbed a tuft of Eddy's stringy black hair and yanked his head up. 'You tell us again!' he barked.

Zasko recognized the man as Ivan Antonovich, Rudov's second in command.

Eddy's head lolled forward as Antonovich hammered his gut with another savage blow. His arms and legs were thin and spidery, but his belly bulged over his waist, like a statue of Buddha. An intricate dragon tattoo snaked its way up his right arm.

As Zasko's eyes travelled across the intricate tattoo, he noticed another odd detail. The man was missing two fingers from his right hand... They'd been severed at the first joint.

'P-p-please, I s-s-swear, that's all I know!' the man pleaded. A spasm ran through his body. His shivering intensified. 'S-s-so c-c-cold... C-c-can't talk!'

Rudov chuckled. 'Yes, I have to keep it cold down here. This is where I store my greatest treasures. The best vodkas in the world, not that *mochá* they serve upstairs.' He stepped over to the shelf and caressed the bottles. His meaty fingers left trails in the delicate frost that coated their glass.

He stopped at one bottle and hefted it from the shelf. It was crafted from gold metal, with a silver star stamped on the front. He pulled a gleaming stopper from the neck of the bottle and took a swig.

'Russo-Baltique,' he said after he'd swallowed. 'It is not to my taste, but this bottle cost me over half a million dollars. God knows how many rubles that is in today's economy.'

Rudov took another long drink. With a sudden twist of his neck, he snapped his head around and spat the harsh liquid into Eddy's face.

Eddy screamed in pain as the alcohol stung the cuts and lacerations that scarred his face.

'Just a taste, Mr. Ashikaga. A taste of more pain to come. Now you shiver from the cold. Soon you will shiver in fear. Fear of what I will do to you if I find out you are lying. Tell me again. Who killed my son, Alexi? Who delivered his corpse to me like a slaughtered cow?'

'M-M-Mark Waters. *Honto ni*, I swear! It was M-M-Mark Waters!' Eddy gasped.

'Who the fuck is Mark Waters?' Rudov bellowed.

Zasko put a hand on the old man's shoulder. 'Please, let me speak to him.'

Rudov looked up, his face flushed with rage. He took a deep breath, then slowly backed away from Eddy.

Zasko slipped his cell phone from his pocket and scrolled through his pictures.

'This man you speak of, Mark Waters... Is this him?' He held up his phone and showed Eddy a picture.

The shivering man nodded frantically. 'Y-y-yes, that's him! That's him! I know him from my yakuza days. W-w-word is he killed Alexi, and his Red Wa p-p-partner too! P-P-Pisac, the Devil!'

Zasko patted Eddy's bruised face. '*Spasibo*. Don't go anywhere.'

He stood up and walked over to Rudov. 'He is telling the truth, but this man's name is not Mark Waters. Before coming here, I spoke with some old comrades in the FSB. Your son Alexi downloaded a file on this man before he was killed.'

Rudov took Zasko's phone and examined the grainy picture. The man in the photo looked to be in his early thirties. His eyes were pale, and his features had a hard, drawn look to them.

'Who is he then?'

'His real name is Thomas Caine. His background is... complicated. The FSB's files are incomplete. But one thing is clear. He is a killer. He is dangerous.'

Rudov's eyes blazed with cold fury as he stared at the phone. 'Antonovich, take our guest to the shipping yard. Lock him in a container. I will decide what to do with him later.'

Ivan nodded and gave Rudov a knowing look. He barked some orders in Russian to the other thug. Then he whipped out a folding knife, and sliced

Eddy's bonds. They hefted the scrawny man to his feet and dragged him toward a pair of metal doors, ignoring his pitiful whimpered protests.

Rudov handed Zasko back his phone. 'Come with me.'

The older man led him to a dark corner of the storage room. Another shelf of vodka was mounted to the wall, next to a painting of the Trinity Cathedral. Rudov slid aside the painting, revealing a small, glowing keypad. He entered a code, and shelves slid aside to reveal a hidden door in the wall behind. It swung open with a hiss.

Zasko followed Rudov into a smaller room. Fluorescent lights flickered on automatically as they entered. Zasko turned, and watched as the door slid shut behind them, locking with a click. A second keypad was mounted next to the closed door on the inner wall.

The chamber was empty, save for a stuffed velvet armchair and a small glass table. A tiny remote control sat on the table, next to a hardwired intercom panel. A digital thermometer was mounted on the wall to their right. The temperature held at minus four degrees Celsius.

A pair of heavy fur robes hung on the wall beneath the thermometer. Rudov grabbed one and threw it over his suit. He tossed the other to Zasko.

'Only three men alive know of this place,' he said, his voice a deep rumble. 'Antonovich, my second in command. Just him, and two others. Good men, men I trust.'

'So this is where you keep them,' Zasko said, flashing Rudov his toothy smile. 'Seems risky.'

The older man nodded, then picked the remote up from the table. He pressed a button, and Zasko heard the hum of electric motors engaging. A frosted glass panel at the far end of the room slid up into the ceiling. Behind the glass stood a towering display cabinet, shrouded in mist.

The mist cleared. Transparent partitions divided the shelves into rows of square cubbies.

Each cubby held a severed head.

'This chamber is not on any floor plans,' the old man growled. 'The walls are soundproof, and no cell phones, no wireless signals of any kind, can penetrate them. Everything is hardwired to my office upstairs. Intercom, temperature, security... everything. In here, we may talk freely.'

Zasko's breath quickened as he took a step toward the case. He clasped his arms behind his back, and paced back and forth, gazing upon the grizzly trophies. Their skin was pale white, and frost crystals hung from their limp, matted hair.

A similar expression graced all their faces, frozen in place by death and ice. Their mouths were twisted into screams, their unblinking eyes wide with panic. Each severed head was a horrific visage of fear.

Zasko's eyes darted over the display of horrors. 'I remember some of these. Others... Well, there have been so many. Not every hunt was stimulating. Some prey are more skilled than others.'

Rudov pointed to an empty cubby near the top of the case. 'There. That is where I want this man's head. Alexi may have been a fool, but he was still my son. I want to see his killer's face in here, alongside the rest of my enemies. You may indulge your... appetites... with the rest of him. But his head is mine.'

'I understand,' Zasko said. 'But these men...' He gestured to the cabinet. 'They were gangsters, informants, petty thieves. Caine is nothing like them. It may be wiser to simply shoot him and be done with it.'

'*Nyet!*' Rudov's voice was hard as steel, and it echoed off the frost-covered walls of the hidden chamber. 'He must be hunted. He must suffer. If I were younger, stronger, I would see to it myself. But you, Piotr... You will bring me my trophy. And when it is over, I will come down here, sit in my chair, and look into his lifeless eyes. I will see that in his last moments, he feared me more than death itself.'

Zasko nodded. 'Very well. I have assembled a team. They are good men, professionals. I have worked with most of them before, in Spetsnaz GRU. Their commanding officers have been well compensated. They will not be missed for a couple days.'

'Good. Then all we need now is the prey.'

Zasko took one last look at the trophy case. He shook his head.

'Caine is not prey. He is a predator, like me. And to catch a predator, you must have one thing.'

The elder patriarch stroked the grey stubble on his chin. 'All my resources are at your disposal. What is it you need?'

Zasko turned away from the case to face Rudov. He licked his lips.

'Live bait.'

22

Beads of sweat dripped down the pockmarked skin of Lau Somchai's face. The short, heavy-set Thai man squinted in the harsh light and raised a hand to wipe his brow. The sky above Pattaya Port was clear and blue, offering no clouds to dim the blistering rays of the afternoon sun. The intense heat reflected back off the metal deck of the cargo ship he was standing on.

A wiry Filipino man wearing khaki shorts and a T-shirt led Lau across the deck toward a large hatch. Rippling waves of heat rose up around them. The boat was old and gray, and every inch was caked in grease and grime. The stench of burning engine oil filled the searing air.

'You not gonna believe this,' the man said. His voice was high-pitched, like a young boy, despite the deep wrinkles in his face. 'These look just like real thing. No one know difference, I swear. We make fortune. And the toys good for kids!'

Lau laughed. 'Sure, for kids. Come, show me.'

They reached the hatch. The wiry man kneeled, unbolted the metal plate, and threw it open. A narrow ladder led down into the cargo hold of the ship.

The man looked back at Lau. 'Where your partner? He no come?'

Lau shook his head. 'He busy. I make deal with you. Got it?'

The man shrugged. 'Okay, come with me.' He scurried down the ladder.

Lau wedged his girth into the hatch and followed, though at a much slower pace. A thick, musty odor hung below decks, but at least the air was cooler than above.

The hold of the ship was empty, save for a single wooden pallet in the center of the dark interior. A white-hot beam of sunlight cut through the open hatch, illuminating the shipping pallet and its contents.

The square platform was loaded with clear

plastic bundles, held together by black cargo straps. The Filipino man whipped a utility knife from his belt and slit one of the straps. An avalanche of the plastic bags fell to the floor, landing in a pile next to Lau's feet.

The pudgy man bent over and picked one up. He tore open the plastic and held the object inside up to the light.

It was a plush toy.

Lau laughed. The stuffed animal in his hands looked like a small blue cat with wide, leering pink eyes. The design was based on a popular cartoon character, though this doll was a counterfeit. It was one of thousands, churned out by third-world sweat-shops across the globe.

'Look just like cartoon,' Lau said, turning it over in his hands.

'Aren't you a little old to play with dolls?' a voice called out from the darkness. Footsteps echoed toward them. The wiry man turned and held his knife up.

'Who there?' he shouted. 'What you doing on my ship?'

A man stepped out of the shadows. He was tall, and his lean body moved toward them with the grace of a natural athlete. He was dressed in brown canvas pants and a navy linen shirt. His sleeves were rolled up to his elbows, revealing tan, muscular forearms.

His face was bronzed and youthful, but the skin around his eyes crinkled with the telltale signs of crow's feet. As he stepped into the beam of sunlight, his piercing green irises sparkled like emeralds. He did not blink, despite the intensity of the harsh light.

Lau, and others around Pattaya, knew him as Mark Waters, a *farang* with a shady past. Expat, smuggler... And to Lau, a partner in crime.

His real name was Thomas Caine.

'We were supposed to meet this afternoon, weren't we, Lau?' His voice echoed through the empty cargo hold.

A shadow of anger flitted across Lau's face. Then he flashed a smile and turned to the Filipino man.

'Ramil, this my partner. Mark Waters.'

The spindly man lowered the knife. 'So you did come. What do you want?'

Caine's eyes darted from Lau to the other man.

'I like to know who I'm doing business with. Your name is Ramil... Ramil Ocampo, right?'

The man known as Ramil smiled. 'Yes. You have heard of me, no?'

Caine nodded. 'I've heard of you, all right. You

did business with Sunil. Running counterfeit toys, like these.'

Ramil clapped his hands together, nodding. 'Yes, yes, they are beautiful, just like real thing.'

Caine's voice hardened. 'Not exactly like the real thing. Sunil got stopped by the Royal Police with one of your shipments. Turns out half the dolls were filled with methamphetamine.' Caine's eyes burned into Lau with an angry glare. 'Ramil here made a side deal with the buyer Sunil didn't even know. But that quantity of meth? He's looking at the death penalty for sure.'

Caine grabbed the doll from Lau. He twisted the blue fabric in his hands, until the stuffed creature's head tore off. White stuffing fluttered to the ground.

Ramil laughed. 'What you talking about, these just dolls. Kids love them! I make in factory. No drugs, no problem!'

Caine held the stuffing up to his nose and sniffed. He dropped the toy to the ground, and examined the other plastic bundles strapped to the pallet.

Lau shook his head. 'What wrong with you, man? We here to make money! Why you always worried? You supposed to be tough guy!'

Caine looked back at him over his shoulder.

'We'll see how tough you feel facing a death sentence in Bang Kwang prison. How long you think you'd last in there?'

Ramil stepped back, away from them. 'Come on Lau, you said we good, you said you make deal!'

Lau raised his hands and smiled. 'Everything fine, we good. Let me talk to my man, okay?'

Ramil cursed in Filipino, then paced away from them.

Caine felt Lau's hot breath on his shoulder as he kneeled next to the cargo pallet. He rapped his knuckles on one of the mottled wooden beams. The sound it made was plastic and insubstantial.

'You embarrass me, *farang*,' Lau hissed. 'So what if he smuggle drugs? We make fortune here!'

Caine ignored him and pulled a small vial of liquid from his pocket. He uncapped the tiny glass vial and spilled its contents onto the beam of wood.

'What the hell you doing?' his partner asked in a whisper. 'What is that?'

The two men watched as the wood sizzled and bubbled. The area touched by the liquid dissolved into a thick gray paste.

Caine stood up. 'Special type of acid. It dissolves only plastics and resins. This pallet isn't real wood, is it Ramil?'

Ramil stopped pacing and shook his fist at Lau, a loud stream of Tagalog curses exploding from his mouth.

'Spare me the bullshit!' Caine snapped. 'It's cocaine. Mixed with some kind of glue or plastic. You poured it into a mold and painted it to look like wood.'

'It look just like real thing... Royal Police never see the difference!' Ramil shouted in English. Then he turned back to Lau and continued cursing in his own tongue. The pudgy man's face flushed red with anger, and he screamed back a reply in rapid-fire Thai.

Caine grabbed Lau and slammed him against the side of the boat.

'What the fuck, Waters? You crazy?'

Caine twisted the fabric of Lau's colorful shirt in his fists. 'I told you before, Lau. No guns, no people, no drugs. Did you know?'

'He is the one with drugs! I your partner, why you no trust me?'

Caine's eyes burned with inner fire, his lips twisted into a snarl. 'Answer me! Did you know?'

Lau shook his head, his eyes wide with fear. 'No, I swear, I not know!'

'You bunch of pussies!' Ramil shouted. 'What the hell wrong with you? We all make big money here!'

Caine let go of Lau. He ran his fingers through his sweat-soaked hair and exhaled.

'Not interested. Find someone else.'

Ramil shook his head. He sneered at Caine as Lau picked himself up and straightened his rumpled shirt.

'It just like they said. Lau the one with balls. Next time, I deal only with him!'

Caine tilted his head and glared at Ramil. 'Just like who said?'

Before Ramil could answer, Caine's cell phone rang.

He ignored it and stared into Ramil's eyes. The Filipino rubbed his scalp, and turned away, muttering something unintelligible.

The phone kept ringing. He slipped it out of his pocket and glanced at the screen.

The number was familiar.

Naiyana...

Before he could answer the call, the ringing stopped.

Caine turned to Lau. 'You know my rules. So does your boss. This...' He pointed at the pile of stuffed animals stacked on the fake pallet. 'This is not happening.'

He climbed the ladder to the upper deck, and slammed the hatch shut behind him.

'*Luk ga-ree*,' Lau muttered.

'You said this was no problem,' Ramil shouted. 'What he mean, rules? He talk to your boss? What boss?'

Lau shot the man a dirty look. 'Anna.'

Ramil sucked in a gasp of breath between his teeth. 'He has the ear of the godmother... the *Chao Mae*?'

Lau looked up at the closed hatch. A bitter smile crossed his puffy lips. He turned and spat on the floor.

'For now. But things change. Someday, I no longer need partner. Someday, I show Mark Waters who boss really is.'

23

Caine pressed the phone to his ear. It rang and rang, but no one picked up. He raised a hand and whistled, signaling one of the yellow and blue taxicabs that sped past the port entrance. The tiny van swerved out of traffic and screeched to a halt in front of the gates to Bali Hai pier.

Caine climbed into the rear seat, glancing left and right at the crowd. His reading of Ramil told him the man was too spineless to try anything stupid, but it couldn't hurt to keep an eye out.

The driver slid the door shut behind him, then hopped back into the driver's seat. *'Pai tee nai krap*? Where to, mister?'

Caine ignored him and listened as the phone continued to ring.

Naiyana... he hadn't seen her since his encounter with the man known as Pisac. The Devil. The Burmese gangster was a high-ranking member of the Red Wa, a criminal organization operating on the northern Thai border. Naiyana was a bar girl. Pisac, along with his Russian Mafia contacts, had targeted her in a human trafficking operation: girls kidnapped to order, auctioned off on a fake dating website.

Naiyana was the closest thing Caine had to a friend. She was one of the few people he'd confided in since his betrayal at the hands of his CIA masters. When she was taken, he went after her. And in doing so, he unleashed the bloodshed that always seemed to follow in his wake. When it was over – when she was safe – she left Pattaya, and returned to her small town.

It was better that way, he told himself. *Safer.*

Safer for her to stay away from him. Safer for him to stay alone.

Suddenly, the phone picked up. Caine heard breathing. Without waiting, he spoke. 'Naiyana! I thought you left town, I thought—'

'Not Naiyana!' The voice belonged to a young

boy. He sounded like he was running, huffing for breath. 'This is Taavi!'

Naiyana's brother Taavi was a local pickpocket and street hustler. His antics had landed him on the local gangs' shit list. Saving the fourteen-year-old boy from a beating was how Caine had met Naiyana in the first place.

'Taavi? What are you doing on this number?'

'Naiyana give me her phone before she leave. She tell me to call you if I get in trouble!'

'Let me guess... You're in trouble?'

'Men are following me. First I think they just perverts, looking for ladyboy tail. I lost them on Walking Street, but now they back!'

'Taavi, where are you?'

'I hide in old building, the flophouse behind Ruby's, where the drug mules used to crash.'

'No, Taavi, listen to me. Stay on the street! You're safer out in the open—'

'Too late!' The boy's voice dropped to a hushed whisper. 'They follow inside! I know hiding place upstairs. Hurry, please!'

There was a click, and the line went dead.

Caine looked up. The driver was staring at him in the rearview mirror. '*Khun phrom?* You ready to go now?'

'You know the backstreet that runs behind Ruby's bar?'

The driver nodded.

'Then step on it.'

* * *

Caine knew something was wrong, even before he saw the crowds blocking the narrow backstreet. A plume of smoke, rising from a decrepit abandoned building, was visible for miles. The cab slowed to a crawl. The driver turned back to face him.

'Too many people, have to stop. You get out here.'

Caine shoved a wad of crumpled baht notes into the driver's outstretched hand. 'Keep the change,' he muttered as he threw open the door and slid off the seat.

He pushed his way through the throng of sweating bodies, as a wave of intense heat rippled from the end of the alley. Caine heard people gasping, and the crackling sound of burning wood.

Finally, he made his way to the end of the cramped, narrow street and stood facing the rear of the abandoned hovel. Somewhere inside, Taavi was hiding.

The building was on fire.

Flickering tongues of orange flame crept up the warped frames of the structure's windows. Thick black smoke hung over the alley, trapping the heat in a cloud of dry, stinging air. The smoke stank of burning rubber and gasoline.

Napalm, Caine thought. This fire was no accident. *This is arson.*

He froze for a moment, his eyes darting around the crowd. They were locals, mostly... bar girls on their way to work, street vendors pushing their carts toward the walking street. It was still too early for the tourists to have crawled from their cozy air-conditioned hotel rooms.

Caine grabbed the arm of a young woman staring up at the blaze. 'Where are the police? The fire department? Is anyone coming?'

The woman narrowed her eyes and jerked away her arm. 'Hey! *Te mue ok bpai, farang!*'

Caine let go and held up his hands. He took a step back. 'I'm sorry. My friend is inside.'

The woman looked him up and down, then shook her head. 'Your friend is drug dealer?'

She gestured toward the building. 'Police no come. Gangs live in there. No one care about this place.'

As she hurried away from him, Caine ran his

hands through his hair, wiping away beads of sweat from his forehead. Something about her tone, her nervous glance as she walked away, made the meaning of her words clear. After years of hiding in Pattaya, Caine knew how the system worked.

Money changed hands. The police, the fire depart-ment... they were paid to stay away. They're going to let this place burn to the ground.

With Taavi inside.

Caine remembered the last time he had seen Naiyana. The look of concern in her eyes. Her kind voice, and soothing words.

You good man. Good friend to me...

Now, Taavi was back. Strange men chasing him, arson... It all felt wrong. It felt like a trap. The hairs on the back of his neck bristled in the super-heated air surrounding the blaze.

Suddenly, one of the rear windows exploded, sending shards of glowing glass into the alley. The crowd gasped again and shuffled back as a column of flame leaped from the opening and crawled up the exterior wall.

Trap or not, Naiyana's brother is inside...

Caine scanned the crowd again. He spotted a ro-tund man in a sweat-stained shirt pushing a metal cart loaded with sliced fruit and bottled drinks. He cut through the alley, heading to the walking street, where hordes of tourists would soon gather.

Caine darted through the crowd, moving toward the cart at a quick jog. 'Water! Hey, do you have water?'

The man stopped and smiled. He fished into the ice, pulled out a clear plastic bottle, and wiped off the droplets of moisture with a dirty white rag.

'*Nam na*,' the man chanted. 'Water, yes. Five baht.'

Caine grabbed the bottle and tore the rag from the vendor's hands. 'Sorry, no time!'

He gave the man a shove, sending him reeling backward. Then he pushed back through the crowd, fighting his way toward the blaze. He doused the cloth with water and tied it over his mouth like a bandana.

He charged up to the building and kicked open the door, sending a shower of glowing ash into the air. He took a deep breath through the cool damp cloth and closed his eyes for a second.

Then he plunged into the inferno.

24

'Taavi!' Caine's voice was hoarse and ragged. The air inside the burning structure hit him like a blast from a furnace. The heat battered him, sapping his strength as smoke and soot swirled around him. Combined with the rippling waves of super-heated air, the haze cut his visibility down to a few feet.

He coughed and stumbled forward, taking shallow breaths through the soaked cloth.

The fire was growing in intensity. The flames would soon devour the old, rickety building. He had to find Taavi and get out before the blaze consumed them both.

'Taavi!' he shouted again. There was no response.

He pushed his way forward. The fire singed his

shirt and pants. He ignored the flame's burning kiss against his exposed skin.

Deeper in the building, a section of the roof collapsed. Caine saw a flash of sparks as the charred debris crumbled to the ground. A breeze wafted through the room. It cleared the smoke for a few seconds, but the fresh oxygen fueled the fire. The flames surrounding him raged higher.

He found himself standing in front of a narrow staircase that led up to the second floor. He grabbed the railing parallel to the stairs. The flesh on his palms sizzled, and the stench of charred skin assaulted his nostrils. He cried out and yanked his hand away. The metal railing was almost red hot. He felt a delayed reaction, a throbbing lance of pain coursing through the nerves of his hand.

'Mr. Waters!' The voice was faint, distant. At first, Caine thought he was imagining things, that the heat and smoke were playing tricks with his mind. Then he heard it again.

'Mr. Waters, up here!'

He gritted his teeth and climbed the stairs. A swirling vortex of heat and flame consumed the second floor. As he approached the middle of the staircase, the wood gave way with a splintering crack. A cloud of glowing embers flew into his face as the stairs collapsed beneath him.

Caine grabbed at the railing mounted to the wall. Again he roared in pain as the heated metal seared into his flesh, but he forced himself to hold tight. The stairs collapsed into a smoking pile of rubble, and his feet dangled inches above the flames.

His hands, now numb and tingling from multiple burns, grasped the railing in a white-knuckled grip. He shifted his weight, pulling himself up the metal bar, moving hand over hand until his flailing feet finally reached the landing on the next floor.

He pulled himself onto the solid platform, gasping for breath in the smoky air.

'Taavi,' he called out. 'Where are you?'

'End of hall... I cannot open door!'

Caine waded through the acrid smoke, moving toward the sound of the boy's voice. He darted down a hallway, as curtains of hungry flame devoured the walls on either side of him. The narrow passage ended at a closed door. He pounded on it with his fist.

'Taavi?' he shouted.

'I'm in here,' the boy cried out. 'I hide in closet, but now I can't get out!'

Caine whipped off his bandana and wrapped it

around the doorknob. The wet scrap of fabric sizzled as it made contact with the scalding metal. He turned the knob and slowly opened the door. In a fire of this size, he knew an explosive backdraft was always possible if a sudden rush of oxygen entered the area.

Inside, the room was a mass of charred wood and thick smoke, but the flames seemed to have died down. Looking up, he saw the roof had collapsed here as well. A thick wooden beam lay at an angle, blocking the narrow door of a closet on the west wall.

'Okay, kid, stay put. I see the problem.'

Caine kicked at the debris on the floor. He found a loose two-by-four that seemed solid and jammed it under the collapsed beam at an angle.

'Stand back! This place could collapse any second,' he shouted through the door. Then he pulled back on the two-by-four.

The slab of wood didn't budge.

Caine coughed as the smoke penetrated his lungs. He planted his feet on the ground and yanked back again. The fallen beam scraped against the floor, moving a fraction of an inch.

Stinging sweat dripped down his face. He coughed again and wiped what felt like acid from his eyes. The muscles in his shoulders rippled and bulged beneath the singed fabric of his shirt. He grunted from exertion as he tugged again, using all his dwindling strength.

The beam shifted, and at last fell away from the door. Caine jumped aside as the heavy slab struck the floor. With a loud crack, the weakened floorboards gave way, and the charred beam plummeted to the first floor. A plume of flame exploded up into the room, but it quickly died. Tendrils of the fire below growled and crackled around the hole in the floor, hungry for the fresh oxygen that had been released.

Caine threw open the closet door. Taavi sat hunched in the back, coughing and gasping for breath. He looked up at Caine with wide, frightened eyes.

'Come on, kid, we're getting out of here.' Caine grabbed the boy in his arms and hefted him off the floor. He coughed and stumbled but managed to keep his footing. He carried the barely conscious boy out into the hallway. Turning left, he headed for the rear of the building. Through the cloud of smoke and ash, he could make out a dusty window at the end of the corridor. He quickened his pace, as the heat behind him grew even more intense. The fire was growing. Soon there would be nowhere left to run.

He reached the window. Setting Taavi down, he wrapped the bandana around his fist and struck the glass. It shattered, revealing the metal platform of a fire escape. Taavi coughed and sputtered as Caine lifted him to his feet.

'Move it, Taavi! Almost there!'

The boy opened his eyes, then clutched Caine's shoulder.

'Whatever you do,' he said, gasping for breath, 'do not tell my sister about this... She will kill me!'

Caine lifted the boy over the windowsill. 'Deal. Now get down there. I'll follow you out.'

The boy nodded and began to descend the metal ladder.

Caine sucked in the fresh air, and waited until Taavi was halfway down. Then he leaned forward, preparing to climb after him.

He felt a vice-like grip on his shoulder. An arm wrapped around his throat and pulled him back into the lethal blaze. He drove his right elbow back, and felt it connect with soft flesh. Whoever had grabbed him grunted and released the hold on his throat. Caine spun around, throwing up his left arm to break the attacker's grasp. He knocked away the hand that gripped his shoulder and squinted in the hazy air.

The figure before him wore a baggy orange jumpsuit. A black visor hid his face, and the hose of an oxygen tank trailed over his shoulder. A yellow metal helmet protected his head.

Pattaya Fire brigade, Caine thought. They finally made it.

Then he noticed what the figure clutched in his hand.

Instead of a fire axe, which was strapped to his back, the firefighter held a slim black pistol.

Caine pivoted sideways as the man fired. The gun made a muted coughing sound, barely audible over the crackling of the fire. Caine saw a tiny metal sliver embed itself into the wall next to him.

The gun was an air pistol. Whoever this man was, he wanted to take him alive.

Caine dipped his shoulders low and lunged forward. Reaching out with his left hand, he wrapped his fingers around the wrist of the man's shooting arm. With his free hand, he tore the visor off his target's face, revealing Caucasian features behind the opaque plastic covering.

Who are these guys?

Had the CIA finally caught up with him after all this time? If not them, who? FBI? Interpol?

He ignored the questions flooding his mind and kept moving, kept attacking. Unlike his opponent, Caine had no oxygen supply or protective gear. He knew that every second he spent in the fire, he grew weaker.

Winding his right arm back, he snapped an open palm strike into his opponent's exposed face. As the man's head snapped back, Caine locked his left arm in a two-handed grip and spun him around. A quick stomp to the instep brought his opponent to his knees.

Caine coughed and stumbled in the caustic air, but he kept his grip on the arm tight. The man screamed as the muscles in his shoulder stretched to the snapping point.

'Who are you?' Caine shouted. 'Who do you work for?'

Before the man could answer, Caine heard loud, crashing footsteps from down the hall. He looked up and saw two more men dressed in the same fire-fighting gear surging toward him.

Twin darts streaked past his face, missing his neck by a few inches.

Caine let go of his opponent's arm. He ducked

down and grabbed the fire axe strapped to the man's back. Wrenching it free, he wound his arm back and hurled it toward the new attackers.

The weapon spun through the air. As the other man raised his pistol to fire, the heavy metal blade buried itself in his chest with a wet thud. The man screamed and stumbled backward. He fell, striking the landing of the collapsed staircase. The brittle, charred wood gave way beneath him, and he plunged through the flames into the inferno below.

Before Caine could savor his victory, another fit of choking wracked his body. He heaved over, gasping for breath. His vision grew hazy. The man on the ground staggered to his feet.

'*Sukin syn!*' he hissed. He pulled his visor and oxygen mask back over his face and stepped toward Caine.

Russian, Caine thought. *Called me a son of a bitch... Probably rules out the CIA.*

He forced himself to stand up. The firefighter swung a right hook at Caine. He blocked it, but the effort left him reeling. He stumbled and fell to his hands and knees. The smoke, the heat... it was all too much. He couldn't breathe, couldn't see...

He felt the heavy rubber sole of the man's boot slam into his gut. What little air he had left exploded from his lungs. He fell to the floor, clawing at the charred wood beneath his fingers.

He felt more hands grab him, flip him over. Something pressed against his neck.

Not a dart... Injector. He heard the hiss of compressed air. They had drugged him.

He looked up and saw the shattered window above.

Taavi... At least he got away. At least he's safe.

As the narcotic coursed through his veins, he was comforted by the thought that he would die alone. The ghosts of his bloody past would claim only him.

Not Taavi. Not Naiyana.

Not Rebecca...

The image of the window faded, replaced by an orange, flickering blur. He closed his eyes and let himself fall into the darkness.

25

The heavy wooden door of the bar swung open, and a gust of freezing wind blasted through the doorway. The men inside – the bar was populated only by men – looked up, as the thick slab of wood slammed against the wall. The crowd's eyes were dark and sullen, their jaws clenched in frowns and grimaces.

A small television hung above the bar counter. The droning of the Russian newscaster on the screen was the only sound in the room. No music played. All chatter had ceased.

A tall, healthy-looking young man stood in the open doorway. His eyes were pale blue and his skin fair, flushed red from the cold outside. A thick wool cap covered his hair, but a few blond locks fell down in front of his eyes.

A military-issue backpack hung from his shoulders, and he held a large canvas duffel bag in his right hand. The bag was almost as big as he was, and the fabric stretched under the weight of whatever was inside.

He turned and closed the door behind him, silencing the howling wind outside. Then he glanced around the bar, an eager but determined look on his face.

He caught the eye of the bartender. The man's craggy features looked as gnarled and aged as the filthy bar counter he hunched over. He swished a dirty gray rag around the inside of a glass mug and glared at the newcomer in silence. Then he tilted his head and nodded toward another door at the back of the room.

The young man adjusted his pack and headed toward the rear door. The other men in the bar turned away from him. They did not look up to meet his gaze as he walked past.

Everyone in the bar knew that those who met in the back room were not men to get involved with. They were not lumberjacks or truck drivers or fur trappers. They were not like the others who lived in the small town.

The men who met in the back all had a certain look in their eye. Even this man, youthful and vibrant as he was, carried that touch of darkness in his fervent stare.

Those who lived in this small mountain town had enough darkness, enough cold and pain in their lives. They had no desire to invite more of the same. So they looked down into their glasses, contemplating their stale beer or cheap vodka as they contemplated anything: with indifference. Or they just stared out the window, at the endless white expanse and the ghostly, snow-covered trees.

The newcomer took one last look around the silent bar, then opened the door in the back and stepped through.

Once the door had closed, a low, quiet chatter arose among the men in the bar. It was not cheerful, but it held some semblance of life. Just enough to forget the men in the back, and the long, dark shadows they cast.

* * *

A cloud of cigarette smoke hovered near the ceiling of the back room. The young man wrinkled his nose as the harsh, stale odor flooded his nostrils. He shut the door behind him and set his bag on the ground.

Commander Zasko sat facing the door. He sat with four other men around a large wood table, the surface of which lay hidden beneath a collage of maps, papers, and aerial photographs.

Zasko and his men all wore identical combat gear. A mottled gray and white camouflage pattern covered their heavy parkas and jumpsuits. The tactical gear was military issue, but they displayed no unit insignias or any other official markings.

The young man was not surprised. He knew this was not an official mission.

The other men were all smoking cigarettes and drinking vodka. They laughed and talked among themselves as they methodically cleaned and checked their weapons.

Zasko looked up as the man entered the room. He leaned back in his chair, and floorboards creaked in protest as his muscular body shifted. Despite the cold, his jumpsuit was unzipped to his waist, exposing a hairy, muscular chest. A metal pendant lay nestled in the thick, coarse fur that covered his upper body. It was the head of a wolf, hanging from a dull metal chain around his neck.

Zasko took a long puff from a hand-rolled cigarette, then stabbed it out in a filthy, cracked ashtray. His dark, penetrating eyes stayed focused on the newcomer.

'You must be Yuri, eh? You are late.' His voice was low and deep, like the purr of a big cat. He filled a small glass with vodka from an unmarked bottle on the table.

The young man nodded. '*Da*, the truck missed the bar. I had to backtrack several kilometers to find this place.'

Zasko pushed the glass across the table toward the man called Yuri. Then he tipped the bottle and began filling the glasses of the other men at the table.

'I know your commander, Vasily. He speaks well of you. Says you are the best shot in FSB Alpha unit. You were awarded the Cross of St George and the Medal of Suvorov, back to back.'

Yuri picked up the glass, but did not drink.

Zasko smiled and raised his glass in the air. '*Za zdoróvye*,' he said, and drank the vodka in one gulp.

Yuri followed and set the glass down on the table.

Zasko licked his lips. 'Well?'

Yuri shrugged. 'This is true. I am fully rated on the Orsis T-5000, VSS Vintorez, Dragunov, of course—'

One of the others, a bear-like man with a shaved head and gray goatee, chuckled. 'All these medals, and before he is out of diapers. Remarkable achievement.'

The other men laughed. Zasko smiled.

'That's enough, Boris,' he said as he refilled his glass. The men's laughter died down. The big man, Boris, glowered at Yuri for a second, then turned away and tossed his shot of vodka down his throat.

'Now then,' Zasko continued. 'What about hand-to-hand? Can you fight up close, without a weapon?'

'I have trained all my life in sambo. Do you wish to test me?' he asked, his eyes shifting from Zasko's smiling face to Boris.

Zasko sipped his vodka. 'Boris, you practice sambo, *ne tak li*?'

Boris stood up and cracked his knuckles. He stood in front of Yuri and looked down at him. 'You practice your whole life, little man?' The huge figure sneered. 'How you find time for this between nursing at your mother's tits?'

Boris stood a foot taller than Yuri, and his girth

made the younger man look like a small child. Yuri looked him up and down, then turned toward Zasko. 'How far do you want this to go?'

Zasko slid a large serrated knife from a leather sheath that hung at his waist. He spun the knife on the table, watching the sharp tip drill into the splintering wood.

'You go until I tell you to stop.'

'I am Spetsnaz GRU, little man,' Boris snarled. 'We feed little FSB boys like you to our dogs.'

The big man lunged forward, his thick, meaty fist exploding toward Yuri's face.

The smaller man sprang into action. He side-stepped the powerful blow and reached across his body, knocking Boris's arm wide with his left hand.

As the giant struggled to recover, Yuri curled the fingers of his other hand into a hook. He raked them across Boris's eyes. The larger man screamed in pain and rage, but Yuri did not stop attacking.

Grabbing Boris's wrist in his right hand, he bent the man's arm backward. With a quick pivot, he sent him tumbling to the floor.

The floorboards shook and rattled as Boris crashed to the ground. Yuri dropped down a split second later, driving his knee into the larger man's elbow. There was an audible crack as the joint shattered from the force of the blow.

Boris howled in pain. Yuri looked up at Zasko. The commander squinted, and his nostrils flared, but he said nothing. The other men at the table exchanged nervous glances.

Yuri grabbed Boris's arm and yanked it upwards. The injured man struggled to lift his body up from the floor in a vain effort to lessen the pressure on his trapped limb.

Yuri struck again, stepping in front of the bigger man and dropping to the ground. He crushed the man's neck in the bend between his calf and thigh as he continued to pull back on the arm. There was a loud pop as Boris's left shoulder dislocated.

He howled again and began tapping the floor with his injured right hand.

'*Pozhaluysta!* Please, you win! I said you win, enough!'

Again Yuri looked up to Zasko. The younger man clenched his jaw and stared into his commander's eyes. Zasko shook his head and smiled. He stood up and stepped over the two entangled men. He looked down at Boris and sighed.

'There was a girl. Katya. You remember her,

Boris, don't you? After our last hunt, you acted... inappropriately.'

'*Da, da,* I remember,' the big man cried. Spittle hung from his lips and pooled on the floor. 'I'm sorry, I had to... I thought it was okay, just once!'

'I understand,' Zasko continued. 'She was beautiful, and we all have our urges, of course. But the man who owns this bar, the man who allows us to meet here? He provides us anonymity, a safe haven for these unsanctioned activities of ours. Katya was his niece. You knew this. I told you to stay away from her. But you touched her. You damaged her, Boris.'

'It won't happen again, Commander. I swear!'

Zasko eyed the knife in his hands. He spun the blade in a circle, balancing it against the rough skin of his palm. He kneeled next to Boris. The big man's face was beet red, and droplets of sweat trickled down his forehead. His eyes bulged.

Yuri tightened his grip, but above his clenched jaw, his frowning eyes betrayed his uncertainty. 'Commander, I—'

Zasko's nostrils flared as he inhaled a deep breath. 'What is that smell, Boris? Have you pissed yourself?'

'*Prosti.* I'm sorry, I swear, I—'

'These people here, they are sheep. But what you

did brings attention to us. To our activities here in town. And worst of all, to our employer. That is something I cannot allow.'

The man struggled to speak, gasping for breath in the powerful hold. Yuri released the man's arm and stood up. Boris gulped air as he staggered to his feet.

'He's had enough, I think,' Yuri said in a quiet voice.

Zasko stared at the young man. His eyes were wide, his pupils dark and dilated. They gave his stare a wild, hypnotic pull. His mouth hung open, revealing the tips of his sharp white teeth.

'It seems our new member has chosen to show you mercy, Boris. Lucky day for you. But you must realize, there is no longer a place for you here.'

The big man nodded, still gasping for breath, the flush receding from his face and neck. '*Khorosho*, fine. I leave now.' He turned and shuffled toward the door.

A loud crack snapped through the room. The coiled black leather of a whip appeared in Zasko's free hand. The long leather braid cut through the air faster than the eye could see and wrapped around Boris's neck like a constrictor snake.

The big man's hands shot to his throat, his eyes bulging as a weak gasp hissed from his lungs.

Zasko spun the leather cord around his body and twisted his waist. The momentum yanked Boris forward. He struggled to free himself from the whip's stranglehold, as he stumbled toward the commander.

With his other arm, Zasko thrust his knife into Boris's gut. The hulking man ceased his struggling, and a gurgle of pain escaped his lips.

Zasko jerked the blade up and twisted the handle of the knife. 'I told you,' he snarled. 'Once you join a hunt, this is the only way you leave.'

Boris crashed to his knees. Blood and innards gushed from the open wound.

'Commander!' Yuri stepped toward them, raising his arms to pull Zasko away from the wounded man. Before he could lay a finger on him, Zasko whipped the knife out of Boris's gut, and whirled the blade around. His arm shot out again, this time pointing the hilt of the weapon at Yuri's face.

The young man found himself staring down the barrel of a small metal tube. The opening protruded from the bottom of the knife's handle. He froze in place and raised his hands in surrender.

'You know what this is?' Zasko asked, his voice dripping with menace.

Yuri nodded. 'NSR-2 Shooting Knife. The hilt is loaded with a single round. Safety and trigger are in the guard.'

Zasko smiled, baring his teeth. 'You know your weapons. This one holds a 7.62mm cartridge. At this range, your funeral would be closed casket. You understand?'

Yuri said nothing.

The wild grin did not leave Zasko's lips. He spun the blade again in his palm. In one fluid motion, he drove the knife into the table and shook the whip loose from Boris's neck. The dead man toppled over onto the floor, his face bloated and pale.

A cell phone on the table began to buzz and vibrate. The other men mumbled amongst themselves and stood up. Two of them grabbed Boris's body and dragged it toward a walk-in freezer.

Zasko slapped Yuri on the shoulder. 'That is the signal. The plane is nearing the drop zone. This unpleasantness is over, but the next time I give you an order, you will not think or debate. You will obey.'

Yuri was silent for a moment. 'Yes sir,' he finally replied.

Zasko coiled the whip and hung it from his belt. 'Very good. Now, my young friend, it is time.'

'Time for what?'

The commander yanked the bloody knife from the table and wiped the blade across his chest. The blood left a bright red streak against the dark mass of hair.

'It is time for the hunt to begin.'

26

Darkness.

It engulfed him.

Moving. Spinning, tumbling.

Falling...

All at once, a black velvety curtain lifted from his senses. Caine's head snapped left and right, but there was too much... too much stimulation for his dulled senses. Light, noise, movement.

A high-pitched whistle screamed through his ears. At first, he thought he was crying out, either in fear or pain. Then he realized his jaw was clenched tight. His heart thumped against his chest, pumping jets of adrenaline through his veins. His senses sharpened, then focused.

Tiny cracks of harsh white light penetrated the darkness. He caught a quick glimpse of gray metal walls. A white cushion hung inches from his face. Dark spatters of dried blood dotted the scuffed and tattered foam. Thick, padded straps dug into his shoulders and chest. His hands were zip-tied in front of him. *The screaming wail was the wind, rushing by outside. The men in the fire*, he thought. *They captured you, drugged you. Put you in this cage... Dropped you from a plane.*

Caine had trained with the Army's Airborne Rangers, and the Air Force's HALO jumpers. He knew he was in free fall. Whatever this strange prison surrounding him was, it was plummeting through the air at terminal velocity. And he was trapped inside, falling along with it...

He struggled against his bonds, but it was futile. The zip-ties held tight. His stomach lurched as the metal box tumbled through the atmosphere. He felt icy blades of cold piercing through the cracks of his prison.

A barrage of confused thoughts assaulted his drug-addled mind. *Where the hell am I? Why the cage? Why didn't they just kill me?*

Who did this to me?

The frantic train of thought screeched to a halt

as the snap of rippling fabric echoed through the tiny box. The straps cut into Caine's shoulders as his body flew upwards. His head snapped forward and bounced off the padding. A jolt of stinging pain coursed through his nose and jaw, but nothing felt broken.

Then all was still... quiet. He felt the box gently sway, as if it was hanging in the air, almost motionless.

No, he thought. *Not hanging. Still falling. Parachute deployed. Must have been automatic, set to an altimeter.*

Someone wanted him alive. For now, at least.

He closed his eyes and forced himself to calm his ragged breathing. His racing heartbeat slowed to a steady, rhythmic pulse. He let his limbs go limp and focused on the cold blackness surrounding him. He inhaled a long, deep breath of cold air through his nose. A few seconds later, he exhaled. He felt his pulse slow even further.

He cursed himself for losing control, for taking so long to stomp down the debilitating tide of panic and fear.

He had been trained to achieve his objectives at all costs. To ignore the rush of stress and emotions one experienced when staring death in the face. The training taught him to beat back the wave of adren-

aline and panic by focusing on a goal, a positive out-
come of some kind. Reuniting with friends or loved
ones. The successful completion of a mission. A purpose, a reason to make sense of the suffering and
pain.

But Caine had none of these things. Betrayed,
alone, on the run... In his heart, he knew his future
was as cold and dark as the cramped metal box and
the frigid air surrounding him.

So instead, he focused on his captors. He had
many enemies. Right now, there was no way to know
who it was that had caught up to him. Who had used
the frightened young boy as bait in their trap.

But as he continued his breathing exercises, he
imagined their shadowy, indistinct faces.

And he imagined what he would do to them the
moment he got the chance.

27

A few minutes later, Caine's body shuddered as the box thudded into the ground. Outside the metal crate, muffled footsteps crunched toward him. There was the clatter of chains, a key turning in a lock. With a loud crash, the metal sides fell away, and sunlight blasted into the open cage.

Caine was strapped to a padded seat. His eyes were closed. He was still, unmoving.

Surrounding him was a vast expanse of harsh white. An icy wind cut across his cheeks like a cold steel blade.

The footsteps moved closer. A figure emerged from the swirling frost. He was short and hunched over. He walked with a slow, steady gait. His feet were clad in thick fur boots, and they plunged deep into the snow with every step.

He wore a thick, tattered parka, its fur-trimmed hood covering his face. A double-barreled shotgun hung from a loose, single-handed grip at his side. He let the tip of the weapon trail in the snow behind him.

As he drew near Caine, the man raised the gun.

'Hey, *privet!*' he shouted. His voice was hoarse and faint beneath the wind. '*Ne bud' glupym...* Do not be stupid! I am here to release you.'

Caine was still. The man in the parka took another step forward.

'*Spyashchaya krasavitsa...* Sleeping beauty. Wake your ass up!'

Caine remained slumped in the chair.

The man pulled back the hood of his parka and leaned over Caine. His face was hard and leathery, his skin marked by the deep cracks and lines of one whose life had seen far too many days of winter. He slid off a glove and pressed a pair of fingers into Caine's throat. Caine's body was cold and stiff. Lifeless to the touch.

'*Otlichno...* Just great. I told those fools the fall would—'

Before the man could finish the sentence, Caine's emerald-green eyes snapped open. He squinted in the swirling white mist, returning the old man's shocked gaze with a predatory glare. His muscles tensed, like a tiger preparing to strike.

The old man's scream expelled a puff of frosted breath. He tried to raise the shotgun, but Caine's bound hands flew up and grabbed the hood of his parka. He pulled down, slamming the old man's face into the top of his skull. There was a loud crack. The man groaned and fell forward. Caine jerked up his knee as far as the straps would allow. He heard the man wheeze as the blow hammered into the tissue surrounding his lungs.

Dropping his hands to the shotgun, Caine gripped the cold metal barrels in his fingers. He jabbed upwards, ramming the gun's stock into the old man's face. As he staggered backward, Caine yanked the gun from his grasp and balanced it against his leg. His fingers were numb and clumsy from the cold, but he managed to wrap them around the trigger. He pointed the twin barrels of the gun forward.

Glancing down, he recognized the weapon as a Bailkai IZH 43. Unlike most shotguns, the Russian-made Bailkai used a barrel selection switch, rather than a double trigger system. He flicked the switch with his thumb, activating both barrels.

The old man shook his head to clear his vision. He looked up and stared at Caine.

'*Ublyudok!*' the man exclaimed, cradling his battered face.

Russian, Caine thought. *Like the firefighters in Pattaya...*

'*Dvigaysya, i ty umresh*,' Caine growled back, speaking the man's native tongue. *Move and you die...*

The man's eyes widened in surprise. He froze in place.

'You speak Russian?'

Caine shivered, but kept the gun pointed straight. '*Da*. Who the hell are you? Where am I?'

'I am Fyodor. You are here... in mountains.' The man spread his arms, gesturing the vast, snow-covered expanse surrounding them. 'Siberia. West of Arshan.'

'You said you came to release me?'

The old man nodded. 'I have knife... Do you mind?' The man took a few steps closer. He was only a few feet away.

Another shiver rippled through Caine's body. He felt frost crackling against his skin. With his hands bound, his shaky grip on the gun was tenuous at best. He raised the barrels, pressing their tips into the man's side. He clenched his teeth to stop them from chattering.

'Nice and easy,' he hissed. 'You know what this gun can do at this range.'

The man looked down into Caine's squinting emerald eyes. With slow, careful movements, he unzipped his parka and pulled it open. A large hunting knife hung from a sheath at his waist. He drew it and slid the tip of the blade under the plastic tie around Caine's wrists.

Caine jabbed the barrels deeper into the man's flesh.

'I said easy...'

With a slow, sawing motion, the man cut through the zip-tie. Caine's wrists split apart. As the blood flowed back into his trembling hands, he dropped the gun into the snow. The old man glanced down. His arm slid toward the fallen weapon...

Caine kicked the man in the gut, knocking him backward. He twisted the latch on his harness, freeing himself from the constricting straps. He tumbled forward out of the chair and sprawled into the snow.

He scooped up the gun and staggered to his knees. Even holding it in a proper grip, his hands still shook from the debilitating cold. He aimed it as well as he could at the old man.

'Your coat... take it off slowly. Throw it to me.'

The man clutched his belly and coughed, still recovering from Caine's sudden attack.

'It won't be enough,' he wheezed. 'Not in this cold.'

Caine gestured with the gun. '*Sdelay eto.* Do it! Now!'

The man shrugged out of the coat and tossed it to the ground between them.

Caine bent down and picked it up. He slipped into the threadbare parka one arm at a time, keeping the shaking gun trained on the man the best he could.

The coat was warmer, but it was torn and threadbare. Patches of insulation had burst from ripped seams, and Caine knew the man was right. The coat was better than nothing, but it would not provide sufficient insulation as the temperature continued to fall.

Caine patted the sides of the coat. He felt a heavy lump in the left pocket. He reached in with a free hand and pulled out a cold metal flask.

'Water?' he asked.

The man shook his head. 'Vodka.'

Caine tossed the flask in the snow. 'Great. Last thing I need.'

An electronic ring sounded from the other pocket. The hi-tech chime seemed out of place in the stark, desolate wilderness surrounding them. Caine reached into the pocket and pulled out a small black satellite phone.

'Expecting a call?'

The old man smiled. 'Go ahead, answer. It is for you.'

Caine pressed the phone to his freezing cheek.

'Yes?' he said.

'*Zdravstvuyte*, hello.' The voice was deep and gravelly. 'Welcome to Russia.'

'Who the hell is this?' Caine snapped.

The speaker continued, ignoring the question. 'I trust you had a relaxing flight?'

'Slept like a baby. What did they give me, etorphine? With a quick shot of naloxone to wake me up on the way down?'

'You sound like you know more about such things than I do, Mr. Waters. Or should I call you Mr. Caine? Either way, I leave these details to my employees. Speaking of which, how is poor old Fyodor?'

Caine glanced up at the old man. The withered figure had wrapped his arms around himself and hunched over in the cold. He shivered and stared with sullen eyes at the flask of vodka half buried in the snow.

'After all this, you sent an old farmer to kill me? If you know who I am, you know that was a mistake.'

The voice chuckled, a deep, rasping laugh that went on for several seconds. 'What? You think I would send a *p'yanyy durak*, an old drunk fool like Fyodor, to kill you? You underestimate me, Mr. Caine. You really don't know who I am, do you?'

'Should I?'

'My name is Sergei Rudov. I believe you met Alexi. My son.'

Alexi Rudov... The name cut through the haze of cold and confusion that clouded Caine's mind. Alexi was a former FSB officer with connections to the Russian Mafia. He and the Red Wa leader, the so-called Devil, were the ones who had targeted Naiyana.

In the aftermath of his bloody vengeance, Caine had framed the Devil and his gang for Alexi's death.

The ruse involved Alexi's severed head, delivered to St. Petersburg, Russia.

The Red Wa were not subtle. Neither was Caine.

The man on the phone continued. 'I must commend you, Mr. Caine. You have caused me great pain and inconvenience. I have spent many months, and spilled much blood, going to war with the Red Wa. Your little present had me convinced the Devil, this Pisac, had killed my son. But now I know the truth. Alexi was a fool to involve himself with such people. But fool or no, he was still a Rudov. Blood for blood, Mr. Caine.'

'So that's what this is about? Revenge? Why didn't you just kill me in Thailand?'

'Patience, my friend. You will die soon enough. But first, you will know fear. You will know desperation. And when death finally comes, you will beg for it.'

'Not likely, asshole.'

'In one hour, I release my dogs. They are military men, like you. They are spetsnaz, special forces. The best of the best. They will track you. Hunt you. They are led by a man of great talent. Perhaps you have heard of him? Piotr Zasko.'

'The Iron Wolf,' Caine snarled. 'I've heard of him... heard he was dead.'

'The FSB's files say the same about you. Piotr is a *khishchnik*... A hunter of men. I assure you, he is very much alive. And he is very much looking forward to meeting you.'

'Zasko's no hunter. He's a degenerate thug, wanted for war crimes in Ukraine. Mutilation of prisoners. Civilians. Women, children...'

'Trophies, Mr. Caine. Some for himself. Some for me. Many of those women and children were the loved ones of my enemies. They died the way you will die. With fear in their eyes. When I step into my private sanctuary, I look upon my trophies. The heads of those Piotr has hunted for me. And do you know what I see?'

Caine said nothing.

'Power. *My* power. We all die, Mr. Caine. To kill a man is nothing. But to take away hope, to steal the will to live, his desire to fight... To make a man die with nothing but fear and despair in his heart... that is my revenge. That is how you will die.'

'Better men than you have tried, Sergei.'

Again the man chuckled. 'You will not escape the Iron Wolf. Mark my words. You leave this world with a scream frozen on your face for all time. And I shall look upon my newest trophy, open a bottle of my finest vodka, and drink a toast. To my life, and your death.'

Caine held the phone close to his face. He expelled a puff of mist into the air and clenched his teeth to stop them from chattering.

'You listen to me, Sergei. They have a saying in Estonia – "a bottle of vodka is a passport to hell." You'd better drink up now. You may be seeing me sooner than you think.'

'There are many hells, Mr. Caine. Yours shall be one of cold and ice.' He hung up the phone.

Fyodor shivered in the wind. The old man gestured to the flask in the snow. 'Do you mind?'

'Knock yourself out.' Caine removed the battery from the phone and slipped the two pieces back into the parka. 'The box they dropped me in, does it have a tracking device? GPS, a transmitter of some kind?'

Fyodor picked up the flask, unscrewed the top, and drank a long swig of the chilled vodka. He coughed, then wiped his mouth. 'I have no idea. I only know that the men Rudov sends here, they always die. The hunters always find them.'

Caine checked his watch. 'They arrive in one hour... fifty minutes now?'

'Yes. The Iron Wolf is never late.'

Caine took a deep breath and examined his surroundings. They were in a clearing, enclosed by towering banks of puffy white snow. The snowbanks sloped down to the west. Miles in the distance, Caine could make out the pointed tufts of fir trees, covered in a layer of white powder. The forest stretched into the distance as far as the eye could see. To the east, the ground turned rocky and rose up to form the base of a mountain ridge.

'You said Arshan is to the east? What is that, a town?'

'*Da*. Small town. It has café. An inn. Train comes one time a week with supplies.'

Caine turned east, surveying the sprawling forest. The sun hung low on the horizon, and a foreboding gray shadow seemed to creep across the snow. Caine guessed it would be dark in a few hours. And when night fell the temperature would plummet.

'Which way do most people go? The forest, or the town?' he asked.

Fyodor shivered and took another swig of vodka. 'Town, of course. Always the town.'

Caine turned to face him. 'Always to town, and they always die. You must have come here in a truck, or a vehicle of some kind, right?'

'Yes, but it is useless to you. They only give

enough gas to make it out here. They bring more gas for return trip, when they meet me.'

'Take me to it. Now.'

With a grunt, Fyodor turned and lumbered through the snow. He took long, slow steps that crunched through the frozen crust, leaving deep prints behind.

Caine followed in his wake, and they disappeared into the frost-filled air.

28

A low howl rose above the rushing wind.

A trio of vehicles burst from the swirling snow and mist. With a mechanical growl, the twin tracks of a massive Ruslan TTM-4902 dove through a snowy bank. The snowcat's massive twin tracks scattered white powder and fallen branches into the air. Screaming past the lumbering arctic vehicle, twin Taiga 551 snowmobiles raced across the frozen ground.

All three were painted with white and grey camouflage markings. They were modified civilian models and carried no weapons or heavy armor. But their presence alone was an imposing sight in the cold, empty desolation of the mountain clearing.

The vehicles circled around the fallen metal box and skidded to a stop. The doors of the snowcat swung open and Piotr Zasko dropped to the ground, followed by Yuri. Arkady climbed out the rear door, as Leonid and Timur dismounted from their snowmobiles.

Each man wore insulated white tactical gear, and black tinted goggles. Their MP-443 pistols slapped against their sides as they lunged through the heavy snow, and they held AK-74 automatic rifles at the ready. Yuri was the exception, carrying the shorter AKS-74U carbine model. The steel barrel and skeleton stock of an Orsis T-5000 sniper rifle hung behind his right shoulder.

Zasko's black, serpentine whip was coiled at his side.

With quick, precise motions, the men fanned out around the metal box. Leonid hefted a short-barreled G-64 grenade launcher and scanned the rocky outcroppings that surrounded the clearing. His eyes darted left and right behind his dark goggles, searching for any signs of motion in the snow.

Timur approached the metal box and rapped the side with the barrel of his rifle. He lifted his goggles from his face and kneeled in the snow. His dark, ruddy complexion and narrow brown eyes marked him as half-Mongolian. The low sun reflected off the snow and ice around them like a blinding mirror, and the icy wind whipped at his face like a curtain of needles. Timur squinted a bit but otherwise showed no signs of discomfort.

A short tuft of frayed nylon cord hung from a thick ring bolted to the cage. Identical bolts were spaced across the sides of the pen. Timur held one of the cords and twirled it in his gloved fingers.

'*Smotri syuda*, look here. Chute is gone. He must have cut it off.'

Yuri tightened his grip on his carbine. He cast a wary glance toward the ice-covered rocks that rose in the distance. 'Do they usually do that?'

Zasko lifted his goggles and stared at the cord. His eyes were wide and intense, and his upper lip twisted into a snarl. 'Never. There is nothing usual about this man. Do not forget that. What else do you see, Timur?'

The trooper began circling around the wreckage of the box. A small GPS unit hung at his belt. It beeped quietly, barely audible above the howling wind.

Timur's brow furrowed. He pointed the unit toward the remains of the metal box. The beeping grew louder. 'He took the chute, but did not disable the GPS?'

Arkady shifted his weight on his legs. '*Komu pohuy*? Maybe he did not know it was there?'

Zasko shook his head. 'Assume he knew it was there. Which means he knew we would be coming to these coordinates. Yuri and Leonid, check the perimeter. Look for tracks, debris, anything he may have dropped. Arkady, stay here and guard the vehicles. Make sure he does not double back and slip out from under our noses.'

Arkady grinned as the other men marched across the snow. '*Da, ser!*' he shouted. 'I hope this prick does come back.' He held up his rifle. 'Then he and I can meet, and we can leave this godforsaken place early.' He turned and traipsed back toward the snowmobiles.

Zasko turned to Timur. He spun his finger in the air. Timur nodded and circled around the landing site, moving outwards in a spiral pattern. After a few minutes, he stopped and kneeled in the snow. A small patch of red droplets glistened above the white crust.

'Fresh blood. And tracks. One set.' He glanced toward the rocks above them. 'They follow the trail up the mountain.'

'He's heading toward town,' Arkady called over his shoulder. 'They always head toward town.'

Zasko slung his rifle over his shoulder. 'It looks that way. Still... best to be sure. If he did head toward Arshan, he will not make it there before dark. There is no hurry. Arkady, fetch Leonid. You two maintain position here. We will check the trail, make sure these tracks do not divert.'

Arkady nodded and trudged toward the men in the distance.

Zasko turned to Timur. 'Well, my friend... let us see where the game takes us.'

Timur stood up. 'This is no game. I read the file, as you asked. You should tell the others.'

Zasko shrugged. 'You, I trust. But no one is supposed to know who our targets are. It is safer that way.'

Timur shook his head. 'Safer for our employer. But as you said, this man Caine, he is not usual. He is not like the others Rudov has sent.'

The commander chuckled. 'You seem quite impressed. Caine is formidable, true. But he is only one man. You saw the blood. He is wounded.'

Timur lowered his goggles, and looked up at the curving, snow-swept trail. '*Da*. And we both know there is no animal more dangerous than a wounded tiger.'

Zasko frowned as they both followed the tracks through the snow.

* * *

Timur stalked toward the edge of a vast gorge that lay beyond the precipice of the mountain trail. The single pair of tracks had led them up and around the mountain, before ending at the location of Fyodor's truck. At least, its former location. The vehicle was missing, and twin tire tracks led farther into the distance.

Footsteps crunched across the snow behind them. Zasko spun around, his gun sweeping left and right across the snow-blanketed field. But it was only Arkady, jogging toward them.

As the man approached, Zasko lowered his weapon and brushed back the thick hood of his parka.

'Arkady, I told you to wait with Leonid!'

Arkady shrugged. 'This is one man with a shot-gun. Leonid can handle himself.'

Zasko slipped his knife from his belt. 'I did not

ask you to think. I ordered you to obey. If you cannot do that, you may join Boris. Is that clear?'

Even in the ice-cold air, the pale look that flashed across Arkady's face was unmistakable. 'Of course, Commander. I apologize, I will go back and—'

Zasko shook his head and returned the knife to its sheath. 'Never mind. You are here now. We have new tracks. We must follow them.'

Arkady examined the ground as Timur continued pacing toward the gorge. He brushed away some packed snow, revealing a black cord strung across the ground. The line was stretched taut, as if it supported a great weight.

'Don't touch it!' Timur hissed. He edged along the length of the line, following it to the lip of the gorge. Zasko held up his hand, signaling Arkady to freeze in place.

'Is it a trip line?' the commander asked, tightening his grip on his rifle.

The tracker shook his head. '*Nyet...* Come, look here.'

Zasko followed Timur to the edge of the gorge. A metallic creak echoed over the icy rocks. Arkady stepped next to them. 'What the hell...'

Three more lengths of the heavy-duty paracord ran through the snow, all stretched tight as piano wire. A battered gray pickup truck hung suspended from the cords, several yards down the wall of the gorge. Thousands of feet below, the icy blue curve of a frozen river snaked through the valley. The slim lengths of cord were all that kept the hanging truck from plunging into its frozen surface.

A muffled cry rose above the wind and the creaking.

'Fyodor,' Zasko muttered. 'That old fool got himself captured. Our target followed him in his footsteps, raided the truck for supplies. Then he pushed it over the edge to throw us off his trail.'

'Why would he not just kill him?' Timur asked, squinting down at the hanging truck.

'He has the old drunk's shotgun. It only holds two rounds. Perhaps he is conserving ammo.'

Timur pulled back his hood and looked over at his commander. 'There are many ways to kill. He does not need a gun.'

Zasko slapped Arkady on the back. 'We will ask Fyodor himself. Arkady, you were so eager to join us. Now you may prove your worth. Go down there and fetch him.'

29

Arkady's feet scraped against the slippery rocks of the gorge as he lowered himself closer to the truck. Tiny rocks rattled down the steep walls, vanishing into the frozen oblivion below.

He played out more rope, dropping another few inches. The sight of the truck hanging below him was a surreal image. The taut paracord was almost invisible against the dark rocks and ice, making the vehicle appear to defy gravity.

He looked up and saw Timur's dark squinting eyes peering over the edge of the crevasse. The heavyset commando was 'on belay' and kept tension on the line as Arkady rappelled down the steep rock face.

'I see something through the rear window!' Arkady called out.

He looked down at the truck again. Frost and dirt smudged the rear window, but again, he spotted a glimpse of motion. A blurry shadow shifted inside the cabin. He looked back to Timur.

'Give me more slack!'

Timur let out some tension in the rope, and Arkady continued his slow descent to the truck. The heavy metal body of the vehicle creaked and moaned as the wind picked up strength. Above them, the sun had dipped closer to the horizon. The bitter chill surrounding them increased.

It was getting later. Colder.

Arkady scooted to his left, traversing across the rocks. He inched closer and dusted the ice crystals off the driver's window.

Fyodor sat in the passenger seat, strapped in place by the seatbelt.

'I see him,' Arkady called out. 'It is Fyodor, he is in the truck!'

'What?' Zasko shouted down. 'Is he alive?'

The shivering old man turned his head at the sound of Arkady's voice. His eyes were wide with surprise and fear. Strips of torn parachute cloth were wound around his mouth like a gag. His wrists were bound with lengths of frayed cord.

'*Da*, alive. Timur, give me more slack – I'm going to try to get him out.'

The half-Mongolian commando frowned. 'Arkady, wait, are you—'

The vehicle groaned again as Arkady tugged on the door. It would not budge. He heard the scuffle of more rocks tumbling down the cliff.

'The door is frozen shut. I need more slack!'

Timur played out more line, and Arkady swung closer to the vehicle. He planted his feet on the rock. Inside, the old man bucked in his seat. The truck shuddered, and more debris shook loose from the rocks.

'Stay still, old man! I'm coming for you! I'm—'

Arkady yanked harder on the door. The metallic screech of rusted metal echoed off the rocks. The door swung open.

Arkady had no time to register the twin barrels of the shotgun bolted beneath the driver's seat. He heard the quick hiss of cord running through a pulley. A split second later, the blinding flash of muzzle fire filled his vision.

Boom!

He was already hit before the explosive roar of the shotgun echoed through the gorge.

Gasping in pain, his feet slipped off the rock wall and his body swung away from the truck.

'Arkady!' Zasko shouted. He turned to Timur. 'Get him up here... now!'

The big man was already hauling up the line. He yanked Arkady's body up across the rocks with short, jerking motions.

Zasko tore the walkie off his belt. 'Leonid, come in! This was a diversion! He covered his tracks somehow, but he must be heading toward the forest. Take a snowmobile, find Yuri. Widen the perimeter. You must pick up his trail! Do not wait for us. We will catch up to you, over.'

'But sir,' the reply crackled back, 'what about the other vehicles?'

'We will take them. We split into two teams, spread the search pattern as wide as possible. Go now!' Zasko hissed. He slid the walkie back onto his belt.

He joined Timur in hauling up the line. Arkady's body rolled over the rock ledge and into the snow.

His face contorted in pain, and he uttered a low groan.

An enormous crimson stain bloomed across the

front of his white jumpsuit. His breath was shallow and ragged.

'*Ya v poryadke*,' he gasped. 'I am okay.'

Zasko drew his knife. He walked over to the taut lines of cord and flicked the long, serrated blade across them, one by one. Each cord made a high-pitched twang as it snapped. The heavy truck groaned louder as it slid down the rocks. A muffled scream drifted up from the cabin of the dangling vehicle.

'The trap was not designed to kill,' Zasko growled.

He stepped over to the last cord. With a loud twang, he severed the line. The truck rolled down the rock face, the scraping of metal and rumbling stone drowning out Fyodor's feeble cries. The vehicle plunged into the gorge and crashed into the ice below.

Zasko paced back over to Arkady and Timur.

The wounded man ripped off his goggles and looked up at him. His panting breath was heavy, expelling the air from his lungs with a wet rattle. 'I am okay! I just need a doctor, a hospital.'

Zasko drew his pistol. Timur stood up and looked away.

'I'm sorry, soldier,' Zasko said. 'I could tell by the

sound, only one barrel fired. If the trap *was* meant to kill, he would have loaded both barrels, to be sure. This was a diversion. He thinks by wounding one of my men, it will slow our pace. He is wrong. The hunt must continue.'

Arkady raised his hands in a futile gesture, his panicked breaths coming faster. 'Wait, Commander I—'

'*Do svidaniya.*'

Zasko did not flinch as the gun roared in his hand.

* * *

Caine moved at a brisk pace through the towering banks of snow. He glanced up and saw beams of sunlight piercing the icy mist between the trees. He noted the steep angle of the dying rays... The sun was setting. Nightfall approached. And as things stood, he knew he would not survive the plummeting temperature.

He forced himself to stop moving. Every instinct in his body screamed at him to run. The fight or flight response triggered by the armed men on his tail was a powerful drive, urging him on. But he knew every step he took was depleting his energy, sapping his body of crucial calories. That energy was vital; his body needed it to maintain his core temperature. As the sun went down, the frigid air would grow even colder. He would need to spend more and more energy to stay warm... to stay alive.

Hope the diversion with the truck worked, he thought. *If not, that was time wasted.*

He took a deep breath and examined his surroundings. He was in a thick, forested grove. The cold air was laced with the sweet scent of pine. Hundreds of the tall, conical trees surrounded him, their needled green branches drooping beneath the weight of accumulated snow and ice.

He dropped to his knees. Using the old man's knife, he began digging at the frozen crust beneath his feet. When he exposed the cold, hard earth below, he stood up and staggered toward the nearest tree. Using the knife again, he shaved thin strips of bark from the trunk, letting them fall on a square of parachute cloth. The shavings would be useless if they became damp from the snow.

When the curls of bark had grown into a large pile at his feet, he gathered them up and dropped them in the hole he had dug in the ice. Next, he pulled the lone remaining shotgun shell from his pocket.

Once again, he debated if giving up the gun had been the wisest course of action. He felt naked and vulnerable without the reassuring weight of the weapon by his side.

Two shotgun shells against a spetsnaz commando team, armed with automatic weapons? His years of bloody experience overrode his misgivings.

Buying yourself some time was more important, he thought.

Using the tip of the knife, he pried the brass primer away from the shell, exposing the wad of gunpowder underneath. He sprinkled the black powder over the bark shavings, then reached into his pocket and pulled out a foot-long red tube. It was a signal flare, scavenged from Fyodor's truck before he had pushed the vehicle over the edge of the gorge.

He lit the flare and touched it to the gunpowder. With a loud hiss, the powder ignited. Smoke began to waft up from the bark shavings. Caine lay down next to the fire and gently blew, stoking the glowing scraps of wood. Soon, tiny flames crackled between the shavings.

He checked his watch.

Ten minutes. Need to finish this up, get moving again!

As the fire continued to burn, he jogged from tree to tree, sawing off the low-hanging branches.

One by one, he tossed them on the fire, letting the heat and flames dry out the bristling green needles. As they crackled from the heat, he waved the scrap of cloth over the pit. The motion broke up the puffs of smoke, masking his presence in the forest.

After the branches were dried and desiccated by the fire, he pulled one out of the pit. Using the knife, he stripped off the roasted needles and shoved them into the sleeves of his parka. He filled every scrap of space he could with the makeshift insulation. His sleeves and pockets soon bulged with the warm material. He jammed more fistfuls of needles into each pant leg and tied off the ankle openings with more cord.

He checked his watch... Twenty minutes had passed.

Have to get moving...

He gathered what was left of the burned branches and tossed them over the burning embers. Then he swept snow and ice into the pit, extinguishing the fire with a loud hiss. He covered all traces of the burning wood under the snow, then stood up and trudged deeper into the forest.

The extra insulation helped and bought him more time. But only a little.

He had to find shelter. The armed men chasing

him were now a secondary concern. The cold was a far deadlier enemy, one that no diversion could outsmart or defeat.

It was the cold that would kill him.

Suddenly, he heard the crack of splintering wood. He froze in place, a familiar tingle on the back of his neck. The same instincts that drove him forward into the icy wasteland now warned him of danger. He could feel it... He was being watched.

The Russians would have found his trail by now. He no longer had time to wipe away his tracks with the parachute cloth or stray branches. But if they were closing in, he would have heard their vehicles approaching. He doubted they could have caught up so quickly on foot.

He listened but heard nothing more. The powdered trees stood silent and motionless in the forest. He looked up. The sun was a few inches lower, the sky a shade darker.

Rubbing his shoulders for warmth, he set off once more through the forest. If he was being followed, so be it. He had to keep moving and find shelter by nightfall.

Otherwise, he would join the trees in their stark, frozen vigil.

30

The cabin lay in the shadow of the frozen trees and a mountain ridge above.

Caine hunched behind a snowbank, peering at the rickety structure with narrowed eyes. He had been watching the site for twenty minutes. In that time, he saw no one come or go from the tiny building. There were no tracks in the snow surrounding the area, and no signs of food or water left out for dogs.

Trapper's shelter, he thought.

Fur trapping was a major source of income for locals in the smaller towns and villages of Siberia. The men who pursued such a trade left the safety of their homes for weeks at a time. They built cabins in remote forested areas like this, situated along their trapping routes, providing shelter for the cold nights during high season.

But this deep into winter, even the trappers would be home, safe and sound in their villages and towns. Their temporary shacks were boarded up, and stood empty and abandoned until the next season began.

Empty and abandoned, like the shack below.

Caine weighed his options. He had no idea how long his distraction might delay the men on his trail. After stuffing his clothes with makeshift insulation, he'd taken a circular path down the mountain. He kept to the rocks and hard ice whenever possible to reduce his tracks.

Along the way, he found a sheer rock cliff that cut down the side of the mountain. Using the remaining paracord and some scavenged metal from the landing site, he fashioned a crude grappling hook. After descending several hundred yards to a frozen stream, he trekked across the ribbon of ice for miles, further obscuring his trail.

None of that matters if you die of hypothermia, he thought.

Night would be upon him in a few hours. To build his own shelter would take time and use up critical energy. Energy he needed to keep his temperature up. To stay alive.

The wind picked up, sending a bitter chill through his parka. Even with the extra insulation, he knew he couldn't survive out in the cold much longer. The temperature had already dropped into the negatives. It would fall even further after nightfall.

Decision made.

He slid down the embankment, making as little noise as possible. When he hit level ground, he moved at a slow pace, to minimize the crunching of his boots across the snow.

Finally, he reached the door of the rickety wooden structure. He put his ear to the warped wood beams but heard no sounds from inside. He creaked open the door and stepped into the cabin.

The low sun cast long shadows across the dark interior of the shack. The windows were open holes, cut into the pine logs that formed the walls. Each was covered with thick plastic sheeting, nailed into the frames. Glass panels were too heavy and fragile for a trapper to lug this far out into the wilderness.

The sparse furniture looked as if it was handmade. A cot stood at one end of the square room, covered by animal skins and a thick fur blanket. Despite his exhaustion, Caine ignored the bed and continued searching the cabin and its grounds for supplies.

Outside, a few yards away from the tiny shack, he found a storage box built from smaller timbers. The wooden pen was about the size of a refrigerator, with a hinged lid. Inside, he found a few blocks of ice, three bottles of filtered water, and a plastic bag full of preserved meat, jerky of some kind.

Must be where the trapper kept his kills before he skinned them, he thought.

Back inside, he slid a small wooden chest from under the cot. Lifting the lid, he found a collection of saws and tools nestled under a folded paper map.

Caine took a sip of water, forcing himself to slow his drinking. This would be all the water he might find for several days... He had to conserve his supplies.

He sat down on the bed and chewed on a piece of jerky. Unfolding the map, he set it down and carefully studied the area. He traced a line that ran south from the mountains.

Railway tracks... Freight line running timber and supplies.

The line intersected the Norilsk mining train route that led south to the port city of Dudinka.

From there, he knew he could arrange passage to a larger city. Then, with a little luck, he could make his way out of Russia.

No!

The voice clamped down on his thoughts of escape, as cold and unforgiving as the bitter frost outside.

Rudov, Zasko... they know your name. They know Mark Waters is a ghost, a convenient fiction.

They know who you really are.

He chewed another bite of jerky, pondering the unpleasant thought. The intelligence community believed he was dead. After his old handler, Allan Bernatto, framed him for treason, he had disappeared. He assumed an old cover identity and sank into the criminal underworld of Pattaya. It was safer to let the world believe the lie.

He hated himself for giving in, for allowing Bernatto to go on breathing. Most of all, he hated himself. He had allowed himself to believe that all the killing and violence, the bloodshed that stained his soul, had been justified. Now he knew the truth.

He was merely a weapon. A tool, used and discarded by powerful men with dark and secretive ambitions.

And then there was Rebecca...

A young operations officer at the CIA. Someone he had grown close to. Someone he had developed feelings for. Like Naiyana, Rebecca had peeled back the darkness that surrounded him, if only for a short time. She had come closer than anyone to seeing the man inside.

If Bernatto found out that Caine was alive and living off the grid, he wouldn't hesitate to act. Caine was a loose end. And loose ends were to be eliminated, by whatever means necessary.

Rebecca, anyone close to him, would be in danger.

He couldn't allow a man like Sergei Rudov to know his secret. It was too dangerous, the threat of exposure too high. Once again, the shadowy tendrils of bloodshed and violence had reached out from his past, grasping at those he cared for with a cold embrace.

Rudov and the Iron Wolf... They would have to be dealt with. Before he could crawl back to his meager, lonely existence, he had loose ends of his own to take care of.

He put down the map and rummaged through the other tools in the chest. He found a collection of old, chipped saw blades, awls, and other small tools. Then his fingers wrapped around the smooth wood handle of a field shovel. He hefted it from the box and held it up in the dim light.

He whistled in appreciation. The short handle and flat metal blade of the shovel were expertly crafted. He recognized its shape... It was a Spetsnaz GRU shovel. The pointed metal head was sharpened to a razor's edge on each side. The tool could be used as a fearsome weapon, and was capable of lopping an opponent's head clean off.

For a moment, Caine wondered who exactly had built this cabin. How had they acquired such a lethal instrument? Then he shrugged, tossed the shovel on the cot, and huddled under the furs. Whoever owned this place, he would be gone long before they returned. He could only allow himself a short rest, just long enough to recharge and regain his lost energy.

After that, the hunt would resume.

His hunt.

31

The tiny cabin glowed a pale green in the amplified moonlight of the night vision scope.

Yuri's breath was slow and rhythmic. He kept the crosshairs steady over the shack's front door, and did not shift or waver. The drooping branches and clumps of hanging snow from a nearby tree masked his position on a rocky ridge.

The sniper hide was closer than he would have liked. At only 500 meters or so, the distance was less than a quarter of the powerful rifle's maximum accurate range. Still, nestled in the darkness and shadowed by the branches of the trees, he was confident he would not be spotted from the cabin's grounds.

With Leonid in the forest below, he was operating without a spotter. Once he began firing, he would have to spend precious seconds reacquiring the target before firing again. Assuming the first shot missed, of course.

At this range, Yuri did not plan to miss.

The red light on the walkie clipped to his belt blinked on. Static crackled in his earpiece. It was Leonid.

'I am approaching the cabin. There are tracks in the snow, about one hundred yards out from the perimeter. No sign of target.'

'Copy that,' Yuri answered. 'I see smoke coming from the roof. He must have a fire burning inside, over.' He spoke in a low monotone. His attention was laser-focused on the night vision scope mounted above the rifle's barrel.

'I copy. Poor little lamb must be cold. I will warm things up for him, over.'

Yuri ignored the man's boast and kept his aim steady. This man they were chasing had already taken out one of their number and managed to delay Zasko and the others. All with only a scavenged shotgun and some strips of cord.

Yuri had never participated in one of Zasko's hunts before. He considered himself a soldier, not a plaything for the demented desires of wealthy oli-garchs like Sergei Rudov.

Lying prone, the chill of the frozen ground pressed up against his body. He felt the wallet in his breast pocket digging into his chest, pushing against the slow, rhythmic beating of his heart.

Before coming to this frozen wasteland, he had slipped a picture inside the slim leather fold. He could see it in his mind's eye... A woman, looking over her shoulder at the camera. He could picture her face, visualize the slightest detail – the sunlight streaming from the window, the sparkling glint it cast in her eyes. The corner of her mouth, tugging her lips into a sly smile.

He wondered what she would think of his activi-ties tonight. Was she awake? Did she dream? Or did she slumber in a drug-induced haze, unconscious in her hospital bed?

It does not matter what she thinks, what you think, he told himself. *You are doing what you must. For your survival... and for hers.*

He forced the doubts from his mind. It was ob-vious that this man they were chasing was not some business rival, or a snitch who had broken the Vor code. This man was dangerous. The commander was rattled, he could tell. Zasko and the others had underestimated their target.

Yuri vowed not to make that mistake.

'Don't get too close,' he answered back. 'All you need to do is flush him out. I'll take care of the rest.'

'*Da*. I'll flush him out, all right. I am in firing position. Stand by. Over and out.'

Whump!

The thump of the GM-94 grenade launcher echoed through the frozen forest. Yuri watched through the scope as the bright projectile streaked toward the cabin. The grenade tore through the plastic covering one of the windows and landed inside the tiny shack.

A brief explosion rattled the cabin's timbers. White-hot flames erupted from the opening. The thermobaric grenade acted like a miniature fuel-air bomb, using oxygen from the surrounding air to create an incendiary blaze.

Yuri heard Leonid fire again. The cabin door collapsed as another explosion shook the building. The shack was engulfed by flames now and appeared as a flickering white blur in Yuri's scope. He saw no other movement... If Caine was inside, it did not look like he would make it out.

'Leonid, I do not see any movement... Do you have anything on the ground?'

'Negative. I think he is, how you say... extra crispy, over.'

Yuri blinked as the blaze grew hotter and brighter in his scope. The white-hot blur obscured his view of the ground surrounding the cabin.

His earpiece cracked to life again. 'I'm moving in,' Leonid said. 'Zasko wants this asshole's head... Can't let him burn up—Urgh!'

The transmission was cut off by the strange, muttered groan, followed by a burst of static.

'Leonid, are you there? Come in, over!'

No response. Yuri pivoted the scope away from the burning shack. He scanned the glistening white ice beneath the dark forest. He saw nothing. No signs of movement. No sign of Leonid.

And no sign of the target.

* * *

Caine heard footsteps crunching closer across the ice. The night breeze carried the man's whispering voice through the trees. The words were indistinct, but it did not matter. Armed men were closing in on his position, as he had known they would.

He lay nestled in the darkness, wrapped in the thick furs from the bed. He clutched the deadly shovel in a white-knuckled grip. Every muscle in his body tensed as he prepared for action.

Not yet, he thought. *Let him get closer. Wait for it...*

He heard the twin explosions of the grenades as they detonated inside the shack. He grinned in the darkness. The heat bloom from the explosions would drown out most night vision optic systems. His enemies would be overconfident and moving blind, if only for a few seconds.

It was time.

He burst from the ice box and leaped into the snow. He'd removed the ice and supplies from the wooden pen earlier. Next, he had lined the cramped space with furs and pillows from the bed inside. It was not as warm as the interior of the shack, but it was enough to protect him from the elements for a short time.

More importantly, it was not where his attackers expected him to be. And in this game, misdirection was one of the few weapons at his disposal.

He darted into a grove of trees and froze, listening for movement. Behind him, the burning cabin lit up the night sky. The crackling flames cast the trees and snowbanks around the blaze into deep, dark shadow.

He ducked low and scurried to another group of trees, farther away from the fire. He heard more footsteps. Someone was moving toward the burning cabin. A figure dressed in white tactical gear emerged from the shadows. The commando stalked closer to the burning structure. Caine watched as the man lowered the grenade launcher and surveyed the area. He held up a radio and spoke in Russian.

Caine leaped from his concealed position and charged across the snow. Swinging the shovel like a baseball bat, he cracked the metal tip into the back of the man's head.

The man grunted and stumbled forward. He lurched around but staggered from the force of the blow.

A second was all Caine needed.

As the man's hands dropped to the rifle slung under his shoulder, Caine snapped the handle of the shovel forward. The wood cracked across the bridge of the man's nose. Without pause, Caine sidestepped and swung the tool in a low arc. The razor-sharp edge of the shovel cut into the man's thigh. He screamed in pain as the metal sliced through his clothes and tore into his flesh.

He stumbled forward and collapsed into the snow. Caine clamped the handle of the shovel over his neck in a choke hold and dragged the body into the trees. He grabbed the man's rifle and slung it over his shoulder as he hefted the heavy grenade launcher in his hands. The man groaned slightly, but did not move. Caine stripped off the man's parka and draped it over his own shoulders.

The man groaned again. Caine glanced down at the AK-74 rifle he held in his hands. A gunshot would give away his position. He stood up and raised the shovel over his head.

Crack!

The explosion of the gunshot echoed through the trees. Caine dropped to the ground as wood splintered and cracked above his head. The bullet shot straight through the tree and buried itself in the snow a few feet from his position.

Sniper, above the trees... Have to keep moving!

Keeping low, Caine raced toward another shadowy grove a few yards away. The explosive fire of the sniper roared again. Caine kept running, as another bullet screamed past his ear, missing his head by inches. It buried itself into another tree, sending a hail of wooden splinters whipping through the air. Caine grunted in pain as he felt a sharp fragment tear through his parka and pierce his side.

He made a beeline for one of the larger trees, a towering larch with a trunk over three feet thick. Skidding to a stop in the snow, he panted for breath. Whoever was targeting him, they had to be using a night vision scope of some kind.

You can use that against him. But first you have to figure out his position.

The angle of the last two shots indicated the shooter was aiming from higher up the mountain, the ridgeline of the cliff he'd descended earlier.

The wind picked up, whistling through the branches of the trees. It sent a light dust of white powder cascading from above. Caine fished the other soldier's mask out of his pocket.

One more shot, he thought. *One more shot, and I can narrow down his position. Assuming he doesn't hit me first...*

* * *

Yuri forced himself to stay calm. He swept the night vision sight across the dark forest below in a smooth, controlled arc. Without a spotter to guide him, his vision was limited to the circle of green light before his eyes. Twice he had picked up the target's movements and fired. But each time the man had escaped into another pool of darkness, or taken cover behind more trees. Once he left the tiny circle of death, it took precious seconds to target him again.

Now, the forest below was still. The soft moaning of the wind picked up. He ignored the gentle swaying of the branches, knowing it was just a by-product of the cold night breeze. In the distance, a lonely howl rose up and echoed through the mountains.

Siberian wolf, he thought. The animals were rare and kept to themselves. They avoided humans and other domestic creatures. They killed only for food, to provide for their family, but rarely fought other members of their pack.

A noble creature... I envy him.

His thoughts were interrupted by a flash of movement in the trees. He centered the scope, moving back to capture whatever it was he had seen in the glowing green circle of night vision.

There... He saw it! The target was wearing Leonid's white balaclava mask, peering out from behind a tree. The man's head bobbed up and down slightly, as if looking left and right.

Yuri exhaled, forcing every last ounce of breath

from his lungs. His finger tightened on the trigger. With a gentle, almost loving caress against the curved metal, he squeezed. The rifle barked once more, and he saw his target fly back into the snow.

As soon as he felt the pressure of the recoil against his shoulder, he flipped the bolt up and tugged back. The action chambered another round of .338 Lapua Magnum ammunition. He re-centered the scope on the fallen target with subconscious precision and squeezed the trigger again. Another round tore into the white mask.

Yuri ceased firing. Through the scope, he saw the figure's head flap and billow in the breeze. He realized with a start that his target had not fallen... The mask was still bobbing up and down. It was hanging from the end of a thin branch, jammed into the snow.

Whump!

The sound streaked toward him. Before he could even move, he heard an explosion, and the targeting scope lit up bright white. Yuri squinted and tore his eye away from the blinding glow of the scope. The trees directly in front of the ridge had burst into flames. The heat and fire played havoc with the scope's optics.

He'd taken out Leonid... He has the grenade launcher!

Yuri crawled backward, retreating from the blaze before him.

He used the mask to draw my fire... He wanted me to give away my position!

Whump! Whump!

Two more explosions shook the snow next to him. The night sky lit up as a wall of towering flames surrounded him. He heard the crack of breaking wood. Branches rustled and shook overhead. Spinning around, he tossed the rifle aside and threw up his hands in a defensive gesture.

The deafening creak of falling timber groaned through the night air. He cried out as a crushing weight fell on top of him. One of the nearby trees had been toppled by the explosion. The blow knocked the wind from his lungs, and he felt a sharp pain in his side.

Der'mo! The silent curse echoed through his mind as he struggled beneath the weight of the tree trunk.

A stinging, dry warmth crept across his skin. A wave of heat was moving closer and closer to his face. The flames were licking at the fallen timber.

The hungry fire crawled along the length of wood, making its way toward his trapped body...

32

Caine sprinted through the snow, gasping for breath in the icy air. The wood shrapnel still protruded from his side, digging deeper into his flesh with every step he took. The twin fires from the cabin and the forest lit up the night sky with a hazy orange glow. He hoped the flames and smoke would block the sniper's line of sight, but there was no way to be sure. The sooner he evacuated the area, the better.

He knew he was moving quicker than he should. The ground was uneven, and slick with frozen snow and icy rocks. In the distance he heard a low, dire howl rise above the crackling of the fire. He did not slow his pace.

Great... now I have the local wildlife to deal wi—

He stumbled, as his foot plunged into deep snow and caught on a gnarled root. Tumbling forward, he struck the icy ground at the edge of an embankment. He ignored the pain, and spread out his hands and legs, trying to stop his body from sliding over the edge. But the frigid night had frozen the snow solid. He shot down the steep, slippery ice like a child on a playground slide.

He skidded to a painful stop in a small clearing, surrounded by an ominous grove of dark trees. The second he stopped moving, he felt an immense pressure on his leg. He heard the snap of cord drawing tight, a rustling whine as it streaked through the branches of the trees above him. His left leg flew up into the air, and he growled in pain as the muscles around the wood fragment pulled tight.

Caine found himself hanging several feet off the ground. A tight noose bit into his ankle. He swayed back and forth, the tips of his fingers dangling inches above the shimmering white frost on the ground.

Grunting with pain and exertion, he bent at the waist, struggling to reach his trapped limb. The movement put pressure on the wood shard, forcing it deeper still into his flesh. He dropped back down, clenching his teeth as a red-hot wave of agony pulsed around the wound.

He froze, listening to the forest around him. He heard the crackling of the fire in the distance. Again, a menacing howl sounded from within the dark forest. Then he heard something else.

Footsteps, crunching toward him.

A figure limped out from the trees and approached him. A dark gash stained the right leg of the man's white jumpsuit, and thick, crimson blood coursed down the side of his neck.

It was the commando, the one he had wounded with the shovel.

'*Nu eto smeshno*, well isn't this funny? My name is Leonid. Let me be the first to welcome you to Russia, motherfucker!'

The man grinned at Caine as he lowered himself down the ice slope. He gritted his teeth and limped closer, wincing with each faltering step.

'You should get that leg looked at, Leonid,' Caine hissed between breaths. 'Cold weather increases the chance of infection.'

The man nodded. '*Da*, you got me good back there. I must return the favor. But you seem to have taken all my weapons. Left me only with this.'

The man slid a long, wicked-looking knife from a

sheath at his side. The blade was black oxidized steel. Moonlight glinted off the narrow silver band that ran along its diamond-sharp edge.

Caine roared and forced himself to bend up again. His grasping fingers could not reach the circle of rope that snared his ankle, and he fell back down, staring at the upside-down figure advancing toward him.

'So I think, I use this to gut you, like wild animal.' Leonid grabbed a tuft of Caine's hair in his fist and yanked his hanging body toward him. He leaned over and stared into Caine's eyes.

'I cut you from your foot to your ass, like the trappers do with the sable and mink they catch. Perhaps I sell your skin as well, to Rudov.'

Caine spat in the man's face.

Leonid let go and stood up straight, wiping the spittle from his cheek. He lashed out with his foot, kicking Caine in the stomach. Caine moaned in pain as the blow struck next to the throbbing wood fragment. He swung backward, spinning around in circles.

Leonid grabbed his leg, stopping his swaying motion.

'Just for that, I take my time. I stop halfway through, drink some vodka, eat my rations. I listen as you beg me to finish the job. Too bad for you, my English not so good.'

Leonid tapped the side of Caine's leg with his knife. Then he sliced through his pants, exposing the skin of his calf to the freezing night air.

'This is for Arkady. Here we go, ass—'

Crack!

The gunshot rang out from the forest. Caine felt the Russian's grip on his leg go loose. He began spinning again, and as he twisted around he saw the commando's body collapse in the snow. Blood streamed from a crimson hole in his forehead.

A dark figure stalked into the clearing. Whoever it was, they were tall and broad-shouldered. Thick winter clothes covered a round, hulking body. A fur-trimmed hood cloaked their face in shadows. Despite the figure's bulk, they moved down the icy slope with ease, without the slightest stumble or hesitation. Then they continued advancing toward Caine, peering over the barrel of an old bolt-action rifle. The barrel of the weapon was pointed at Caine's swaying head.

'*Kto ty?* Who the hell are you?'

The words were muffled by the parka's hood and a thick scarf. The voice had a strange, unfamiliar accent, and was higher pitched than he would have expected.

'I'm not Russian!' Caine shouted.

The figure took another step closer, brandishing the rifle. 'What you doing here? Why all these men in woods?'

'I'm not with them,' he answered, wincing in pain as the swaying motion tugged at his wound. 'More men are coming. We have to get out of here!'

The figure stood motionless, silent.

Caine squinted, trying to make out a face behind the shadow of the hood. 'Men are coming, do you understand? Danger!'

The figure lowered the rifle and pulled back the hood.

Caine looked up into a wide, tan face. Narrow lips, chapped from the cold and wind, pursed in annoyance. A pair of dark, squinting eyes regarded him from above a small, flat nose. A short bob of dark hair framed either side of the broad, impassive face.

It was a woman.

'How I know you not dangerous?' she asked in her broken English.

'I'm the one hanging upside down,' Caine answered.

'You not Russian. American?'

Caine hesitated for a moment. 'Who are you?'

The woman slung the rifle over her shoulder and slid a knife from inside her parka. 'I the one who cut you down. Long as you not Russian.'

Caine nodded. 'Yes, American. I'm American.'

The woman gave a satisfied grunt. She stepped toward him and severed the trapline with a quick slash of her knife.

Caine fell to the ground. He gritted his teeth once more as his wounded side slammed into the ice.

'You hurt,' she stated.

'It's fine,' Caine gasped. 'I can make it.' He staggered to his feet and took a step. He immediately collapsed to his knees, another wave of pain shooting through his abdomen.

The woman shook her head. 'You no see trap. Now you hurt. You not smart.'

'You got me there,' Caine gasped.

The large woman hefted him to his feet and slung his arm over her shoulder. 'I help you. You say more men come?'

'Yeah. More men come.'

The direful howl once again resonated from the depths of the forest.

'Are those wolves?' Caine's words were slurred.

His limbs were heavy with pain and exhaustion. The cold and lack of rest were taking their toll.

The woman shook her head. 'No. Not wolf.'

Caine's head lolled as the powerful woman dragged him through the snow.

'Good,' he mumbled. 'One less thing hunting me.'

'Half wolf,' the woman said.

'What?'

She smiled. 'Don't worry. They with me.'

Caine opened his mouth to ask her what she meant, but his eyes rolled back into his head. His head slumped forward and he slipped into unconsciousness.

33

A sliver of orange sun cut through the cloud-covered
horizon. Dawn was approaching, but the forest was
still cloaked in darkness and shadows. A thin haze of
smoke drifted across the ice and snow. The air
smelled of burned timber and gasoline.

The pair of Taiga snowmobiles screamed across
the frozen ground, sending a spray of ice and powder
in their wake. The vehicles skidded to a stop. Timur
dismounted and stalked forward, sweeping the area
with his rifle. He advanced toward the charred remains of the cabin.

He stopped moving, held up his right hand, and
waved forward, signaling the all-clear.

Zasko climbed off his Taiga and strode out into the snow. He sniffed the air.

'Thermobaric grenades. Leonid was here.'

Timur kneeled in the snow, and scanned the area with a cool, unblinking stare. 'I see his bootprints. The target's prints as well. But I don't think Leonid got him.'

'Why do you say that?'

Timur stood up. 'Both sets point that way,' he said, pointing toward a thick copse of trees in the distance. 'And Leonid is walking with a limp.'

Zasko drew his pistol. 'See if you can pick up his trail. Find out what happened.'

'*Da, ser.*' Timur marched off toward the trees.

Zasko narrowed his eyes. He surveyed the dead, blackened trees that protruded from the smoky haze. 'I told Rudov,' he muttered to himself, barely a whisper. 'You are nothing like the others we have hunted.'

He heard the crack of snapping wood behind him. He spun around and raised his pistol.

A figure stepped out of the smoking trees. He coughed and stumbled toward Zasko, raising his hands.

'Do not shoot. It is me.'

Zasko lowered his weapon. 'Yuri?'

Black soot and ash covered the sniper's white clothing. His right sleeve was torn open, and the skin of his arm was pink and bubbling... third-degree burns.

Yuri stood before him. One of his blue eyes was swollen shut beneath a mass of burns and scar tissue.

'What the hell happened here? Report!' Zasko demanded.

Yuri took another step toward Zasko. 'Who is this man?'

'What are you talking about?'

'The target? Who is he?'

Zasko holstered his weapon. 'His name is unimportant. If you remember your training, you will—'

'*Bred sivoy kobyly!* Enough with the bullshit!'

Zasko glared at him. 'Fine. No names, but as I said, this man is not our usual prey. He is highly trained. Former US Special Forces. Then CIA, Special Operations Group. I do not have all the details; much of the report was classified or missing. But I understand his kill record is... impressive.'

The wounded man glared at Zasko with his one good eye. 'Special Forces? He lured us here. Surprised Leonid somehow, took him out. He almost killed me.'

'Calm yourself, soldier. You are hysterical.'

Yuri took another step closer. His lower lip quivered. 'And Arkady? He is dead as well, no?'

'Yuri, I said calm down. That is an order. Do not make me—'

'You still give orders? In less than twenty-four hours, this man has cut our number in half. You have led us into a slaughter!'

Yuri charged forward, grasping at Zasko's throat with his bruised hands.

The commander sidestepped the attack, and his arm shot up. His whip was clutched in his fist, held in a loose coil. The circle of leather looped around Yuri's right arm. With a quick tug, Zasko spun the man around, throwing him off balance. Grabbing the back of his parka, the older man jerked down, and Yuri fell backward into the snow.

A glint of steel appeared in Zasko's free hand. The knife twirled around his fingers. Before Yuri could move, he felt the cold kiss of its blade against his neck.

He ceased his struggling. Zasko stared down at him, his eyes wide, his face a cold, blank mask.

'Why are you here, Yuri? Why did you join our little hunt?' he asked in a low growl.

'I needed money. That is all.'

'Money for what?'

Yuri glared up at him for a moment. Then he blinked. The rage seemed to drain from his face.

'My wife. She is ill. The hospital says she needs new medicine. Expensive medicine. I'm not here for you, or this idiotic game. You can cut off this man's head without me.'

'The head is for Rudov. They are his trophies. Me? I only want his heart.'

Yuri squinted at his commander. 'What?'

'I will cut it from his body. Then I will savor it, bite by bite. And when I am finished with my meal, I will know I am victorious. I will take this man's strength and make it my own.'

'You are insane.' Yuri spat out the words as if they left a bad taste in his mouth. '*Psikh*.'

'That is what I do to my prey, Yuri. And that is what Sergei Rudov will order me to do to you, if you abandon the hunt.'

'And if this man kills you first?'

Zasko shrugged. 'Fear of death is the spice that makes life worth living. But if I die, Rudov will send someone else for you. And for your lovely wife. She will suffer for your cowardice, my friend.'

Zasko stood up. 'The target took out your good eye. You're useless as a sniper now. I should kill you for insubordination, but I need the manpower. The hunt must continue.'

He held out his hand. Yuri knocked it away and staggered to his feet.

'*Tut!* Over here,' Timur called to them. 'I have the trail!'

Zasko took a deep breath, then turned to face the tracker. 'Which way did he go?'

Timur pointed toward the dark forest that ran down the slope of the mountain. 'Deep into the woods. And he is not alone.'

Zasko slid his knife back into its sheath. 'What?'

The stern-faced man nodded. 'Sled tracks. Dogs. Heavy boots. Someone was helping him.'

Zasko smiled. 'As I said, spice. The thrill of the hunt is the chase.' He turned back to Yuri as Timur ran over to them.

'We bring the snowmobiles. Timur, you're with me. Yuri, you will follow.' The older man looked the younger man in the eye. 'Do you understand?'

Yuri nodded. 'I understand. But we are only three men. After what I have seen... I do not think—'

Zasko bared his teeth and thumped his chest. 'What? Our prey is wounded, and tired. We are spetsnaz! We have superior numbers, and superior firepower. Are you telling me we cannot take down one man, here in our own homeland?'

Yuri watched as Zasko and Timur mounted one of the snowmobiles.

'It is time to finish this,' the commander grunted. 'We move out, now!' They sped off down the mountain.

Yuri took a deep breath and watched his exhale turn to mist in the cold air. He crawled onto the other vehicle and followed their trail into the shadowy darkness of the forest.

34

Caine shot up in bed. His fingers grasped at thin air, searching for the gun he normally kept on his nightstand.

There was no gun. There was no nightstand. Just a crooked table next to the bed. A couple books, with Russian lettering on the spine, lay stacked on the table. His flailing arm knocked a small framed picture off the pile of books.

Then he remembered.

The snow, the ice... the men hunting him. Feverish glimpses of the moonlight sparkling off the frost-covered trees. The howling of the dogs as the woman dumped his body on the sled. Charging through the depths of the forest, the cold night air rushing across his face...

He remembered seeing cabins, like the one he had escaped from. Men sitting around a fire, more sleds, and other vehicles.

A settlement of some kind.

He looked around the room. He was lying in bed, inside one of the cabins. The timber walls and plastic windows seemed identical to the previous building. A pool of heat gathered under the covers near his feet. He threw aside the thick blankets and found a brass pot with holes punched in the lid, sitting near the foot of the bed. He sat up and lifted the lid off the pot. Several large stones lay inside, radiating warmth.

Must have been heated by a fire, he thought. *Where am I?*

He realized the throbbing pain in his flank had subsided, replaced by a dull ache. His fingers traveled across his skin... He felt the ridge of a scar, and stitches holding the wound closed.

He picked up the photo he had knocked over. The image was surrounded by a simple wood frame. The color and detail in the print had faded with time, but he made out two Asian women, laughing and embracing in a park somewhere. They looked like they were in their forties, and they wore long, billowing pastel dresses. To Caine, the dresses looked like *hanbok*, traditional Korean gowns.

His memory of the woman in the woods was vague and feverish, but he could swear she was one of the women in the picture.

The door to the cabin opened. Caine tensed and set the picture back down on the table. It was her, the woman, still wearing her heavy parka. She stepped into the cabin, shut the door behind her, and walked over to the bed. She was carrying a cast iron bowl on a tray, and she set it down on the table next to him.

'I treat wound. Stitches. Here, eat. Soup, good.'

She held the bowl out to Caine. A hand-carved wooden spoon was stuck in a mass of black noodles and stewed meat of some kind. The broth was thin and cloudy, and filled with what looked like shredded cabbage. He took the bowl and spooned the mixture into his mouth. To his surprise, the soup was served cold. The noodles were satisfying, but the meat had a strange, gamey taste.

'It's good,' he said. 'What's this made from?'

The woman chuckled. '*Naeng-myeon*. Soup, you

eat. Good for you. No egg, no kimchee. *Mianham-nida.* Sorry.'

Caine continued to slurp the liquid into his mouth. Whatever it was, it was food. His body had rested. Now he needed sustenance.

'You saved my life,' he answered. 'I can do without the kimchee. Who are you?'

The woman gave him the faintest hint of a smile. 'My name Bora. Bora Ryu. You American? Your name John? John most popular American name, yes?'

Caine nodded and spoke between spoonfuls of the cold broth. 'Yes, I'm American, but my name is Tom.'

The woman chuckled. 'Tom. Like Tom Sawyer. Famous book. Good American name.'

Caine finished eating and set down the bowl. The woman handed him a steaming cup of liquid. 'Tea,' she said.

He took a small sip. The warm liquid tasted of herbs and honey. It soothed his parched throat as he drank.

He cradled the cup in his hands, warming his fingers.

'You're Korean?' he asked.

She nodded and sipped from her own cup of tea.

'Joseon.' At Caine's confused look she added, 'The Democratic People's Republic of Korea. North Korea to you.'

Caine's mind reeled. *What were the odds of running into a North Korean woman in the middle of a Siberian forest?*

'North Korean? How did you get here?'

The woman sighed. 'Government send me here. I work for Russians. Timber, lumber, from forest. I am... I was arrested in Pyongyang. Government send me away. Send me here.'

She took another sip of tea, then licked her lips. 'They make me slave. Me, and others like me.'

'Other North Koreans?'

She nodded. 'Other men. I only woman. But we all slaves.'

Of course, Caine thought. *The old work gulags, set up by Brezhnev and Kim Il-sung in the late sixties.*

At the height of the Cold War, the DPRK sent prisoners to work as cheap labor for the Russians. Then came the fall of communism, and the economic decay in North Korea. Now, ordinary laborers were rounded up and sent to work in the dismal and dangerous Siberian saw mills. The pay was meager, and the North Korean government confiscated most of their wages. Institutionalized slavery was one of the beleaguered nation's few profitable exports.

Conditions inside the mills were bleak, and exposure to the outside world was strictly controlled. Still, some of the laborers were desperate to travel to the camps. They saw it as their only chance to escape the iron fist of their decaying home.

'I thought the workers in those camps weren't allowed to leave,' Caine said. He watched her reaction as he took another sip of tea. Whoever this woman was, she had dispatched the Russian commando in the woods without a second thought. She had knowledge of traps and was clearly a skilled hunter.

His killer instincts slithered through his mind. *If she thinks you're a threat, she could be dangerous.*

Bora stared at the picture next to the bed. Her eyes seemed to lose focus, and her wide brow furrowed. 'There was fighting, a riot. Happen years ago. Many men died. Russian guards, and many of my people. Some escaped, to China, or to the cities, the South Korean Embassy. I... I and others, we wanted none of that.'

'You didn't want to be free?' Caine asked.

She tilted her head. 'We free here. We grow food, we hunt. Build cabins, keep to ourselves. For me, that is free enough. I am old. I know I cannot go home. But I don't want to go to China, or South Korea, or even America. I stay here. Alone, in the woods. It is good.'

'But you're not alone. You said there were others. I saw them, I think.'

She nodded. 'A few. Old men, felt same as me. We stay here, we keep to ourselves.'

'So that was your cabin I found? Sorry about—'

She shook her head, cutting him off. 'Not mine. Abandoned by Russian trapper. I use it when I go into forest. When I want to be alone.'

Again, her eyes drifted to the picture.

Caine thought for a moment. 'How long have I been sleeping here?'

Bora took another sip of tea. 'Not long. Few hours. Your body cold. You need rest.'

There was a knock at the door. Bora set down her cup and heaved her body out of the chair. The floorboards creaked as she walked toward the door. She swung it open halfway. Caine saw a quick glimpse of two Korean men. They were older than Bora. Their short beards were dotted with flecks of gray, and the skin around their eyes was a mass of wrinkles.

They spoke in hushed tones. Bora followed them outside and shut the door behind her.

Caine slid out of bed. He peered out the plastic window and saw Bora and the men traipsing toward another cabin. He could hear her shouting, arguing with the others as they crossed the snow. Then they filed into the shack, and the door slammed shut behind her.

He searched the cabin for his shirt and belongings. If Bora was right, if he had been sleeping for hours, then he could not afford to stay here any longer. The old woman seemed to know her way around the woods. But no matter how careful she had been, it was only a matter of time before Zasko's team picked up their trail.

And when that happened, Bora and her friends would no longer be alone. The violence that followed in his wake, the curse he had brought upon Naiyana, and everyone else who got close to him... it would follow him here as well.

Bora and her friends were refugees, survivors of a horrifying ordeal. They were living out their last days here in peace and solitude. But now, they too would be caught in the crossfire.

He threw on the parka he had taken from Leonid. The GRU shovel was standing by the door, in a puddle of water from the ice that had melted off its blade.

Caine hefted the weapon and slid it through his belt.

Better for everyone if I just leave.

He patted the pocket of the parka, confirming the satphone and battery were still held within. Then he stalked toward the door, prepared to venture out in the bone-chilling cold once again.

35

Zasko lay prone on the snow, invisible within the drifts of white powder that surrounded him.

He squinted through the twin lenses of his binoculars and watched as a pair of men ambled through the trees. One of the men broke off and entered a small cabin, built from fallen larch trees. A whisper of gray smoke drifted from the chimney that poked above the dwelling's roof. Several other cabins nestled in the forest below. They all appeared to be handmade.

Zasko heard a soft crunching in the snow. Timur crawled next to him. The commander lowered the binoculars and glanced over at his tracker.

'Have a look,' he said in a low voice, handing the binoculars to his comrade.

Timur was silent as he peered down at the settlement hidden in the woods.

'What do you think?' Zasko asked.

'Five, maybe seven men. Could be Mongolian? The cabins look handmade. Judging from the condition of the wood, I'd say they've been here for some time... at least two years.'

The commander stroked his goatee. 'All this time, all these hunts. Yet I've never seen this place.'

Timur lowered the binoculars. His dark, squinting eyes were unreadable, but his mouth dipped in a grimace. 'No man ever made it this far before.'

Zasko nodded. 'True. But our target's lucky streak is about to end. Come.'

They crawled backward, moving away from the hill that overlooked the cluster of cabins. Zasko stood up and dusted snow from his winter gear. He and Timur walked over to Yuri, who was cleaning his weapons on a plastic tarp. The younger man looked up with his good eye.

'What did you find?'

'Our prey is down there. He has taken refuge in a small camp, a settlement of some kind.'

Yuri examined the barrel of his pistol, then snapped the slide closed. 'Settlement? What kind of settlement?'

'Who knows? Escaped prisoners, refugees perhaps. It does not matter. They are no match for us.'

'That's what you said about the target. Before he cut our team in half.'

Before Zasko could reply, an electronic chirp sounded from the pack on the snowmobile. Zasko turned to Timur. The GPS unit on his belt began beeping.

'The satphone,' Timur said. 'He's activated it.'

Zasko stalked over to his pack and pulled out the phone. He looked at the display.

'Timur, get a fix on his position,' Zasko snapped. He held the phone to his ear. '*Zdravstvuyte*. Hello, Mr. Caine.'

'Piotr Zasko. The Iron Wolf.' Caine's voice crackled over the line.

'Only a few men know my real name,' Zasko answered. 'Have we crossed paths before?'

'Doha, Qatar. 2004. You were working with the GRU.'

'Ah, yes. Preventing the spread of radical Islam. The work was quite... messy. I remember it well.'

'I remember lots of bodies. Lots of missing pieces.'

Zasko made a clicking sound with his tongue. 'Early days, my friend. I was not yet the hunter I am today, I acted... impulsively. Took whatever trophy caught my fancy. An ear, a finger, teeth... Trinkets of flesh and bone.'

'And now?'

Zasko turned away from his men and paced a few steps across the snow. 'Now, Mr. Caine? Now I hunt for the same reason all creatures on this earth hunt: to feast on my prey. To devour all a man has to give and grow stronger from the taking. The heart, my friend. A man's power, his very soul, lives in the heart.'

Static filled the line. For a moment there was silence. Then Caine chuckled.

'You're a piece of work, Zasko. But you're going to have to try harder if you want to take a bite out of me.'

There was a click, and the line went dead.

Zasko cursed and marched back toward Timur. 'Do you have a fix on his position?'

The tracker nodded. 'He's not in the cabins. The reading is a few kilometers west of here. Satphone went dead again, but we can look for tracks.'

Yuri stood up and slid his pistol into its holster. 'So his name is Caine? This *Caine* took out three of us while he was alone. Now he may have help from these so-called refugees.'

Zasko shot Yuri a smoldering look, but a moment later nodded in agreement. 'You are correct. Perhaps I have underestimated this prey of ours.'

Zasko straddled his snowmobile and began dialing a number on the satphone.

'What are you doing?' Yuri asked.

Zasko glanced up at him as the phone began to ring. 'I am calling in a favor. After all, every hunting party needs its dogs.'

36

The roar of the snowmobile was a distant buzz, faint and indistinct beneath the wind and the crackling ice in the swaying branches. Caine's ears picked up the sound. He listened for a moment...

It was growing louder. Closer.

Damn, he thought. *Zasko must've been closer than I thought.*

He sprinted as fast as he could, charging toward the densest grouping of trees he could find. The noise grew louder. They had almost reached his position.

Taking cover behind a thick tree trunk, he flipped down the hood of his stolen parka and took aim with his AK-74. The rifle's magazine was half empty, and the man he had taken it from, Leonid, only had one spare.

He swept the rifle left and right, peering over the sights through the snow-draped trees. The wind was growing stronger, and tiny ice crystals filled the air with a blue-white haze.

He wasn't sure how far he'd traveled since sneaking out of Bora's cabin. He had listened at the door, heard the men argue with the woman outside. He didn't speak much Korean, but he didn't need to – he could hear the fear and concern in their voices. He was an outsider, and she had brought him into their sanctuary.

As always, death followed on his heels. For himself, and now everyone in the camp.

They were right to be afraid.

He had gathered his things and snuck out of the cabin, leaving before Bora returned. He knew Zasko would have tracked his position after the satphone call. With any luck, they would ignore the camp and continue in their pursuit of him. Once they picked up his trail, the hunters would not stop to investigate a few refugees. At least, not until he was dead.

He had hoped he would have more time, could cover more distance, before the men caught up to him. According to his map, he was still far from the train tracks. But somehow, they were here. This would be his last stand.

The snowmobile burst through a snowbank. Caine tracked the vehicle with the rifle as it charged though the trees. A lone, dark figure sat on the roaring vehicle. A thick, fur-clad arm reached up and waved at him as she skidded to a stop.

The rider was Bora Ryu.

Caine lowered the rifle. 'What the hell are you doing here?' he shouted.

Bora dismounted and shuffled toward him in the snow. Her hunting rifle was slung over her back, and she was bundled in her thick fur parka and scarves.

'Men in village scared. They want you to leave.'

'They're right. I told you, more men coming. They want to kill me, and they will hurt—'

Bora grunted and silenced him with a wave of her large arm. 'O, *ib damul-eo*. Be quiet. I always know this day will come. We will have to fight again. We hide long enough.'

Caine shouldered his rifle. 'No, Bora. These men, they're too dangerous. They're not prison guards or fur trappers. They're soldiers. Assassins. They'll kill you without a second thought.'

Bora shrugged. 'If I die, I die. If these men kill you, they come for us next. Time for hiding is over.'

Caine said nothing. He could not deny the truth of her words.

Suddenly, Bora looked up at the sky. She hurried over to Caine and pulled him to the ground, rolling them both under a mound of snow.

'Hey, what the—'

'Shhhh!' she hissed, covering her lips with a finger.

A second later he heard it. The thumping of a helicopter, swooping low overhead. The vehicle roared above them. Then the sound grew faint as it flew into the distance.

After a few minutes of silence, Bora nodded. They stood up. Caine brushed the cold snow off his hair and skin.

'A helicopter out here can only mean one thing,' he said.

Bora stared up at the sky, as if she could still see the distant aircraft on the horizon. 'More men.'

'Yeah, more men. You still think hiding is a bad idea?'

'Why these men after you?' she asked.

'They tried to hurt someone... someone I cared about. So I hurt them first. Now, they want revenge.'

'Who they hurt? Girlfriend, wife?'

He shook his head. 'A friend. Someone important to me. That's all that matters.'

Bora's eyes became wide and unfocused. She stared across the snow, a blinding white plain stretching into the misty horizon. 'I had friend back home,' she said, her voice a throaty whisper. 'Someone I care for. Someone important.'

'The picture?' Caine asked, remembering the photo in the cabin.

The woman jerked her head up, as if pulled from a trance. Her wide, dark eyes focused on his face. She nodded.

'These men follow you now,' she said, her voice louder. 'Then they will come back for me, and the others?'

Caine exhaled a puff of mist and scanned the trees. Then he looked her in the eye. 'That's probably true.'

She adjusted her scarf and checked her rifle, making sure a round was loaded in the chamber. They walked side by side toward her battered snowmobile.

'Then we must kill them first. Bad idea, good idea... it does not matter.'

Caine couldn't help but laugh.

He shook his head and smiled. 'I admire your

optimism. But if we're going to have a chance at surviving this, we can't fight them, out here, in the open.' Caine looked up, keeping a wary eye on the horizon. 'We need to choose our battleground. Familiar terrain, someplace we know better than they do.'

Bora straddled the snowmobile. The engine sputtered to life. 'I know place. Two hours away. I take you there.'

Caine got on the back of the vehicle and wrapped his arms around the large woman. 'Where are we going?'

Bora glanced over her shoulder at him. Her dark eyes and wide nose peeked over the edge of a gray scarf that covered her mouth.

'I take you to the place I escape. The sawmill.'

She turned away and revved the engine. 'The killing place,' she shouted over the noise of the motor.

The snowmobile leaped forward, and they plunged deeper into the forest.

37

The sawmill lay nestled in a mountain valley, on the edge of a vast frozen lake. A bridge of rough timber logs straddled a frozen river that snaked down from the mountains and fed into the lake. The entrance to the mill stood at one end of the narrow platform. On the other side, the dirt road that led to the bridge was buried under a dense crust of snow.

A rusted, gnarled fence of corrugated metal and barbed wire surrounded the mill's grounds. The metal was bent and crumpled in some areas, leaving gaps in the fence. Torn banners, emblazoned with Korean characters, fluttered from poles mounted along the fence.

Caine peered through the shattered windows of

a building on the northern edge of the complex. He had a clear view of the fence and the other buildings, surrounding a field littered with trash and debris. An abandoned truck, its chassis stripped for parts, sat on blocks in the middle of the yard. Scattered piles of old timber lay near the rusted hulk. The arm of a loading crane loomed over the grounds. Its tattered cargo sling hung from a rusted cable that creaked and swayed in the wind.

Caine kept a watchful eye on the field as he took inventory of their weapons and ammo. He had laid out what remained of their arsenal on an old, rotting conveyor belt. The circular track slanted down from the roof and ran through the crumbling building. Its worn, frayed rubber surface was pelted with bird droppings and debris carried in by the shifting winds.

He began stripping down the rifle he had taken from the commando back in the woods. Using a rag and some graphite powder provided by Bora, he cleaned and lubricated the bolt and bolt carrier at the top of the weapon. He was grateful that Bora had been able to scrounge up the fine, powdered lubricant. Liquid oil was useless in the sub-zero temperatures outside. It could freeze, causing the gun to jam.

As he worked, he glanced down at the other armaments on the belt. In addition to the AK-74, there was Bora's hunting rifle, a bolt-action Mosin-Nagant. The old Russian workhorse was chambered in 7.62 Rimmed Rifle and was as rugged as it was accurate. Other than that, Leonid's grenade launcher, with two remaining thermobaric rounds, was all they had left.

A loud clatter rumbled through the building. Bora entered the room, rolling a dented metal barrel across the concrete floor. She grunted as she stood it up next to two identical barrels. Then she rested her hands on her knees and panted for breath.

'This all the fuel that is left. I know where guards hid supplies. Everything else gone, other barrels empty. After workers fight and escape, Russians leave this place, never come back. Mill close down. We make raids from forest. Take what we can, what we need to survive.'

Caine finished reassembling the AK, then slapped a full magazine into the receiver. He pulled back the charging handle. It moved with smooth, mechanical precision. He glanced over at the trio of fuel barrels.

'Diesel?' he asked.

'Mmmm,' she grunted in the affirmative as she picked up her old rifle.

'I cleaned it for you,' Caine said, glancing down the sights on the AK.

Bora examined her gun and gave him a suspicious look. 'Clean? Gun not dirty.'

'There was some salt corrosion on the bolt face.'

The old woman shook her head. She worked the bolt action and peered into the chamber. 'Gun work better a little dirty. No fix what not broken.'

Caine smiled. 'Whatever you say. Look, I appreciate all you've done. I owe you my life. But these men... they'll be coming soon. You really should go.'

Bora looked up at him from the rifle. 'I told you. No more hide. I fight.'

'Bora, if you stay here, I can't protect you.'

The woman barked a short laugh as she emptied a pouch from her belt. Brass cartridges rolled across the conveyor belt. She began loading them into the rifle, one by one. 'Protect me? I the one save you, remember?'

'There's no shame in hiding.'

The woman shook her head. 'What you know of hiding? You stay and fight? Then I stay and fight.'

Caine loaded one of the spare grenades into the launcher. He flipped the weapon closed. The remaining grenade stood upright in front of him. He stared at it for a moment, lost in thought.

'Before these men targeted me, before they hurt my friend... I *was* hiding. In Thailand.'

'Hiding from who?'

Caine was silent for a moment. He sighed and stared out the windows. 'It's hard to explain. Long story.'

Bora slung her rifle over her shoulder. She rested a hand on Caine's shoulder. He looked up at her, surprised by the gesture.

'You can only hide so long. Back home, my friend, she very special to me. What we had, how we feel... Government say we illegal. She thought she could hide. Hide how we feel, what we were. But men still came. Men still hurt us. They will always come.'

'I'm sorry,' Caine said. 'What happened to her?'

Bora dropped her hand. She stared at him for a moment. She expelled a puff of icy breath, then looked away. 'Dead now. Arrested. Firing squad. I was big, strong. So they send me here.'

'Bora, I—'

'No more hiding.' She checked her rifle again. 'If I die here, I die fighting.'

Caine looked out the window again. His emerald eyes zeroed in on the loading crane. Icicles hung from its long, narrow arm. Its base was buried in a towering drift of snow.

'Bora, the equipment here, do you know how to power it up?'

She nodded. 'Generators underground. I know where.'

'What about all the ice? How did they clean it off the crane, and the other equipment?'

She gave him a strange look. 'They use chemical. Looks like salt, they spread it over ice, and ice melts. Why?'

De-icer, Caine thought. *Ammonium nitrate.*

'Do you know where they keep this chemical?'

She nodded. 'They keep it with generators. I take you there.'

Caine glanced at the barrels of fuel. His lips curled into a grim smile. 'Lead the way.'

38

Yuri held up his fist and waved forward. He advanced down the bridge, stalking toward the mill. With every step across the rough timbers, he swept his rifle left and right. He scanned the horizon, searching for any sign of movement behind the crumbling fence. Beneath them, the river was solid and unmoving. It was a ribbon of gray ice, curving toward the mill, and to the frozen lake beyond.

He glanced to his left. The men summoned by Zasko moved with him in a loose formation. Unlike the spetsnaz team, their uniforms were non-standard. They wore a motley collection of green and tan camouflage gear, layered with civilian winter clothes.

Their weapons were just as varied... a random assortment of rifles, shotguns, and pistols.

Yuri knew these were private contractors, a disparate collection of retired VDV troopers and law enforcement. Now they worked for the security companies that provided protection and muscle to the rich oligarchs. And they occasionally dabbled in off-books operations for the Kremlin. Yuri had worked with such men before, during the Ukrainian crisis. The media had called them 'little green men', referring to the unmarked green uniforms they wore during that conflict.

Someone must have owed the Iron Wolf quite a favor, he thought. Within hours of Zasko's call, the men had been rushed to their position via helicopter.

There were six of them, split into two teams of three. Yuri was leading one team across the bridge, in a frontal assault. The rest had been assigned to Timur. They were moving through the trees, toward the rear of the complex.

'Do you see anything?' It was Zasko, speaking through the walkie. The man's voice crackled in his ear. The commander had taken Yuri's sniper rifle, and was positioned across the lake, up in the woods.

'Negative,' Yuri answered, keeping eyes on the fence ahead of them. 'No sign of target.'

'GPS signal is steady,' Timur chimed in. 'But there is no movement.'

A soft clanging noise drifted through the air. Yuri cocked his head, listening. It sounded like metal, scraping against the wood timbers of the bridge. 'Wait, I hear something.'

He held up his hand in a closed fist. The other men stopped.

'What is it?' Even over the walkie, Yuri detected a note of impatience in his commander's voice.

He turned off the walkie and put his fingers over his lips, quieting the men around him.

He waited in silence. He heard the noise again...

Clank... clank...

The other men peered around, trying to pinpoint the location of the sound.

'What the hell is that?' one of them asked in a hushed voice.

It was coming from underneath them. Kneeling, Yuri shouldered his rifle and bent his head over the edge of the bridge.

Beneath them, the ice had crumbled and melted. A small hole revealed the dark, frigid water beneath the surface. A pair of metal drums bobbed up and down in the water, brushing against the wood beams of the bridge.

Yuri's good eye opened wide in surprise. One of the barrels listed sideways in the water, revealing a mechanism wired to the side. He recognized the device instantly – one of Leonid's thermobaric grenades. Wires ran from the explosive round to a radio and some other electronics, duct-taped to the side.

Yuri leaped to his feet. 'Bomb! Run!'

The green men paused for a split second in shock. Then they followed him as he charged down the bridge toward the mill.

He had made it a few yards when the bomb detonated. The shockwave threw him to the ground. He caught a quick glimpse of a billowing cloud of fire and saw two of his men tossed through the air like rag dolls. Their bodies struck the cracking ice. The smooth white surface had shattered into chunks from the explosion's shockwave. The bodies sank into the dark water below.

Yuri and the remaining survivor picked themselves up. Behind them, the remains of the bridge crumbled into the dangerously frigid waters as well. Their route back was gone. Retreat was no longer an option.

'*Prodolzhay dvigat'sya*. Keep moving!' he shouted.

The two men raced forward, charging toward the open gates of the mill.

Crack!

A gunshot tore into the wood under their feet, sending splinters into the air. Yuri scanned the horizon. The shot came from a high angle, but beyond that, he had no idea where the shooter might be hiding.

A crane rose above the metal walls of the fence. A cluster of old timbers hung from its rusted claw.

That's where I would hide, he thought. He sent a wild burst of gunfire toward the cab.

Crack!

Another shot rang out. The mercenary by his side dropped to the ground. A fine red mist stained the wood timbers beneath them.

Yuri ignored him and kept running. The main gates of the complex – two massive sheets of corrugated metal marked with Korean lettering – stood closed. A chain was strung between them, but the metal sheets were bent and twisted, a five-foot gap left between them. Yuri dove through the opening as another shot cut through the air. Cradling his weapon in his hands, he skidded behind a pile of timber and took cover. Another bullet thudded into the wood.

'I'm inside but I'm pinned down,' he shouted into his walkie. 'Sniper, cannot see their position.'

'Draw their fire. I will find them,' the commander responded.

Timur's voice crackled over the radio. 'I have movement on the GPS, the satphone. It's heading toward our position, at the rear of the mill.'

'Caine must be trying to escape!' Zasko's voice rose in pitch. 'Move in, now!'

Yuri peered around the corner of the logs. He spied an abandoned truck near the center of the mill. Taking a deep breath, he raced toward the rusted hulk. He slid the last few feet across the ice, as another shot sparked off the metal frame of the vehicle.

'I hope you have the sniper's position,' he whispered into the radio, 'because I'm running out of—'

Before he could finish his sentence, a pair of explosions shook the camp. A section of fence on the north side of the complex collapsed. A white Taiga snowmobile burst through the wreckage and tore into the complex.

Timur piloted the vehicle into a long skid. The vehicle juddered to a stop, and he sprayed the nearest building with gunfire. His squad of green men took up position beside him. The remains of the building's glass windows shattered under the onslaught of their combined fire. Finally, Timur stopped shooting.

Silence fell over the frozen yard.

Timur dismounted and stalked toward the building in a low crouch. His men followed. One of the green men advanced and took up a position next to the battered door. The mercenary pumped his shotgun and fired, blasting a hole through the wood panel.

Nothing happened. The man kicked open the door. Timur gestured to the other two men and pointed at the entrance. They stalked forward, disappearing into the building.

'Timur is moving in. Do you have the sniper?' Yuri whispered.

He heard a low, throaty chuckle in his ear. '*Da*, I have them in my sights. I can see the fat cow plain as day.'

Crack!

Yuri heard the familiar retort of the T-5000 rifle echoing across the field. Peering around the corner of the truck, he saw a heavyset body wrapped in thick winter clothes tumble from the crane. It struck the snow-covered ground and rolled to a stop. Yuri squinted, trying to get a clear look at the body.

Zasko's voice crackled in his ear. 'Sniper down. Join Timur. Flush out Caine.'

'Wait,' Yuri whispered. 'Something is wrong.'

He stepped out from his cover, and advanced on the body.

39

Dark pools of shadow covered the floor of the abandoned building. A shaft of sunlight pierced the icy gloom, beaming through a hole in the rusted metal roof. The soft rumble of the conveyor belt was the only sound echoing through the cavernous interior.

Timur crouched low behind some old machinery. Using hand gestures, he silently directed his men to flank him. Obeying his orders, they fanned out and moved along either side of the turning belt. Looking down, he stared at the tiny blip moving on the GPS tracker's screen.

Whoever it was, they were right on top of his position.

The conveyor belt chugged in a circle, moving around the room in a clockwise direction. The machinery was old and rusty. A thin haze of smoke belched from the motorized drive wheels, and the room stank of chemicals.

Timur glanced at the nearest mercenary. The man rounded the corner of the circular belt and stood up. He looked over at Timur and shook his head.

Nothing.

Timur checked the GPS again. The signal was still moving through the room. It appeared to be coming up behind them, moving in to flank their position.

He spun around and raised his rifle.

There was no one there.

One of the other men kicked over a stack of dented old fuel barrels. As they crashed and rolled across the floor, he fired his weapon into the shadows behind them. Bright orange muzzle flash glowed in the dim light. His bullets thudded into more empty barrels.

Timur stared at the conveyor belt. The top of the belt was empty, save for some twigs and debris that had fallen in from the ceiling. A dead bird moved past his face. Frost glittered on its decayed feathers and lifeless eyes.

Crouching lower, Timur peered under the metal track.

He saw a tiny plastic object, lashed to the underside of the conveyor belt. It slowly turned toward him, pulled along by the motion of the belt. A red light blinked on its surface.

It was the satellite phone.

'Stand down. He is not here,' Timur whispered.

'*O chem ty govorish*'?' The closest mercenary whispered back. 'He must be here... The GPS...'

Timur tore the phone from the tape and held it up. 'He knew we were tracking it. This was a diversion – he led us here on purpose.'

He heard metal scraping against the floor. Looking up, he saw the fuel drums the other man had kicked over, still rolling back and forth across the concrete.

The drums were empty. The air reeked of chemicals...

The distant crackle of gunfire erupted outside the building.

'Move out! Now!' he shouted. He spun around and charged toward the nearest window. Something whistled through the air toward them. He caught a fleeting glimpse of a small cylinder arching through the hole in the roof. It bounced on the ground and rolled across the stained concrete floor.

Timur leaped toward the shattered window. Before he could clear the opening, he heard an explosion and felt the air ignite around him.

* * *

Caine peered down at the tiny figures stalking across the snow. From his perch high above the icy ground, he heard the crackling of gunfire. He watched as one of the commandos and his men approached the abandoned building. He watched them ready their weapons, saw the puffs of mist their breath left in the cold air.

Suddenly, a gunshot rang out. Above him, he heard the bullet ricochet off the metal of the crane. The chunky, heavyset figure tipped over and plunged to the ground. He ignored the falling body. It had done its job. He kept his attention focused on the empty building.

The men advanced inside.

Won't be long before they find the satphone, he thought. He rested the short barrel of the grenade launcher on the rough curve of a log and eyed the large hole in the roof.

He only had one round remaining. Missing the shot was not an option.

Caine hung suspended high above the camp, tucked in the bundle of logs hanging from the crane. He and Bora had hollowed out an opening in the middle of the timbers, and Caine had slipped inside.

They had planted the dummy on the crane arm. It was a simple diversion – just an old parka and coveralls stuffed with twigs and debris. If the men below figured out where Caine's shots were coming from, he could only hope the dummy would draw their fire. With any luck, he'd have enough time to take them out before they zeroed in on his true hiding spot.

The hanging logs were an unsteady perch, as they bobbed and swayed in the breeze. He leaned further out from his concealment and aimed the grenade launcher at the building below.

More gunfire erupted beneath him. The bullets thudded into the heavy logs. Caine heard wood splinter and saw tiny chips of bark and timber spray through the air around him.

So much for the diversion, he thought.

He shouldered the heavy launcher and grabbed

his rifle. Crawling out from hiding, he used the cargo sling's cables to steady himself as he stood atop the swaying logs.

Glancing over his shoulder, he saw another spetsnaz commando standing in the snow next to the dummy. Whoever it was, they were aiming their rifle up at his position. Caine fired a wild burst toward their position on the ground. As the figure below backed off, he dropped the rifle and balanced on top of the pile of logs. He aimed the grenade launcher again, squinting as the hole in the roof spun into view.

He pulled the trigger.

The weapon fired, sending its heavy projectile arcing through the air. The grenade struck the top of the building, a few feet from the hole. Caine held his breath as the shell bounced, then rolled across the sloped metal surface.

It dropped through the hole and plunged into the darkened interior.

An explosion shook the metal walls of the building. Then the fuel he and Bora had spilled inside ignited. Even this high off the ground, Caine felt a blistering wave of heat, as plumes of fire burst through the roof and windows. He saw a tiny burning figure dive out the front of the building, and roll to a stop in the snow.

Another burst of gunfire struck near his feet.

Caine returned fire, but it was impossible to aim from his precarious position. He saw the commando circling beneath him, lining him up in the sights of his weapon.

Climbing farther up the cargo harness, Caine grabbed at the main cable that hung from the crane. He shimmied up the taut steel line and reached for the metal bars of the crane arm. As he grabbed the bar, his feet slipped off the cable. More bullets ricocheted off the crane. The commando stalked forward, pointing his rifle up at the beams of the crane arm.

Caine looked down, eying his attacker's position. *That's it, just a little closer...*

The soldier took another step forward.

Caine's flailing legs came to rest on a small red metal box. The rig release hung between the main cable and the sling that held the timbers. He kicked at a lever that protruded from the side of the box. The logs jerked slightly, but nothing happened. He stomped down again, but the release was frozen and stiff.

The commando's rifle fired, and Caine felt a

dagger of pain as a bullet grazed his leg. More gun-fire sparked against the metal bar next to his numb fingers.

He clenched his teeth and let go of the bar, let-ting his body slide down the cable. His foot slammed into the release lever, striking the metal rod with his full weight.

With a loud clank, the release popped and the sling cables screamed through the pulleys. As if in slow motion, the huge, heavy timbers rolled apart and tumbled through the air.

He heard the man below scream.

The sound was cut short by the crash of the mas-sive logs slamming into the ground.

40

Caine descended the crane using a ladder mounted to the tower. He took cover behind the metal structure. Peering around the corner, he surveyed the smoking building and the pile of fallen timber.

No one was moving. No other men entered the grounds.

He clicked on his walkie. 'Bora, do you copy? Are you there?'

Static hissed through the speaker.

Cursing, he checked his rifle, and found the magazine was empty. He eyed the pile of timbers once more. He jogged toward the body of the soldier pinned beneath the heavy logs. Glancing left and right, he scanned the grounds of the mill, but he saw no one else. The abandoned building still crackled and burned. The blaze sent thick black clouds of smoke billowing into the cold air. The charred remains of the commando who dove through the window lay motionless in the snow.

Caine returned his attention to the fallen soldier before him. The man's rifle was pinned under one of the enormous logs that lay across his torso. Both his legs and ribcage had been crushed by the heavy wood. His face was pale and still.

Caine spotted a spare magazine clipped to the man's belt and yanked it free. He ejected the empty one from his rifle and tossed it into the snow. Then he slammed the fresh one into his weapon.

He reached into the corpse's parka, searching for a pistol or secondary weapon. His grasping fingers found a wallet, tucked into an inner pocket. He pulled it out and flipped through its contents.

There was no identification inside, only some crumpled ruble notes and a black and white picture of a woman. Caine held up the picture and examined the woman in the photograph. She had light hair, dark eyes, and an inviting smile. He flipped over the scrap of glossy paper. The back was labeled *Irena* in scrawled black writing.

The body beneath the logs shifted. The man

began to spasm and cough. Caine stepped back and raised his rifle. The commando spat up blood and made a strange gurgling sound.

Caine's finger froze on the trigger. There was something unsettling and familiar about the noise the man was making. It took him a second to recognize the sound.

He was laughing.

'What's so funny?' Caine grunted.

The injured man coughed again. A fine red mist spattered the snow next to his face.

'Th... That's the second time you drop tree on me.'

Caine was silent for a moment. He peered at the man over the barrel of his rifle. 'Last night, in the forest. You were the sniper?'

The man offered a weak nod, as more blood trickled from his mouth.

'*Da*, that was me. No more sniping for me now, eh? I half the man I used to be.'

He turned his head to look at Caine with his one good eye. The other was still shut, hidden beneath a mass of swollen flesh and scar tissue.

'Hope you're not expecting an apology, kid,' Caine muttered. 'I think we both know you're not walking out of here. Tell me what I want to know, and I'll make it quick, at least.'

The man gasped a short, high-pitched wheeze of pain. 'I don't know much. This is my first hunt. Zasko, these men... I know it was wrong, but I was desperate. Irena... my wife. She is sick. I did it for...' His voice trailed off.

Caine lowered the rifle. 'I don't have time for a sob story. Where's Zasko now?'

The sprawled man shook his head as best he could. 'He was in the tree line, across the lake. He must have repositioned, or he would have shot you by now.'

The woods, Caine thought. *Bora was in the woods, flanking the men on the bridge.*

'*Pozhaluysta*,' Yuri gasped. 'Please... Irena... leave me her picture.'

Caine glanced at the crumpled photograph in his hands. 'You said she's sick. What does she have?'

'They call it Wilson's disease,' Yuri croaked. 'Her liver will fail soon.' The man gasped. 'Difficult to treat. Only medicine that will work... is very expensive. That is why I took this job, why I come here.'

Caine eyed the coughing, bleeding young man. Keeping his distance, he kneeled and pressed the scrap of paper into his open hand. The soldier's fist closed tight around the photo.

He closed his eyes. 'Thank you.'

'What's your name?' Caine asked.

'Yuri. Yuri Duskin.'

'And your wife... Irena Duskin?'

The man stared at Caine. 'Why do you ask?'

'I have friends... smugglers. They have access to pharmaceuticals. I'll see what I can do.'

The walkie on Caine's belt squawked and crackled. Keeping the rifle trained on Yuri, he grabbed the radio and pressed the talk button.

'Bora, is that you? What's your position?'

There was silence. Then a man's voice came through the speaker.

'Bora? I take it that is the name of your refugee friend?'

The Iron Wolf.

'I remember the reports about what happened here,' he continued. 'A revolt, a riot in the sawmill. Now I know who those people in the forest really are.'

'Let her go, Zasko. Rudov's not paying you to hunt North Korean refugees.'

'True, but there is plenty of meat on her bones. Plenty of trophies, so perhaps I shall—'

'You said you want my heart,' Caine snarled, cutting him off. 'So come and get it.'

'Meet me on the lake. Under the cliff, to the east... You will see me there. I will release your friend, and we will finish this.'

'Fine.' Caine lowered the walkie. He glanced down at the wounded commando.

'The refugee camp... did Zasko report its location?'

Yuri shook his head. '*Nyet*. He will not report it. Not until the hunt is over. He does not want the authorities to know we are here.'

Caine nodded. He clipped the walkie onto his belt and aimed the rifle at Yuri with both hands. 'It's time.'

'If you can help Irena... The medicine she needs, it is called Cupramine. Please believe me, I am not like Zasko. Not like these other men.'

Caine blinked. The wind picked up, blowing particles of ice across the frozen ground. He squinted, shutting out the stinging cold as it howled around him.

'I used to tell myself the same thing,' he said. 'Sometimes I even believed it. But look around. No saints out here today.'

Yuri nodded. He clutched the picture tighter and closed his eyes.

Caine pulled the trigger. The quick burst of gunfire echoed across the frozen field, and through the empty buildings.

Then he turned and stalked across the blood-spattered snow, moving toward the abandoned snowmobile.

* * *

Caine ducked low behind the handlebars of the snowmobile as he raced across the smooth glassy surface of the lake. Behind him, the lumber yard continued to burn. A dark cloud of smoke hung over the camp. Orange flames crawled up the fence and devoured the remains of the mill.

Ahead of him, white mountains hugged the lake in a cold, rocky embrace. They rose up to the east, forming a gray, frozen bluff. The remains of a waterfall trickled down the rocks, beneath a shimmering layer of ice. It sent a steady flow of frigid water tumbling below the lake's frozen surface. Cracks radiated from the impact of the waterfall, crisscrossing the ice like a spider's web.

Caine could barely make out two dark figures, standing on the ice a few yards from the falling water. The sun was moving behind the mountain, and a dark shadow crept over the entire area. The air became colder as the wind picked up in strength and howled around him.

As he drew closer, he saw Bora, her hands tied in front of her. The towering woman dwarfed Zasko, but Caine could see his shadowy form standing behind her. As he moved closer, he saw the glimmer of a blade, pressed against the woman's throat.

You shouldn't be here. The whisper of experience slithered out from its lair, hidden between his nightmares and memories of death. *This is a trap. You should run, leave while you can...*

Caine's instincts had saved his life on more than one occasion. He rarely ignored them. When the killer inside him spoke, he listened.

Not this time, he thought. *I need to finish this. For Bora, for Naiyana and her brother... even for Rebecca. It won't be over until Rudov and the Iron Wolf are dead.*

He skidded to a stop a few yards away from them. He dismounted the snowmobile and stood up, holding his rifle at his side. For a few moments there was silence. Then the mournful howl of the wind picked up, swirling around them.

Bora squinted at him and shook her head. 'You really come? You still can't see trap!'

Caine said nothing.

'Your friend is right, Mr. Caine.' Zasko's voice was

muffled behind Bora's thick winter clothes. 'A man with your reputation for survival? I was certain you would cut your losses and run. Make your way to the railway tracks and leave this place.'

'And I was sure you'd try to pick me off from high ground,' Caine said. 'Be an easy shot from up on that bluff.'

Zasko chuckled. 'I must confess, that was indeed my plan. But your friend here flushed me out from my sniper hide. When I moved to another position, I found myself caught in one of her ridiculous snares.' He shook his head. 'Vines, ropes, and a shovel. You two are quite the pair. I cut myself free, of course, but my rifle fell into a crevasse. Speaking of which, put your gun down on the ice. Now.'

Caine bent at the knees and lowered his rifle. He glanced up at Zasko... He could see the man's dark eyes, peering at him over Bora's shoulder. For a moment, he considered trying to pull off a snapshot. But he knew it would be next to impossible to hit the man before he—

Zasko dug the blade deeper into Bora's neck. She grunted as a droplet of crimson blood trickled along its blade.

'Slowly, Mr. Caine. Do not test me.'

Caine set the gun down on the ice and stood back up.

'Now, kick it over here.'

Caine glared at the man and shot him a quick grin. 'Yeah. Not gonna happen.'

He kicked the rifle behind him. It clattered across the ice.

Zasko pushed Bora forward. They walked across the ice toward Caine.

'Yes, it is better this way. You truly are remarkable prey. Face to face is the only way to kill a man such as you.'

Caine stepped toward Zasko, closing the gap even further.

They stood a couple yards apart. The wind died down, and again there was silence. Zasko's dark eyes burned into him. The man licked his lips. 'When I consume you, your strength, your pain, all that you are will become a part of me.'

'Choke on it,' Caine said, clenching his fists.

The other man nodded. 'Very well... then let us begin.'

Blam!

The muffled shot of a pistol exploded behind the woman. Bora's eyes opened wide, and a gurgle of pain escaped her lips.

Caine charged forward, his senses shifting into high alert. He saw Bora fall away from Zasko as though she were moving in slow motion. He closed the distance between them and reached behind his back. Zasko raised his right arm, the one that he had hidden behind the woman. Caine spotted the lump of black metal clenched in his fist... A Makarov pistol!

A savage grin spread across Zasko's face as he aimed the gun at Caine.

41

Caine's fingers grasped the weapon behind his back. He darted left as he swung his arms out in front of him. He continued charging toward Zasko, watching the pistol rise toward him.

Too slow, he chided himself. *Not gonna make it!*

Bora fell to the ground but deftly rolled over onto her back. She lashed out with a kick, striking Zasko with one of her thick, powerful legs. His knee buckled, and he stumbled forward. The gun roared in his hand, but the shot went wild.

Caine felt a lance of white-hot pain slice across his right leg. The bullet tore clean through the flesh of his thigh and buried itself in the ice below. A spiderweb of cracks spread beneath them.

Caine fought through the pain and swung the shovel out in front of him. The sharp head slashed across Zasko's forearm, then struck the pistol. The weapon flew from his grasp and slid toward the crumbling ice beneath the waterfall.

Off balance from the powerful swing, Caine struggled to recover. Zasko was faster. The man lunged forward and Caine heard a loud crack pierce the air. A whip unfurled from his opponent's right hand. The black leather cord wrapped tight around Caine's throat. With an angry bellow, Zasko yanked on the whip, trying to draw Caine toward him. He spun his knife around his fingers, preparing to strike.

Caine dug in his heels and leaned back. The muscles in his neck and throat bulged as he resisted his captor's strength. He spun his body sideways, throwing Zasko off balance and forcing him to take a step forward. Looping his left arm around the whip, Caine turned again, pulling Zasko closer. He raised the sharp head of the shovel, preparing to strike with an overhead stab.

Zasko made a quick snap with his arm, and the whip dropped away from Caine's neck and arm. It flew back, and Zasko grasped it in a tight coil. Caine surged forward, jabbing with the pointed tip of the shovel, but Zasko sidestepped the blow. With a lightning-fast movement, he used the circle of leather cord to tangle Caine's weapon arm. Spinning his body around, he used his momentum to drag Caine down to the ice.

Caine felt his feet skid beneath him, his weight now jerked off balance. He slammed into the frozen surface of the lake, and the wind exploded from his lungs in a pained gasp.

He heard the ice crackle around them. More cracks appeared, a series of thin white lines branching out beneath him. Caine rolled to his right as the other man stamped down onto the ice. His foot sank a few inches as the ice gave way beneath him. Frigid water began pooling up through the cracks.

Caine swung out his legs in a sweep. The blow knocked his opponent off balance. Zasko fell sideways, striking the ice with another heavy thud.

Caine rolled on top of the man and raised the shovel over his head in a two-handed grip. Even as he drove the weapon down, Zasko thrust a knee into his abdomen, tearing the stitches from the agonizing wound.

Caine gasped and the shovel bit into the ice a few inches from Zasko's head. Using the momentum of the missed blow, the Russian flipped Caine onto his back and straddled him. He slashed at Caine's arm, forcing him to release his grip on the shovel. Zasko swept the weapon away from them. The knife spun around his fingers, then stabbed down at Caine's throat.

Moving on pure instinct, Caine threw up his forearm, blocking the attack. Grabbing the man's knife hand with his other arm, he pummeled his opponent with a series of knee strikes. Zasko didn't budge and continued to drive the knife downwards. His lips curled into a leering, maniacal grin.

Caine felt blood dripping from the torn stitches in his side, and the new gash in his leg. His vision grew hazy, as the blade inched closer to his neck.

'The hunt is nearly over,' Zasko gasped, panting for breath. 'I shall cut out your heart and roast it over a fire out here in this frozen hell. And when I have cleaned my kill, stripped your body to the bone, I will lead more men into that silly cow's encampment.' He nodded toward Bora, who lay unconscious on the ice. 'We will burn their cabins to the ground, shoot any refugees we find. And the more blood I spill, the more medals they shall pin on my uniform.'

Caine blinked. The blade sank another inch closer... its tip hovered above his heaving throat.

Something strange about the knife, he thought... He squinted, focusing on a tiny metal protrusion in the grip. He grasped the hilt of the knife, forcing the blade sideways, away from his face.

As soon as his fingers touched the hilt, a look of concern flickered across Zasko's wild, animalistic face. Grunting with exertion, the man twisted the blade at an angle, keeping the hilt from pointing back at him.

That's it, Caine thought. *NR-S2, shooting knife.*

The ice continued to crack beneath them. More white lines radiated from the two men, a mosaic of hairline fractures in the smooth white surface of the lake.

Caine shook his head... his vision cleared.

Clenching his jaw tight, Caine forced the knife sideways again. The blade shook and hovered between them, neither man able to drive home a killing blow.

Zasko narrowed his eyes and glared at Caine. Even in the frigid cold, beads of sweat dripped down both their faces.

'You cannot win,' Zasko finally gasped. 'It is only a matter of time.'

'I don't care if I win,' Caine snarled. 'As long as you lose.'

Caine lifted his head off the ice. He slammed his forehead into the bridge of Zasko's nose. The man pulled back and roared in anger. For a split second, his hold on the knife weakened.

It was just enough.

Caine twisted the handle down, pointing it toward the ice. His prodding fingers found the slim metal trigger, mounted to the guard.

He fired the weapon.

The bullet exploded out of the handle of the knife and struck the ice. A final, deafening series of cracks and pops sounded beneath them. Caine felt himself rolling, falling backward.

The ice had broken.

As he plunged into the lake, a blinding white agony flooded every sense in his body. The frigid water felt like a sea of icicles, piercing his flesh from every direction. He ignored the pain, fighting his way through the sudden burst of instinctive panic. He reached out and felt Zasko's body tumbling beside him as they sank into the gelid depths of the lake.

He wrapped his arm around the man's throat and pulled him deeper into the water. His sinking body carried them both into the freezing blackness below.

Above them, he saw the cracked sheet of ice, lit from behind by the setting sun. It was a massive plain of glowing white, stretching as far as his eyes could see. Then the soft glow receded. Darkness surrounded him.

Zasko struggled but Caine kept his arm locked tight around the Russian's throat. Tiny bubbles of oxygen exploded from the man's mouth as he kicked and fought. Their descent began to slow, as Zasko's kicking legs drove them back up toward the surface.

As they fought, Caine saw a dark shape, tumbling toward them in the cold shadows. It was the snowmobile, plummeting past them in the water.

Caine hooked his leg under the handlebars. The heavy vehicle acted as an anchor, dragging them deeper and deeper down, farther into the icy depths. A white haze crept around the edges of his vision, blotting out all detail. His heartbeat slowed, as his body succumbed to the murderous cold that engulfed him.

Zasko's struggling grew weaker. The deathly chill was stronger than both of them.

Before his vision went dark, Caine looked up. He saw a faint gray shadow, moving across the other side of the glowing sheet of ice.

Bora... she's hurt.

Naiyana... Rebecca... you can't go yet. Rudov...

It's not over...

He felt his arms go limp. He released his hold on Zasko. The body drifted away from him, spinning in a gentle circle as it floated into the distance. Beams of sunlight from above lit the man's face. His eyes were open, staring. They were as dark and lifeless as a shark's. His lips looked rubbery and bloated. His mouth was frozen in a twisted scream.

The body drifted into the shadows of the murky water and disappeared.

Caine struggled to free his leg from the snowmobile. His limbs felt leaden. Dead weights. He no longer felt cold, or pain. He no longer felt anything.

He closed his eyes. One last bubble escaped his lips. Then he opened his mouth, and felt the icy water rush down his throat, filling his innards with a billion stabbing needles of cold. It was the last sensation he felt before the white blur faded to a pinpoint.

He was gone.

Free.

42

Caine gasped. The light was blinding. He blinked as the intense glow overhead faded to a dull, cloudy gray. He coughed and his body shuddered as water exploded from his throat. The liquid trickled down his cheeks.

The cold... He shivered as the cold hit him like a punch to the gut. He gasped again and clutched his body with his arms.

He was lying on his back, looking up at the bleak, empty sky. He heard footsteps walking across the ice. A heavy parka was draped over his body.

He turned and saw Bora, kneeling beside him.

His lips quivered as he struggled to speak.

Shivers ran up and down his spine. 'You... You pulled me out?'

The woman nodded. Her face looked pale and tired. Her lips were thin and drawn and had taken on a bluish tint.

Caine sat up. 'You're h-hu—' Caine paused, unable to speak from the cold. 'Hurt,' he finally sputtered. 'Zasko, shot...'

She reached out and put her hand on his chest. Her thick, powerful arm forced him onto his back again.

'You rest,' she demanded. Her voice was low and hoarse. 'Very cold. Your body in shock.'

Caine realized it was her parka that she had draped over him. She wore only a thermal knit sweater and her winter coveralls. The sun was a thin orange sliver, hidden behind the mountains. Soon, the killing cold would return.

She stood up and Caine saw the puddle of red left behind where she had been sitting. It was a brilliant splash of crimson against the pale blue ice.

He looked behind him. The dark pool of water lapped against the edges of the broken ice. 'Zasko?' he asked.

The woman stared at the water. 'I watch you

fight. Even match. You both almost die. Then you both fall in. I pull you out. Fight over.'

Caine shook his head. 'Not an even match. I had an advantage.'

Bora squinted at him. 'He almost kill you. What advantage you have?'

Caine grinned as another shiver ran through his body. 'I had backup.'

Bora smiled. A booming laugh exploded from her mouth. Suddenly, she gasped in pain and dropped to her knees. She grabbed her side. More blood pumped from her wounds.

Caine threw off the parka and forced himself to stand up. Bora had tied a bandage around the wounds in his leg, but each step still shot a spasm of pain through his muscles.

'Bora, we have to get out of here, make it back to your camp. It's not that far—'

'No, no.' The woman shoved his hands away. 'Not far, but too far for me.'

'The sun is going down... It's too cold, you'll die out here.'

Bora closed her eyes. 'Then I die. Everyone dies. The camp, the people living there, they are safe. I go in peace. See my friend again. That is where I belong.'

A strange look of peace drifted across her face. She grabbed his hand. 'Running, hiding, surviving... I do these things for long time. Maybe whole life.' She looked up at him. 'They not the same as living.'

Caine stared back at her in silence. 'Right now, surviving is all I have,' he finally answered.

Bora smiled. 'Now, maybe. When you old and tired like me, you feel different.'

Caine clutched his body as he shivered in the cold. The woman had done her best to dry him off, but his clothes were soaked by the icy water. Frost crystals began to form in his hair and nipped at his skin.

She nodded toward the smoking ruins of the mill in the distance. 'You go now. Back to mill, back to fire. Get dry, warm. Then follow the lake, around mountains. Train tracks not far.'

Her hand fell away from him as she slumped down on the ice. She looked up at the sky. 'Stars come soon. Beautiful sky. I watch them one last time. Before I sleep...'

Her words were slurred, barely a whisper. Her eyes closed.

Caine took a step backward. He felt lost, uncertain... Zasko was gone. His men defeated. Caine had won. He had survived.

Now what?

You know what, the killer inside him answered. *This isn't over.*

He stood over her, clutching her tattered, worn parka in his hands. 'Thank you, Bora,' he said.

She did not answer.

Caine shrugged on the heavy coat. He shoved his hands into the pockets, lowered his head, and turned around. He trudged forward, leaving her body and the shattered, blood-stained ice behind him.

He did not look back. Her body was soon lost in the shadows of the setting sun, and the shroud of icy mist that filled the air.

* * *

Sergei Rudov paced across the cold concrete floor of his vodka cellar. He pressed his ear to the satphone and listened as it rang.

No one answered.

'*Chert!*' he shouted and hurled the phone toward the nearest shelf. It struck the row of frosted bottles with a loud crash. The glass vessels shattered, spilling their precious clear liquid across the shelf. 'Where the hell is he?'

Two of his men followed in his footsteps. They

exchanged nervous glances, then one of them kneeled and took off his suit jacket. Using the jacket, he began to dab at the growing puddle of liquid.

The other man slipped a cell phone from his pocket. 'Sorry, boss. I get someone to clean this up, right away.'

Sergei spun around and pulled his thick fur robe tighter. '*Nyet!* Find Antonovich... tell him I must speak with the Iron Wolf immediately. No more excuses!'

'*Da*, yes sir!' The man spun around and headed toward the stairs. Rudov glanced down at the shivering man mopping up the spilled vodka. 'What the hell are you doing? Go with him. I want Antonovich on the phone, now!'

The man leaped to his feet and jogged after his partner.

Rudov shook his head. He grabbed a bottle of vodka from the shelf and pulled off the top. He took a long drink, then wiped his lips. Only a few lights were on, angular shadows cloaking the cold, cavernous basement. The club upstairs was closed for the evening, leaving the storeroom dark and silent.

He walked to the back of the room and slid aside the painting. Entering the code, he watched the fake shelf slide away. He stepped through the door into his private sanctuary, closing the door behind him. He took another sip of vodka and picked the remote up from the glass table.

The glass panel at the far end of the room slid up, revealing his trophies. Rudov sighed and slumped in his chair. The chill in the air cooled his rage. He stared at the frozen grimaces of fear and terror before him. As always, his trophies soothed him. It had been days since he had heard from the spetsnaz commander. The hunt should have been over by now. Caine should be dead. Perhaps he was just impatient... These things took time.

Rudov glared at the empty space in his trophy cabinet. He took another swig from his bottle and grunted. 'Next time I come here, I will have a new trophy.'

The intercom on the table crackled to life.

'Careful what you wish for, Rudov.' The voice held a sharp, cool edge, like frost on the blade of a knife.

The muscular old man leaned forward. His icy blue eyes narrowed, and his jaw clenched. 'Who the hell is this?'

'I'm disappointed, Sergei. You spent all that time and money to hunt me down, and you don't even recognize my voice?'

'Caine.' He spat the name as if it left a bitter taste in his mouth. 'I take it you have beaten the Iron Wolf?'

'I saw his face, Sergei. After he died, I looked into his eyes. Do you want to know what I saw?'

Rudov said nothing. He slammed the bottle on the table, stood up, and paced toward the door.

'Fear, Sergei,' Caine continued. 'Zasko died with fear in his eyes. The same way you will.'

Rudov barked a short, angry laugh. 'Do not be so sure. So you have bested the Wolf. Survived the hunt. Congratulations. I have other men in my employ. Men who make Zasko look like a saint. And I will send them all. For you, for the boy. And for that Thai whore hiding in her *kusok der'ma* village.'

He punched a code into the keypad next to the door.

Nothing happened. His eyes narrowed. '*Kakogo cherta?*' he muttered. 'What the hell...'

'I had a little conversation with your second in command. What was his name, Antonovich?'

Rudov shook his head and punched in the code again. The door remained closed.

Caine's voice continued to echo through the room. 'It was a bit hard to understand him. Broken jaw will do that. But he told me only three men know about your little sanctuary down there. Your trophy room.'

'The code,' the man hissed. 'You changed the code.'

'Guess it makes sense,' Caine continued. 'If you're going to keep evidence of multiple homicides in your possession, you don't want an ambitious rival gaining access.'

Sergei pounded on the door, his thumping blows echoing through the room. In the back of his mind, he knew it was a futile gesture. No one outside could hear.

'Solid concrete walls, soundproof, no cell signals in or out. Everything hardwired, right? Cameras. Intercom. Temperature control. Must be getting cold in there by now.'

Sergei glanced up at the wall. The digital thermometer showed the temperature dropping rapidly. Already, it had fallen from zero to negative ten degrees. Each breath sent a puff of mist into the air. A shudder wracked his spine.

'My men will find me,' he said. His words were slurred by the shivering of his body. Even the thick fur robe he wore was not enough to fend off the chill. The cold crept into his bones. 'If you are on the intercom, you must be here in the building. They will kill you, and free me.'

'Wouldn't count on that, Sergei. They'll find Antonovich and the others long before they find you. By then, it will be too late.'

Sergei watched as the temperature dropped to negative twelve degrees. The numbers continued to fall.

His face contorted into a mask of rage and hatred. He pounded on the door with both his fists. '*Ty sukin syn!* You son of a bitch, I will kill you! I will tear off your head with my bare hands, I will—'

'Russo-Baltique,' Caine said.

Sergei ceased his ranting. 'What?'

'The bottle on your desk. Russo-Baltique. Good stuff? Looks expensive.'

Sergei took a deep breath. 'I can pay. We can come to an arrangement. I—'

'I poured myself a glass. I'm drinking a toast. To my life and your death. But look on the bright side, Sergei. You got what you wanted.'

'What are you talking about?'

'When they finally pry open the door to your chamber of horrors, your men will find a new trophy inside.'

The thermometer ticked down as the temperature continued to drop. Sergei sank to the floor and leaned against the metal door. His shivering was uncontrollable now.

'G-G-Go... Go to hell,' he gasped.

'Going after Naiyana and her brother was a mistake. But this? This is for Bora.'

'*Kto?* Who is—'

'Goodbye, Sergei.'

The intercom went silent.

'Caine, wait!' The old man's pitiful wail bounced off the walls and echoed through the room. He clutched himself tighter, desperate for warmth. 'Please, we can make a deal!'

There was no response. The digits on the thermometer kept falling, lower and lower. Colder and colder.

The frozen faces in the trophy cabinet stared down at Rudov, welcoming him into their ranks.

43

Caine pulled the parka's hood over his head and turned away from the snow-covered street.

To his left, sheets of ice floated across the dark, glossy water of the Fontanka River. Ahead of him, in the distance, spotlights blazed off the azure domes and golden spires of the Trinity Cathedral.

A siren howled in the darkness. Across the river, a pair of white and blue police cars wove through traffic, screaming past the quaint riverside buildings. Caine turned left and ducked down an alleyway. He knew the police were not looking for him, but he felt uncomfortable in the open streets of St. Petersburg. Rudov and the Russian Mafia's reach went deep into the local government. He knew it would be wise to leave the city before the old gangster's body was discovered.

As his boots crunched across the snow, he removed the satphone from his coat pocket. He dialed a number from memory. It was the second time that day he had called her...

A singsong voice answered the phone in Thai. '*Hal-loh?*'

'It's me,' Caine grunted. 'Put her on.'

'She busy. You tell me what you want, I let her know!'

'Tell her to pause her damn Korean dramas and pick up the phone.'

The voice muttered an unintelligible curse. '*Ro sak kru*, hold on.'

Caine continued walking down the alley, glancing left and right to make sure he was alone.

He heard a sharp intake of breath, a gasping wheeze on the other end of the line. 'Now what?' the old woman demanded. 'You seem to have a knack for interrupting my favorite shows.'

Anna. The *Chao Mae*. A godmother in the *chao pho* crime families. His partner Lau worked for her, and as much as he hated to admit it, Caine owed her some allegiance as well.

'Sorry,' Caine replied. 'You okay? You don't sound good.'

'I'm not the one wandering around Russia in the winter.'

Caine left the alley and crossed through an empty parking lot. Above him, the stars twinkled in the cold, clear sky. The wind began to pick up, sending an icy chill across the river.

'Your information about Rudov paid off. Thank you.'

He could hear her sipping tea on the other end of the line. 'Sergei was a sick old bastard. It takes a certain kind of person to hold on to power as long as he did. I'm sure he got what was coming to him. But then again, I'm not one to judge.'

Caine said nothing. He and Anna maintained an uneasy alliance, but he suspected the old crone was just as capable of monstrous deeds as Rudov, or any other gangster.

'You mentioned you could arrange transportation for me?' he said, breaking the silence.

A rasping laugh crackled over the phone. 'Well, well. So eager now to make use of my shipping contacts. Lau tells me you cost us quite a bit of money the other day. You embarrassed him in front of Ramil. Made him lose face.'

'When you asked me to work with Lau, you knew my terms. No drugs. No guns. No people.'

The woman sighed. 'Yes, yes, I remember. Very well. There's a cargo vessel leaving Neva Bay this evening. Lau will get you details. Be on it. You'll be back in Pattaya in a few days.'

Caine took a breath. He glanced up at the stars.

'There's something else,' he said. 'A woman, Irena Duskin. She's being treated in a hospital in Seversk for liver disease.'

'*Khîi*,' the old woman cursed. 'I just missed the opening of my next show.'

'Ramil has legitimate pharmaceutical connections, doesn't he?'

'Perhaps,' the woman muttered. A sly tone crept into her raspy voice. 'But I'm not interested in charity cases. Who is this woman? What's so special about her?'

'That doesn't matter.'

He heard her inhale from her cigarette. She coughed and wheezed on the other end of the line. 'And what is it you want?'

'I need a drug called Cupramine, as much as Ramil can get. I'll text you the hospital details. Have him send it to her. All of it.'

The woman clucked her tongue. 'I take a cut of

your profits, so getting you home, helping you with Rudov... That's just good business. But I see no profit for me in this.'

'Anna—'

She cut him off with a loud sigh. 'Oh, very well. But in return, you will owe me another favor.'

Caine gritted his teeth. 'Fine. Same rules apply.'

'Still think you're on the side of the angels, eh?' the woman cackled.

'I told you before, I don't believe in angels.'

'Long is the way, and hard, that out of Hell leads up to light.'

'What are you talking about?' Caine snapped.

'The quote is from a book. *Paradise Lost*, I believe. Perhaps a little above your head?'

Caine was silent.

'You think a few good deeds can wipe away a past like yours?' the woman rasped. 'I've looked into your eyes, Mr. Waters. And I know the eyes of a killer when I see them. As a gambling woman, I'll wager you won't be hearing the heavenly choirs anytime soon.'

'Neva Bay,' Caine muttered. 'I'll be there.'

He hung up the phone. The wind picked up. Flakes of white snow began to fall. The ivory powder swirled through the air, obscuring the stars above.

Caine lowered his head and jammed his hands deep into the pockets of his coat. He quickened his pace across the empty lot. It was getting colder.

He still had a long way to go.

He disappeared into the darkness. Behind him, his footprints remained in the snow. The lonely trail followed him into the still silence of night.

* * *

MORE FROM ANDREW WARREN

The next book in the Thomas Caine series from Andrew Warren, *White Tiger*, is available to order now here:

https://mybook.to/WhiteTigerBackAd

ACKNOWLEDGMENTS

Diving into Thomas Caine's mysterious past was always a creative goal of mine, and I'm so excited to explore Caine's 'untold' adventures while hiding off the grid. I'd like to thank the following for their very generous help with this book.

As usual, thanks must go to Sam Carver for serving as Caine's armorer and giving me some insight into the weapons and hardware at the Iron Wolf's disposal. Mr. Carver also provided some fascinating background details for this particularly sinister villain.

Thank you to Michael from the Orion Team Goodreads Group. Michael very kindly shared his knowledge of cold weather survival techniques, based on his experiences in the Canadian armed forces.

Thank you to Kronos Ananth and Bodo Phundl (AKA the Typo Assassin) for their help proofreading this manuscript.

To paraphrase the great Stephen King, what I got right is thanks to them. What I got wrong is thanks to me.

Again, I'd like to thank my editor Vic Britton and the entire Boldwood Books team for helping me to bring this 'duology' of a prequel to vivid life.

And, as always, a very special thank you to my wife, Mimi.

Finally, thanks to you, the reader, for taking the time to read this book. Without you, none of this is possible! I hope you will join me on Thomas Caine's next adventure.

ABOUT THE AUTHOR

Andrew Warren is the international bestselling author of the Thomas Caine thriller series. Andrew was born in New Jersey and has over a decade of experience in the television and motion picture industry, where he has worked as a writer, story producer, and post production supervisor. He currently lives in Southern California with his wife and trusty dachshund sidekick.

Sign up to Andrew Warren's mailing list for news, competitions and updates on future books.

Visit Andrew's website: www.andrewwarren-books.com

Follow Andrew on social media here:

- [f] facebook.com/andrewwarrenbooks
- [o] instagram.com/andrewwarrenbooks
- [BB] bookbub.com/authors/andrew-warren
- [butterfly] bsky.app/profile/aawarren.bsky.social

ALSO BY ANDREW WARREN

Thomas Caine Thrillers

Tokyo Black

Red Phoenix

Fire and Forget

Code Green

Hell and Ice

White Tiger

THE *Hit* LIST

Every crime has a story...

**THE HIT LIST IS A NEWSLETTER
DEDICATED TO PULSE-POUNDING,
HIGH-OCTANE ACTION THRILLERS!**

**SIGN UP TO MAKE SURE YOU'RE ON
OUR HIT LIST FOR EXCLUSIVE DEALS,
AUTHOR CONTENT, AND
COMPETITIONS.**

**SIGN UP TO OUR
NEWSLETTER**

BIT.LY/THEHITLISTNEWS

Boldwood

Boldwood Books is an award-winning fiction publishing company seeking out the best stories from around the world.

Find out more at www.boldwoodbooks.com

Join our reader community for brilliant books, competitions and offers!

Follow us
@BoldwoodBooks
@TheBoldBookClub

Sign up to our weekly deals newsletter

https://bit.ly/BoldwoodBNewsletter

www.ingramcontent.com/pod-product-compliance
Lightning Source LLC
Chambersburg PA
CBHW010700100726
47900CB00010B/2736